SHATTERED DEFENSE

CASSANDRA GREY

Immortal Works LLC
1505 Glenrose Drive
Salt Lake City, Utah 84104
Tel: (385) 202-0116

Cover Art by Ashley Literski
http://strangedevotion.wixsite.com/strangedesigns

ISBN 978-1-953491-27-5 (Paperback)
ASIN B09GP5XZSP (Kindle)

To the thousands of victims of serial killers through the ages whose lives were senselessly taken—and to the killers themselves, so many of whom were driven by demons they never saw coming.

To Patrick Lindsay, a capable attorney who read this book during production and lent his valuable knowledge to make sure all the legal machinations were accurate. (No one wants a mistrial on a debut novel!)

To my daughter, who provided the barest kernel of this story one afternoon in the kitchen as I was preparing dinner. And to my other children and grandchildren who believe I can do anything.

CHAPTER 1

I t was a usual early winter evening at the Sinclair on Tanger.
Until it wasn't, that is.

The commonplace man in the Grecian blue Patagonia ski jacket finished filling his black Ford Expedition SUV and screwed the gas cap back on. Thrusting his hand inside his pocket, he pulled out his keys.

And that's when all hell broke loose.

As soon as he yanked the handle to climb back into the SUV, a snowboard flew at him from inside the SUV through the open doorway, slamming into the man's nose with astonishing force. Blood splattered everywhere. His guttural screams sliced through the frigid air as he crumpled to the pavement next to his vehicle, thrashing in agony. Startled customers ran to him.

Within an instant, the would-be rescuers realized they had it all wrong. The passenger's side door flew open. Out scrambled a young teenage boy wearing nothing but bloody boxer shorts. Flailing his arms and screaming at the top of his lungs, he ran barefoot across the icy concrete, burst through the glass doors, and collapsed into the arms of an alarmed woman. The impact sent her cup of Coke into orbit.

Almost by reflex, the employee at the register picked up a cell phone and jabbed 9-1-1. And he wasn't the only one.

Outside, a handful of customers threw themselves on top of the floundering man. In the distance, sirens screamed toward the station.

Andrea Harrison shivered involuntarily as she slung her coat across the back of the chair; the mountainous environment of Utah's Park City was a stark contrast to Los Angeles this time of year. She was still yanking off her gloves when her boss, Sloan Tate, swept through the office door and pulled it shut so abruptly that it startled her. He sank into one of the leather wingbacks before setting his coffee mug on the edge of the desk.

"Welcome back, Andie." A slight grimace tugged at the corner of his mouth. "Look, I hate to pounce on you like this, especially on your first day back at the firm from vacation, but have you seen the news?"

Andie dropped into her chair. "Nope. What's up?"

"Night before last, a thirteen-year-old kid was snowboarding over at the Canyons, lost track of time, got separated from his friends, and decided to hoof it home. It got dark way sooner than he anticipated, I'm sure, and after working up a sweat on the board I think he was so cold he didn't think he'd make it home. So when a nice-looking older guy in a black SUV offered him a ride, all that great advice about 'stranger danger' flew out the door, and he climbed aboard."

"Seriously?"

"Seriously." Sloan took a gulp of coffee before continuing. "I'll spare you the really disgusting details, but the guy got him out on a dark, deserted road just north of town and sodomized him pretty brutally. We're not quite sure what happened after that—or why—or what this guy had planned, but he drove around for what seemed like hours to the thirteen-year-old, hurling threats at this kid the whole time. The guy had a heavy-metal CD blaring nonstop—the kid said he didn't recognize the group—and he told the kid he was dead if he tried to make a move. So the kid stayed hunkered down in the back seat with his snowboard, held hostage by the child locks on the back doors." Sloan took another sip of coffee.

Andie ran her fingers through her cropped auburn hair, fighting the feelings of disgust that roiled from her knotted stomach and into her throat. She steeled herself for the rest. "And then what?"

"We got lucky—that's what. This guy didn't start out with a full tank—in any sense of the word, if you know what I mean—and ended up having to stop for gas. By then, the kid in the back seat was pretending to be asleep. So our guy at the pump didn't notice, or couldn't see through the heavily tinted windows, that his captive, complete with snowboard, had managed to get into the front seat. No sooner had our guy screwed the gas cap back on and opened the door for the next leg of the adventure than his nose connected with the end of the snowboard. It's amazing what a jolt of adrenalin will do to an athletic thirteen-year-old who has been violated and is scared out of his wits."

As she blew out a slow sigh, Andie suddenly realized she'd been holding her breath.

"Our guy saw stars and was on the ground pressing his hands to his face when our thirteen-year-old flung open the passenger door and bolted across the gas station parking lot. Since he was wearing only a pair of bloody boxers and was screaming at the top of his lungs, he managed to attract plenty of attention. A couple of heroic citizens strong-armed our assailant while a woman in a Honda, along with a handful of others, dialed 9-1-1. There was a lot of blood—apparently his nose was broken—and things got a bit messy, but he's being held without bail right now on every charge north of Sunday. And he wants *you* to represent him."

Andie's heart turned to lead, and a throbbing pain inched up the back of her neck. "Do I even *know* this guy?"

"I doubt it. He's not from around here—at least, there's no indication he is. His SUV had Oregon plates—but, of course, the plates were stolen. They originally belonged to a clean one-owner 1988 Ford Taurus that had apparently been parked in an elderly woman's driveway just outside of Portland for a couple of months. She hadn't left the house on her own in all that time—her daughter shuttled her back and forth to the grocery store once a week and to the random doctor's appointment—and she didn't even notice the plates were gone until a cop poked around, trying to find the vehicle.

"The VIN has been scratched out of the SUV with some sort of power tool, and they're getting ready to do some additional searches on the other serial numbers under the hood. But there are bumper stickers on the back for a gubernatorial election in Louisiana and a really garish sticker from Dollywood, so who *knows* the genealogy on that one. Of course, the registration certificate in the glove compartment is issued to a man from North Carolina who died three years ago. The address on the certificate turns out to be a blueberry bog along a country road in Maine. Never been a house anywhere in the vicinity. This guy's done his homework."

"Why *me*? Are you *sure* he asked for *me*?"

"No mistake. He was demanding that the police call you before they even got him cuffed and into the patrol car. And it's not like he sat in an interrogation room and ran his finger up and down the column of attorneys listed in the phone book and picked your name at random. He knew your name, and he was ready. He was spitting blood from a wicked nosebleed and spitting out your name at the same time. He has refused to say a word—won't answer any questions—until he has legal representation. You. He wants *you*. He put down an astonishing retainer—one we really can't afford to turn down, one I consider nothing short of a miracle with the economic hits this firm has taken in the last year. Anyway, when I showed up at the jail and told him you were out of town until this morning, he just gave me a blank stare and shrugged his shoulders, letting me know that wasn't his problem. We haven't even been able to arraign him, because he wouldn't let anyone else represent him—not even temporarily."

Andie's thoughts raced. "I don't get it, Sloan. How does he know *me*?"

"Believe me—no one gets it. I'm suspecting he runs in some pretty rough circles—and I figure he has a friend or acquaintance you defended in the past. Maybe just did a little homework on good attorneys in town—you know, just in case. Never hurts to be prepared. But we're going to figure that part out later, because this morning we've got to get you down to the jail and then over to the court so the cops can officially charge this guy."

"Do I even dare ask about the kid he assaulted?"

"He's being released from the hospital this morning; he was treated for minor injuries and is being tested for HIV. I'm sure they haven't even scratched the surface when it comes to emotional wounds. And I'm just as sure that a huge part of his ability to even stay vertical will come from knowing that this animal is behind bars. For good. He didn't even *want* his snowboard back. Couldn't stand the thought of it."

Sloan's normally strong voice trailed off. "It's been all over the news since yesterday morning. I'm sure you can imagine the vigilante attitude that has gripped the town. We're not even *close* to it yet, but I'm sure impaneling an impartial jury in this neck of the woods will be next to impossible, counselor. Like I said, welcome back."

Andie closed her eyes and took a deep breath. "So this is it."

"*It?*"

"*It.* The one they always talked about in law school. The one where you have to defend someone you know is guilty. Someone you don't want loose on the streets. Someone you want to shove in a cell, then lock the door and throw away the key. And if I do my job *well,* I'll buy freedom for a pervert who brutalized a little boy."

"No, Andie." Sloan was on his feet now. "Your *job* is to make sure this man—every man—receives the fairest possible trial and is afforded the rights guaranteed him by the Constitution. Those rights do not include the ability to do harm and avoid the consequences. Your *job* is not necessarily to win his freedom. You know that."

"I *do* know that, Sloan. But what about the rights of the boy he attacked? How can I jump in with both feet and work my ass off to protect the *rights* of a guy who would do something like that? Hell, Sloan—that could have been *Beau.*"

A sudden tightness in Andie's throat made her feel like she was being choked, and hot tears burned her eyes. The rapid fierceness of her reaction surprised her; after more than a year, she thought she was over the worst of it. Beau may be dead, but at least he didn't die like this.

Sloan's voice was quiet. Almost tender. "Yes, Andie, it could have been Beau. It could have been that freckled kid who mows the lawns out front. It could have been any of the hundreds of kids that roam the halls over at the junior high school...any one of them would have been one too many. And I want you to be absolutely clear on your *job*—you make sure that once this monster is dressed in prison blues and has a permanent cell to call home, he can't look back and accuse you of not doing everything necessary to make sure he was treated fairly and with respect. That's all, Andie. I don't expect you to get him off. *No one* expects you to get him off."

"*He* probably does." Andie swiped at the tears that hovered at the corners of her eyes.

"No, he doesn't, Andie! This isn't a your-word-against-mine deal. He was caught in the act—okay, maybe not in the *act,* but might as well have been. You've got a terrified and injured kid bolting out of the man's SUV in nothing but his bloody shorts, and he's not a toddler who's too young to testify or identify his attacker. He can tell anyone who'll listen *exactly* what happened to him, and he can identify the guy. I'm sure when the police finish processing the SUV, there will be all kinds of body fluid evidence. You've got two guys who kept this man pinned to the ground at the side of his vehicle while they waited for the cops to show up. And you've got a handful of other witnesses from the Sinclair who watched the whole take-down. No. This guy doesn't expect to get off. He might have a few tricks up his sleeve that he hopes will reduce the severity of his sentence, but I can guarantee you he doesn't expect to get off. There's no way."

Andie massaged her temples to ease her aching head. "But *why me?* I know two Salt Lake attorneys right off the top of my head who love this sort of case—and you *know* who I'm talking about. How about I agree to meet with him, represent him through his arraignment, but then pass him off to someone who's going to get a lot more glee out of this case than I will?"

"You can try, but I don't think he'll go for it. He wants *you.* He didn't come across as someone who was going to change his mind on that point. Besides that, Andie—and this is an awkward spot for me—I won't hold a gun to your head, but you know what this firm has been through financially for the last year, and you know how badly we need this case. Well, not the case, but the dollars attached to it."

"I know that, Sloan. I can't say I'm excited, but you know I'll back you up."

"Thanks. I never really doubted that you would. And, listen, Andie—you don't have to do this by yourself. I've already briefed Jackson and Grace, and they're both prepared to serve as co-counsel. As cut-and-dried as this appears, there's always strength in numbers. Besides that, I don't want you going down to the jail by yourself."

Sloan opened the door and waved his now-empty mug in Andie's direction. "Go for it—and I wish you luck. But in the meantime, grab Jackson as soon as he gets in. You've got to get down to the jail and start the ball rolling."

CHAPTER
2

A ndie squirmed in her seat, dreading the upcoming meeting with her new client, as Jackson Shepherd eased into a parking space at the jail reserved for court personnel, switched off the ignition, and turned to her. "This blows." He checked the rearview mirror, touched his finger to his tongue, and smoothed out one of his eyebrows. *Oh, great,* thought Andie, *and I didn't even pluck this morning.*

With a roll of her eyes, she nodded. "Hey, at least he didn't ask for *you.* About now, I'm starting to second-guess my career choice."

"Yeah, what's *that* all about? I didn't know you ran in those kinds of circles."

Jackson recoiled as Andie delivered a playful punch to his arm. "That's just it—I *don't.* I seriously can't figure out how he got my name. I owe payback to someone, that's for sure."

"So, we're agreed—we're just going to introduce ourselves, hand him our cards, race through the preliminaries, and arrange to meet him at the courthouse for the arraignment?"

"That's the plan." Andie gripped the door handle so hard her hand ached. "I don't want to spend any more time in there than absolutely necessary. As soon as he's been arraigned, I *might* try to talk him into switching up—going with Skabelund or Howell in Salt Lake. This is exactly the kind of case they both love. Lots of publicity. You don't get to be a household name without taking on clients like these whenever the opportunity presents itself. Plus, if Skabelund thinks there's enough media hype in the wings, he might do it pro bono. Could save this client a lot of money—and that might be enough to incentivize him to take another attorney."

"Does Sloan know? That you want this guy to go with someone else?"

"He does. I told him first thing—the second the thought occurred to me."

"And?"

"He doesn't like it; you know how badly the firm needs an economic shot in the arm right now. My passing this guy off to one of those hot-shots would be a real blow to Sloan. Besides, he doesn't think the guy will go for it. Apparently, this guy was shouting my name while he was being cuffed and read his Miranda rights. That's the thing that has me so baffled. He knew my name. He knew just who he was going to hire. It's like he knew he was going to get caught, and he figured out his strategy ahead of time. And he picked *me*. That really freaks me out."

"Face it, Andie. You're one of the best. If the guy did *any* kind of homework once he blew into town, he knew who to ask for."

Andie felt the heat of color in her cheeks. "You know, Jack, since the day I passed the bar I've tried to give it my all. I guess there are some who think I'm one of the best up here. But how on earth would *he* know that?"

Jack shrugged as he reached for the door leading to the cell block. "Who knows? I guess word gets around among these guys. Or maybe he really is a local, and we just haven't figured out the connections yet. Or maybe you've defended one of his friends or family members and he sat in court watching you at your best."

"Yeah, Sloan wondered the same thing. Well, my new goal in life is to pass him off as quickly as possible."

SHE'D BEEN through this exercise too many times to count, but Andie still stifled a mild panic when she heard the inner doors at the jail click shut behind her. She was locked in every bit as much as the criminals who leered at her on her way to the interview room. All those humid afternoons in her law school classroom never hinted at how it would feel to be locked in a room with a person who thought nothing of robbing a child of his innocence in the most brutal way possible—locked in a room without a rapid escape.

The prisoner was on his feet before the guard touched his badge to the keypad. And his eyes were riveted on Andie.

Frozen in place by the icy dread that clutched at her, Andie hung back while Jack moved around her, hand extended. "I'm Jackson Shepherd. I'll be serving with Ms. Harrison as co-counsel in your defense." Even as the man took Jack's hand, his eyes never left Andie's face.

Jack shifted uncomfortably, still in the powerful grip of the handshake. "And...you are?"

"Andrea Harrison, counselor at law," the man almost spat. His penetrating gaze seemed to bore through Andie's carefully controlled expression. Andie finally stepped into the room, allowing the door to lock behind her.

Andie kept one hand wrapped tightly around the handle of her briefcase, the other in the pocket of her jacket. "Yes, I'm Andrea Harrison. And you are?"

"Oh, I *know* who you are." He wasn't what Andie was expecting —not in the least. Standing a little over six feet tall, he was muscled and athletic; trying to imagine him without his facial injuries, she realized he was even a little good-looking. He exuded a sort of power —or maybe it was just a sense of control. The biggest surprise for Andie was his age; considering the peppering of gray through his dark hair and the lines that played around his eyes and mouth, he looked like he was somewhere in his fifties. He was well manicured and carefully coifed, even after being rolled around on the pavement at the gas station. He looked for all the world like a dad, a grandpa. He didn't remotely resemble the doughy, sick-looking, leering child molesters that had danced across the front pages during her lifetime.

No wonder thirteen-year-old Jameson Harper had climbed into the SUV so readily.

Andie felt a wave of chills race up her spine. "You know, I'm a little confused. You know me, but I don't know you. I don't even know your name. Have we met?"

"Let's just say your reputation precedes you."

"Well, I'd like to thank whoever recommended me; lots of our business trades on word of mouth and personal recommendation. Who was that?"

He just stared in response.

Jack cleared his throat and lowered himself into one of the metal chairs at the small table. Grateful to get off her wobbly legs, Andie sat down next to him.

The man in the orange jumpsuit stayed on his feet—now, Andie realized with sodden dread, he was in the power position. He wouldn't make this easy.

She tried not to show her discomfort as she drew in a deep breath. "Look, sir, I'm going to ask you to take a seat. We don't have a lot of time here this morning; they're waiting to take you over to the court for an arraignment—the procedure during which you are officially charged."

"Don't patronize me," he growled. "I know what an arraignment is."

"Should I take that to mean that you've been involved in the criminal system before?" Andie asked. *Great. A repeat offender.*

No answer. He simply narrowed his eyes, his look changing to one of pure contempt, his stare so penetrating it was almost painful.

"All right," she said, trying to sound a lot more powerful than she felt, "if you know what an arraignment is, then you also know that the number-one factor in my ability to help you is your willingness to talk to me. And that needs to start with you telling me your name. Your driver's license is forged. You had an array of credit cards in your wallet, all under the same fake name. In other words, I can't get your name from your ID or even from the cops. You're going to have to tell it to me—and I'd suggest you give me your *real* name, or I'm genuinely unable to help you."

"You *have* to help me. I retained you as my lawyer."

"If I don't have the basics—something as simple as your name—you've limited my ability to help you. I'll have no choice but to decline the case, and you'll have to find someone else to take it."

The silence in the room was suffocating. He finally pulled out a chair; the metal legs grating against the gray tile floor sounded like fingernails being dragged across a chalkboard. He lowered himself into the chair across from Andie and Jack, never averting his stare from Andie's eyes. After what seemed like hours, he spoke it with defiance and force. "Barlow."

"Is that your first name or your last name?" Jack asked, a pen poised above his legal pad.

"Brock Barlow." Still locked in Brock's gaze, Andie heard the pen scratching against the legal pad as Jack took notes. Andie's hands were clasped tightly in her lap as she tried to still the trembling.

"All right, Brock. Has anyone explained the charges that will be filed against you?"

"No. I refused to talk to anyone until you were here."

Andie lowered her eyes to escape Brock's piercing stare. Jack pulled out the notes they had quickly scribbled before leaving for the jail. "Let's see. They're going to charge you with kidnapping, reckless endangerment, aggravated sexual assault in the first degree, forcible sodomy, and attempted homicide. Do you understand the charges?"

"Isn't that a bit of overkill?"

"I don't know," Jack enunciated, his frustration obvious. "You tell me."

"Endangerment—sexual assault—sodomy. Aren't those sort of the same thing? Why all the drama?"

A small yelp leapt out of Andie's throat before she realized it. "Actually, there are specific differences between each of those charges according to the statutes," she said, refusing to make eye contact. "Would you like us to get the statutes and go over them with you? I know they're available in the office here. We'd be happy to explain the specifics."

"Not necessary. Won't change anything."

"But part of our responsibility is to make sure you understand the charges against you. If you don't, it can cause very serious complications down the road."

"Oh, you mean I could get the whole thing overturned?" Brock shot a sinister smile in Andie's direction. "Oh, that would be too bad. Especially for an esteemed attorney of *your* reputation." Sarcasm hung heavy in the air.

Andie straightened up in her chair and fixed him in her line of vision. "Look, Mr. Barlow, I'm done playing games here. What you allegedly did is very serious, and the charges against you are very serious. And if you're guilty and you escape punishment because of legal technicalities, it's not as sad for me as it is for the boy you allegedly violated. I'm here for one reason only: to make sure your rights are protected and you receive the fairest possible trial. I can't say right now that I believe you are innocent. And based on the way you've been acting since we got here, I'm not sure I can continue to defend you."

Brock lunged across the table in one fluid motion and grabbed Andie's arms in a crushing grip. As one guard frantically fumbled to unlock the door, Brock commanded, "You *will* represent me." Jack leapt to his feet and tried to pull Brock away as two guards rushed into the room and restrained their prisoner. As he was being cuffed, Brock snarled, "I paid good money to retain you. You *will* do your job, and you *will* help me."

Andie stepped to the door and leaned against the frame. "You just assaulted me, Mr. Barlow, and I now have every right to refund your retainer and walk away."

Jack picked up her briefcase and handed it to her. "Look, Mr. Barlow, neither Ms. Harrison nor I want to represent you if this is how you're going to behave. And we don't have to—get that? There is no law saying we have to accept the retainer and defend you. Let me translate that for you: you're on your own if anything like this happens even one more time. Sit down, cooperate with our questions, and refrain from touching either of us again. Or we're off this case."

"Oh, there's no danger of a repeat performance on that end," the guard said, pushing Brock into the chair and fastening the cuffs to it. "We'll be right here. And I don't think your man is going to be real mobile anymore, if you know what I mean."

Brock's head whirled around. "You can't stay here. I have the right to confer with my legal counsel privately. You're violating my rights."

"Well, your attorney here has some rights, too, mister, and that includes not being assaulted by you."

"Fine. I'll behave."

"You've got one more chance. After that, you surrender your rights."

"Unlock my cuffs."

"Nope. That's our insurance policy. You're one with that chair so your attorney over there can breathe a little easier."

The guards made their way through the door, and the sickening click of the lock reverberated in Andie's ears. She swallowed hard to push the bile back down her throat. Sizing her up, Jack pushed her chair over to where she stood by the door. With a respectable distance between her and the table, she sat down quietly.

"Okay, let's start over," Jack said. "Do you understand the charges that are going to be filed against you?" Andie gratefully realized that Jack wasn't cutting Barlow any slack.

"Yes."

"No questions at all?"

"No." That's why there were two of them in the room with Barlow; Jack was a witness to the fact that Brock claimed he understood the charges.

"How are you going to plead?"

"Not guilty, of course." Even after all her experience, Andie was stunned. *With all those witnesses—including the boy you assaulted—*

you're going to try to convince a jury that you didn't do what you're accused of?

"Duly noted," Jack grumbled. "We'll see you in court in a few hours."

Barlow twisted in his chair, straining against the confinement of the cuffs. "That's all? You're not going to give me any advice or anything? This isn't what I paid for."

Andie stood. "It seems your mind's made up, so what kind of advice were you hoping for, Mr. Barlow? I'm new on this case—was out of town until last night—but from what I *do* know, I'd likely advise you to plead guilty—or maybe you could plead not guilty by reason of temporary insanity—and then we can work on ways to get you the fairest possible sentence. Since your victim has identified you, and is old enough to be considered a very credible witness, I'm not sure a plea of not guilty is going to be very successful as—"

"No!" Barlow exploded, cutting her off. "I will *not* plead insanity!"

"Well, we've got a lot of work ahead of us, and we've got a lot to discover, but I wouldn't dismiss that so easily, Mr. Barlow."

"I am not insane!" The veins stood out like thick cords on either side of his neck.

"No one is saying you're insane," Jack countered. "But it can be argued that *something* temporarily clouded your judgment and caused you to attack a thirteen-year-old boy. That *thing*—whatever it was—is often called *temporary insanity*. Hence the word *temporary*. We're not saying you're insane."

Barlow thrashed against the restraint of the cuffs, reddening with agitation. Andie turned to the guard on the other side of the barred door. "I think we're finished," she mouthed quietly. He released the lock with his keypad, and Andie stepped out of the room, the relief palpable as it washed over her. Jack was close on her heels. Despite her annihilated mental defenses and her desperate desire to run away as fast as she could, she clamped her jaw and focused on her breathing as she walked methodically down the passageway between cells to the set of doors that led to freedom.

"Andie, are you okay?" Jack asked as he pulled the door open for her.

She snipped, "I'm fine," contradicting the swirling anguish inside.

CHAPTER 3

Andie bent over her desk, her forehead cradled in her arms. She was too mentally exhausted to focus on much of anything.

"That bad?" Sloan asked as he leaned his shoulder against the doorframe of Andie's office. She cautiously looked up in response to the sound of his voice.

"Oh, worse."

"Have you been to court yet?"

"No, we go at one." Her head dropped back down as she moaned under her breath. "It was a nightmare, Sloan. He stared at me. He refused to tell me how he knew me or why he insisted on me representing him. Hell, he even refused to tell me his name until I threatened to decline the case."

Sloan shook his head. "Like I said, he's probably hooked up with one of the guys you've defended in the past. Someone who thinks you're the best thing since ketchup. I wouldn't stress out too much about it."

"That's not all," Andie said, rubbing her throbbing temples. "He grabbed me."

"What?" Sloan stiffened with anger. "That's why I sent Jackson with you! What happened?"

"We were trying to explain the charges, which he hadn't heard, and he was acting like an ass. I told him if he didn't cooperate, I was not going to defend him. He was on me like white on rice—I thought he was going to break my arms." Andie pushed up the sleeves of her jacket; ridges of bruising bore witness to the assault.

"Use that at the arraignment if you have to. I'm fairly certain they'll either order him held without bail or will set such an obscenely high bail that he won't see the light of day anytime soon—but if you have to, let them know he poses a danger to others, including you, and that everyone is best served if he stays behind bars for now."

"I'll do that if *Jack* will stand next to him while I'm saying it." Sloan smiled.

"There's more, Sloan. This guy seemed very well-versed about the legal process. I suspect he's been involved in the criminal system before."

"That doesn't necessarily mean much, Andie—maybe it's nothing more than too many episodes of *Law and Order*."

"Maybe...but I got some powerfully weird vibes. He really gave me the creeps. And I think it was because of more than what he did to that boy. I could almost swear he's a repeat offender. There's something about him. I was unnerved before I even stepped into the interview room with him."

"Did Jack get the same vibes?"

"Not exactly, but he was none too happy himself. The guy was arrogant. Manipulative. I think he's twisted in some really fundamental way—but he went nuts when we suggested he cop a temporary insanity plea. And I mean *nuts*. I'm surprised you couldn't hear him yelling clear over here. We obviously hit a nerve. This isn't going to be easy, Sloan."

"The great cases never are."

"Lucky me."

AN HOUR LATER, Jack collapsed into a chair across the desk while Andie sorted through everything that had happened while she'd been out of the office. It occurred to her she should focus on whatever she could do to help Brock Barlow, but she didn't want to. There'd come a time—too soon—when she'd have no choice, but right now she wanted to focus on *anything* else.

"I've been on the phone with Conlin down at the court," Jack said. "I had to talk to him about something else, and while I had him on the line, I explored what we could do to save Jameson Harper the trauma of having to be in the same room with the man who assaulted him. There are options."

"Remote testimony?"

"Yeah, that's probably the most viable one. Conlin said they don't like to use it because there's some amount of legitimacy in a witness having to face not only the accused, but everyone else in the courtroom too—the jury, the judge, the attorneys, even the people in the gallery. Makes it less likely that a witness will fabricate a story. But this case isn't exactly routine. Forcing a thirteen-year-old to face the guy who brutalized him seems like nothing more than cruel and unusual punishment."

"I can't argue that." Andie closed the file she'd been reading and leaned back in her chair. "And there's powerful precedent for children being allowed to testify, and even be cross-examined, remotely. Grace has tried a few cases in family court where kids weren't made to face their abusers."

"We might want to consider that," Jack said, rising from the chair and moving toward the door. "Want to grab some lunch before the arraignment?"

Suddenly conscious of how queasy she felt, Andie shook her head. "I'll just meet you at the court."

"Okay. But meet me in the lobby—don't go past the checkpoint until I'm there. I know Barlow will be cuffed and manacled, but I don't want any repeats of this morning."

Andie winced. "You're not alone." As Jack headed down the hall, Andie pulled a yellow legal pad out of the top drawer and scrawled across the top, *Harper—remote testimony*.

It had started.

JACK AND ANDIE sat stiffly on the front row of the gallery. It was well after one, but Judge Stevenson was still hearing summary motions for a case that had not been finished when the court adjourned for lunch. Other than a handful of other attorneys waiting to stand before the judge, there were only a few observers scattered on the benches, most of them clustered toward the back. Despite the cold weather outside, perspiration beaded up on Andie's forehead and dribbled down her back in response to the stifling air in the courtroom.

The door at the side of the room swung open, and there he was: Brock Barlow, still clad in orange, manacled and chained at the wrists and ankles, and flanked by a pair of steely guards. Again, his eyes immediately locked on Andie. It was clear he wasn't going anywhere —in fact, he'd been reduced to nearly the lowest possible condition as far as human dignity was concerned—but a look of smug arrogance and defiance still washed across his face. A chill raced up Andie's spine, and she averted her gaze as the guards walked Barlow to the prisoners' section of the courtroom. She heard the scuttle as they situated him in a straight-backed chair and settled on either side of him.

The two attorneys in front of the judge droned endlessly as they wrapped up their motions. Andie kept her head lowered while she moved her eyes barely enough to glance cautiously in Barlow's direction. He looked like a wild beast lunging against the leather restraints of a captor. Straining against the cuffs that bound him to the metal arms of the chair, he pressed forward—leaning as far as he possibly could toward her. His eyes, narrow and menacing, stabbed at her. The man seethed with hatred. Sitting there, stealing a wary look at him beneath hooded lids, Andie absorbed all that hate—if he wanted so desperately to have her defend him, why was he so hateful toward her? The wave of fear that washed over her caused physical pain.

A crack of the gavel signaled the end of the case before the judge, and the two attorneys fluidly gathered up their files. Conlin rose to his feet, cleared his throat, and produced enough volume to be heard beyond the back wall of the gallery. "The State of Utah versus Brock Barlow."

Judge Stevenson peered over the top of his reading glasses. "Is the defendant present?"

Andie stood. "Yes, your honor." He was present, all right—still straining against the cuffs, still looking as though he would break free and crush her in his bare hands at any moment. Still leering with hatred, he owned the air that surrounded Andie. She stood frozen.

Jack nudged her. It was time to do the dance...stand in front of the table, face the judge...stand within reach of Brock Barlow. Andie moved stiffly to the very edge of the real estate she was expected to occupy. The guards on either side of Barlow freed him from the chair and in one smooth motion cuffed his hands behind his back and steered him toward Andie. His ankles cuffed and manacled, he lurched like Frankenstein as he stumbled forward in an attempt to take long strides. Brady Young from the county attorney's office stood and walked toward the front of the room.

Word had spread rapidly through the jail after Barlow had grabbed Andie that morning, and the guard positioned himself squarely between the two of them. Andie cautiously breathed out a sigh of relief.

Judge Stevenson looked up.

"Let's see here, Mr. Barlow. Looks like you're being charged with kidnapping, reckless endangerment, aggravated sexual assault in the first degree, forcible sodomy, and attempted homicide. That's quite a litany. Let's take them one by one and—"

"No need," spat Barlow.

The crack of the gavel split the air. "I can appreciate that you've got an opinion, Mr. Barlow, but you need to follow procedure. I'm afraid you've temporarily lost the right to address me, so your attorney will speak for you." The judge looked like he was trying to rub the last vestiges of a wicked headache from his forehead.

Barlow snapped his head to the side and glowered at Andie.

The judge looked directly at Andie. "On the charge of kidnapping, how does the defendant plead?"

"Not guilty, your honor."

"On the charge of reckless endangerment, how does the defendant plead?"

"Not guilty, your honor."

A derisive laugh bubbled up from the depths of Barlow's gut. Again the crack of the gavel. "Mr. Barlow, I'm going to ask that you remain silent while the charges are read and your attorney pleads. If I have to remind you again, I will have you removed from the courtroom and we will proceed without you."

Barlow glared at the judge with silent contempt.

"On the charge of aggravated sexual assault in the first degree, how does the defendant plead?"

"Not guilty, your honor."

"On the charge of forcible sodomy, how does the defendant plead?"

"Not guilty, your honor."

"And on the charge of attempted homicide, how does the defendant plead?"

"Not guilty, your honor."

The judge directed his gaze at Brady. "Well, I can't say that I'm particularly surprised. What are your recommendations, counsel?"

Brady cleared his throat. "We recommend that the defendant be held without bail, your honor. The defendant has demonstrated unstable behavior during his incarceration. In addition, when he was arrested, he was driving a stolen vehicle with a fake registration, and he carried a forged driver's license. We believe he poses a considerable flight risk, especially since from what little we know about him, we don't think he lives in this area. And the seriousness of the charges causes us great concern; even if he doesn't flee, we believe he poses a significant danger if he is not behind bars."

Barlow visibly stiffened but didn't seem surprised.

"Ms. Harrison?"

Andie stepped slightly to the side. "My client has pleaded not guilty, your honor." The bile rose in her throat. "As his guilt has not been proven, we'd like to recommend $300,000 cash bail."

Barlow suddenly leaned into the guard, pushing him toward Andie. Again he taunted her with his black, unfeeling eyes.

"The seriousness of these charges is significant. The defendant is hereby ordered to be held in the Summit County Jail without bail until he is turned over for trial." The judge pounded the gavel to emphasize his ruling, and the guard next to Barlow steered him toward the door. A sneer spread across Barlow's face as the pair of guards shoved him through the door and into the hallway beyond the courtroom.

Andie swallowed hard.

Game on.

ONCE BARLOW WAS on the other side of the closed door, Brady Young approached Andie and placed a tentative hand on her shoulder. "Look, I know we're on opposing sides, and I *really* don't want to do anything to threaten the integrity of this trial, so just consider this conversation in the spirit in which it's intended. Bottom line is, I'm not even sure what we've got here. We're at a total loss. I don't even know where to start."

Andie stifled the urge to laugh. "Oh, don't look at me! I can't shed any light on the guy."

One of Brady's eyebrows shot up in a quizzical expression. "We figured you knew him. We heard he asked for you by name and paid an almost unprecedented retainer to make sure that happened."

"Where'd you hear that?"

"One of the arresting cops told us he was spitting your name out the entire time he was being arrested—seemed a lot more interested in making sure he got you to represent him than in what was going on. Said he was so intent on retaining you that he had to read the Miranda three times just to make sure the guy had heard it all. He wasn't even sure then, but when he started a fourth time, the guy got combative just to show how annoyed he was."

"And the retainer? Who told you about that?"

"Oh, come on. You know people talk."

Andie suddenly realized *she* didn't even know how much of a retainer Brock Barlow had shoved in Sloan's direction to secure her. Sloan hadn't talked a dollar amount. Neither had Barlow. "Well, you figured wrong. I've never seen this guy in my life. Sloan figures he's in tight with someone I previously defended—that he might even have observed me in court before."

"Great. So we've got a freak show at the Sinclair station, a victim who's old enough to tell what happened, and a couple of involved citizens who strong-armed our man and held him captive until the cops got there. And that's about the extent of it."

"Hey, at least *you've* got a victim who can talk and a couple of witnesses. That alone can sew up the prosecution, and you know it. *I've* got nothing more than an uncooperative, belligerent client who refuses to give me any solid information and who's relying on my reputation—an uncooperative, belligerent client I've never seen before in my life."

"Well, when you put it *that* way, I guess I'm not so hard up." Brady smiled. "Look, I've only got a couple of clerks to help me on this one, but if we find anything out that might shed some light on this guy, of course the disclosure laws stipulate that I have to let you know. I highly doubt you'll be able to parlay anything I find into a stunning defense."

Andie laughed. "Yeah, I doubt that too. The evidence thus far is fairly compelling."

CHAPTER
4

Andie stomped her feet on the bristly mat on the porch of the Harpers' white clapboard house to chase the powdery snow from her boots. No one had shoveled the front walk since last night's storm, but the Harpers probably had lots of other things on their minds right now. She rang the bell again; they were expecting her.

Andie suddenly wished Jack had come along, but they both decided that Jameson might be overwhelmed by two attorneys...and that a woman might be less threatening, given the nature of his assault. So Andie it was, by herself, dreading the prospect of making a young boy—someone Beau's age—relive what was undoubtedly the worst thing that had ever happened to him.

"Hello. You must be Ms. Harrison." Samantha Harper absentmindedly smoothed the front of her wool slacks and extended her hand.

"Please, call me Andrea. And thank you for agreeing to speak with me today. I know this must be extremely difficult for Jameson—and for you and your husband."

"He...his life has been turned upside-down," Samantha Harper responded, wiping at the corner of her eye. "He'll never be the same. None of us will. Jameson has a ten-year-old sister, and I'm terrified to let her out of my sight. And there is no husband—he left with his secretary a few years ago."

Andie felt the color creep up her neck. *Just like my father. Simply left.* "I'm sorry; I shouldn't have assumed. I can't imagine how distressed you must feel."

"Jameson already told the police everything," the woman said, narrowing her red, puffy eyes. "And he also told the people at the hospital everything that happened. I'm not sure why he has to repeat it again."

"There are a number of reasons, Ms. Harper. What happened to your son was an extremely shocking and painful ordeal. He might remember things now that he couldn't really process right after it happened. We often find that perspectives can change in a matter of just a few days, and it's our desire to get the most complete information we can. And you should know that while we have been able to study the police report, we are not given rights to see any of the medical records or any of the information your son provided at the hospital. All of that is protected by law."

Resigned, Ms. Harper signaled Andie to follow her. They walked into a living room bathed in the light that streamed through a wall of two-story windows. Andie couldn't help noting the irony—pools of natural sunlight illuminating a room, a house, where the blackest evil imaginable had sunk its teeth into the very heart of the family who lived there.

As Andie draped her coat over the arm of the couch and situated herself at one end, Jameson Harper appeared hesitantly in the doorway. Andie was startled—though Sloan had described him as athletic, he was a slight, almost fragile-looking boy, appearing closer to ten or eleven than his thirteen years. His hair was almost black— could it have been dyed?—and a scattering of freckles played across his nose. He wore the T-shirt and jeans every kid in Park City seemed to wear; nothing about him really stood out.

Andie stood and acknowledged him as he slipped into the room. "Hi, Jameson; it's nice to meet you. My name is Andrea Harrison, and I'm an attorney. I'd like to ask you a few questions about...what happened to you." Sitting back down, Andie picked up her yellow legal pad; it was another attempt to put Jameson at ease—no high-tech equipment.

Jameson briefly glanced at her and lowered himself into the other end of the couch, next to the chair in which his mother sat. Andie detected an almost imperceptible nod...Ms. Harper's permission for her son to describe the indescribable. Jameson settled into the corner of the couch, which seemed to swallow his delicate frame. "Okay," he muttered, so quietly Andie wondered at first if he had really spoken. He raised his head; his chestnut-brown eyes seemed enormous.

"Let me start by saying how much I appreciate your willingness to talk to me," Andie said, concentrating on keeping her voice soft and quiet. "I know how difficult it must be for you to even think about it, much less talk about it."

"I can't...*stop* thinking about it. It's *all* I think about."

"I'm sure that must be true, and I'm sure it must be very hard. But if we're going to get to the bottom of what happened, it's important to hear your version. Do you feel like you can talk to me?"

He searched his mother's face before finally turning to Andie. "Yeah, I guess so." He interlaced his fingers and buried his hands between his thighs. He clenched his jaw so tightly that his facial muscles rippled.

"Why don't you start by telling me where you were that afternoon and how you got into the SUV."

Jameson shifted nervously and tapped his foot softly against the frame of the couch. Tears appeared at the edges of his lids and hung on his lashes. "I, um, had gone snowboarding at the Canyons with some friends—Eric Myer and Cam Sullivan—but they wanted to leave earlier than I did, so I stayed and made another couple of runs. When I finished, I tried to call my mom, but she didn't answer. Since it was still light, I decided I could just walk home."

Andie detected the softest of moans escape Ms. Harper's slightly parted lips. A look of stricken guilt splashed across her features. Andie could almost hear the ceaseless dialogue that undoubtedly tormented her every waking hour like a relentlessly looping recording. *If only...if only....*Jameson paused and swatted at the tears tumbling down his cheeks.

"You're doing great, Jameson. What happened then?"

After another glance at this mother, he took a deep breath. "I was walking along the highway, and I didn't realize how far it really was. Like, it always seemed so much closer in the car. I'd been boarding most of the day, and I was trashed. My board was really heavy. It was getting dark, and I was starting to get really cold."

"Did you call your mom for a ride then?"

"I tried, but she still didn't answer. I saw the gas station at the top of the hill and thought I'd call again when I got there—inside, where I could get warm—but...I didn't...make it that far." With that, he covered his eyes with his hand.

Andie waited while Jameson softly wept. She quickly made a few notes on her legal pad and jotted down a few reminders about other questions. When Jameson still didn't speak, she cleared her throat. "Then what happened, Jameson?"

It took him a minute to respond. "That...guy...drove up in this big SUV. He had kind of been following behind me. I had heard him sort of slow down, and I'd turned around a couple of times to look at him. I couldn't figure out why he was driving so slowly on the highway. Then he pulled right up next to me and asked me where I was going." Andie saw him shudder. "He told me he worked sometimes with Coach Nelson at the school and asked me if he could give me a ride home."

"Had you ever seen him with Coach Nelson?"

"No."

"Did Coach Nelson often have other men working with him?"

"Not really...but he knew Coach Nelson's name, so I thought he must have been telling the truth."

"Are you on one of the teams at school?"

"Yeah, the wrestling team. Coach Nelson helps with the wrestling team sometimes. I just started. Featherweight."

"But you'd never seen this man with Coach Nelson?"

"No, but I had seen him at the gym. I'd never seen him with Coach Nelson, or with the other wrestlers, but he hung around the locker room a few times last week. He seemed nice. So I was tired and cold and it was getting dark, and I knew my mom would be worried, so I got in the SUV. He told me to get in the front seat but to put my board in the back." This time he covered his face with both his hands and rested his elbows on his thighs. Ms. Harper cried softly.

"What happened then, Jameson?"

"I kind of knew I was in trouble right away, because he didn't ask me where I lived. He just gunned it down the highway and went right through the light at the intersection where he should have turned to get to my house. He kept going, really fast, and I asked him where we were going. He said, 'To hell.' I reached for the door handle to jump out even though he was speeding down the highway. He grabbed my other arm and told me if I tried anything stupid I'd be sorry. I...I just wanted to get out and go home."

"Did you tell him that?"

"Yes!" Now burrowed down into the corner of the couch, Jameson almost wailed. "I told him I was sorry I got in the SUV and I just wanted to get out and that he could keep my board and I would walk the rest of the way home—that he didn't have to drive me. He told me I was never going home again." His face was flushed a deep ruddy color, and tears flowed freely; Ms. Harper visibly winced. Jameson looked directly at Andie. "He just kept on driving."

"Where did he take you?"

"I'm not sure what the road is called, but it's off all by itself. It had a ton of snow on it and it hadn't been plowed. At first I thought he might get stuck, and that maybe I could get out and run away, but he didn't get stuck. It...it was dark by then. I just kept thinking about how to get away. I remembered all the times my mom told me never to get in the car with someone I didn't know, and I felt really stupid for making such a dumb mistake. But I was more scared. Really scared."

He cried, his words catching in his throat. Glaring at Andie, his mother asked Jameson if he wanted to stop and give the rest of his statement later. Andie nodded her assent.

"No. I want to get it over with."

Andie took a deep breath. "Then what happened, Jameson?"

"Ms. Harrison, is this really necessary?" Ms. Harper moved onto the couch next to her son. "Does he really have to go over this again?"

"I don't need all the details, Jameson. But do you think you can just tell me the sequence of events—generally in what order things happened?"

The hiccupping sounds in Jameson's throat slowed and gradually stopped. "Um, yeah. I think I can do that. He pushed me into the back of the SUV and came back there with me. He held my shoulders down with his hands, and he shoved his knee really hard between my legs...and that's when...he...um, attacked me. He tore off my clothes...really rough...and he hurt my arm. I was screaming, and he told me if I didn't stop he would kill me. So I stopped screaming, but I think he was going to kill me, anyway. I screamed when..." The crying started again. He finally looked up. "When he...it hurt so bad!"

Ms. Harper gathered him up into her arms and stared hard at Andie.

"When he was...done...he climbed back up to the driver's seat and told me to stay in the back. He told me to stay down so no one could see me and he told me I couldn't put my clothes back on. I told him I was really cold, and he said, 'Not as cold as you're going to be when I choke the life out of you and throw you out into the snow.' So I knew he was still going to kill me, even if I stopped screaming and even if I did all the things he said.

"I couldn't stop thinking of how to get away. I stopped screaming and crying because I was trying to figure something out. Instead, I started praying. All I could think was how sad my mom and sister would be if he killed me. I wondered how long it would take someone to find me. I worried about my friends. I worried about Eric and Cam and how they would feel for leaving me at the resort. I wondered if I..." Jameson simply stopped talking.

"What?"

"I wondered if it would hurt. To die, I mean."

Andie felt a large boulder in the pit of her stomach. Her throat was tight. It was a story of outrage she couldn't wrap her head around. The skin on her upper arm crawled where Barlow had grabbed her at the jail. He was filthy, and he had touched her too. And he had brutalized this innocent child beyond all reason.

"Jameson, obviously, you got away. How did that happen?"

"He drove for a little while until he got to the other side of town. Then he started swearing about not having enough gas. He pulled in to that Sinclair and told me to stay in the back and to lie down. He got out and locked the door and looked through his wallet for a credit card. At first I did what he said, but then I noticed the windows were tinted and he couldn't see me. So I slowly got up and pulled on my boxers and crawled up to the front seat. I moved really carefully and kept watching him in case he looked closer."

At this point, he sat up straighter—to pull himself out of the corner of the couch where he had been cowering just minutes before. It was almost as if he felt some justified pride in his plan to get away. Andie's throat relaxed, and she scribbled as quickly as she could on the legal pad. "What then, Jameson?"

"I managed to get my board into the front seat. I put the end of it right where he was going to get in. When he unlocked the door and opened it, I slammed it right into his face. He flew back and fell down. I unlocked the door next to me and ran as fast as I could into the gas station. I screamed the whole way. I just wanted people to help me so he couldn't get me back into the SUV."

Andie looked up. Jameson's cheeks were stained with tears. "As soon as I ran through the door of the gas station, I found a lady who looked nice and I just hugged her. Some people ran up to me and asked me what had happened, and I was crying and laughing at the same time, and I told them that someone had tried to take me and that he had hurt me and wanted to kill me but that I had gotten away. I think people believed me, because here it is winter, and I was just wearing my boxers, and they were all wet with blood. I think someone called the police because they came right away. And two men held the guy down until the police got there so he couldn't get away. It was pretty awesome, kind of like on TV."

There was no question. Jameson Harper's experience had been completely traumatic. But Andie felt just a little relief over an ending that could have otherwise gone so completely wrong. And from the way he looked, Jameson saw his rescue—the smart escape that he himself figured out and executed—as the only catharsis in the entire experience.

"Jameson, is there anything you might have forgotten? Anything he might have said that you haven't told me?"

"Um, no, I don't think so."

"From what he said and did, are you *sure* he intended to kill you? Or do you think he was just trying to scare you so you wouldn't attract attention—so he wouldn't get caught?"

Ms. Harper spun and stared in disbelief at Andie. "What? How on earth—You heard what my son said. How can you even *doubt* the intentions of that animal?"

Andie paced herself carefully to maintain calm. "What *I* think is not important, Ms. Harper. The critical thing is what *Jameson* thinks —how Jameson interpreted the experience then, and how he sees it now. If he is certain Brock Barlow intended to kill him, then that's what the court has to go with."

Ms. Harper fairly screamed, "Unbelievable! Whose side are you on, anyway?"

Andie involuntarily bit down hard on the inside of her cheek until she tasted the coppery, slightly salty flavor of blood. "I have listened carefully to Jameson, and I believe what he has told me. But it is my responsibility to represent Mr.—"

"*What?*" Ms. Harper leapt to her feet. "*You are defending the man who did this to my son?*"

"Ms. Harper, I apologize for any misunderstanding. When I called you and asked if I could speak with Jameson, I explained I'm the defense attorney in this case. I should have been clearer; I thought you understood what that meant. Didn't the prosecuting attorney explain to you who I was and what I was doing? He should have."

Ms. Harper was fuming. *"What? No! At least, I don't think he did. Maybe he did. But I've been so upset...defense...I thought you were defending* Jameson!" She grabbed Andie's coat off the arm of the couch and thrust it at her with such force that Andie had to struggle to stay on her feet. *"Get out of my house! Now! Or I will call the police!"*

Andie began to apologize again for any misunderstanding, but Ms. Harper was flapping behind her with such energy that Andie thought it best to get out as quickly as she could. Just as Andie reached the door, Ms. Harper lunged forward, grabbed the legal pad out of Andie's hand, and flung it far behind her. Andie dived for the pad and grabbed it before hurrying out the door. As she stepped onto the porch, Andie heard Ms. Harper slam and lock the door behind her.

Wanting to put some distance between her and Ms. Harper, Andie drove to the end of the street and turned the corner before easing to the curb and jamming her Honda into park. She rolled down the window and gulped cold air until her lungs burned with the effort. Her stomach lurched, and she was afraid she was going to vomit.

It wasn't Ms. Harper's rage that so sickened her, though that was difficult enough. It was the haunted look in Jameson's eyes—the slightest tremble of his lip, the way he fidgeted nervously as he pressed himself more tightly against the cushions. It was the way he spoke so deliberately, so slowly, fighting with every syllable to move away from the edge of a panic that threatened to pull him into a bottomless abyss. More than that, it was the fact that she was defending the man who had plucked him off an ordinary highway and brutally stolen every shred of innocence—a man who had danced a terrifying jig around a little boy, forcing him to confront the prospect that his own mortality was chillingly tenuous.

Her sobs took on a peculiar rhythm as she tried to imagine a frail boy—naked, chilled to the bone, pressed against the rough texture of the SUV carpet, searing pain punching like a hot poker and penetrating to the very core. Had he *really* known what was happening? Kids now knew so much more at such an earlier age. Would Beau have known? Would he have volunteered his life by climbing into that SUV, just because he was tired and cold and didn't want to bother her? An icy dread clutched at the center of Andie's heart. No, Beau died at his own hand instead in the spindly branches of a winter-worn tree, innocence intact. And he was gone. Forever gone. In his own way, so was Jameson Harper.

CHAPTER 5

"Listen, Sloan, I can't defend Brock Barlow. I had my reservations before, but I just interviewed Jameson Harper, and there's no way I can stand in that courtroom and launch a defense. The guy makes me sick. I really need you to drop Barlow and return his money."

"Look, Andie, I know the evidence is compelling—"

"You don't get it!" she nearly screamed. "It's not the evidence. Actually, it's not just *compelling*—it's *damning*, and there's no way to get past it. I don't think Brock Barlow has even the slimmest chance of beating this, no matter how good an attorney he has on his side. It's not that. I love a good challenge, and I'll put on the gloves and face almost any kind of fight. For me, it's the fact that he is the worst sort of monster imaginable. I know I've defended plenty of people who were guilty. I know that's my job. But this guy is a special sort of fiend, snatching an innocent kid off the side of the road to brutalize and kill. I cannot live with the thought of spending one more minute to make his situation any easier."

"Was the boy articulate?"

"Absolutely," Andie snapped. "But not just articulate. He was terrified. Haunted. Defeated. Faced with the sheer anguish of remembering something every single minute that he would give anything to forget. I'm sure the physical pain will eventually subside, but the emotional pain will tear him apart for years. He's wrecked, Sloan—he's wrecked, and now I'm trying to help the man who wrecked him. Your concern is that boy's viability as a witness. My concern is his viability as a human being, and I'm not sure how viable he is."

"You've taken on some pretty tough cases in the last couple of years, Andie, and you've done remarkably well. I dare say, in fact, that's how Brock Barlow 'knew' you. Word travels. I told you this before, and I'll tell you again—no one, not even Brock Barlow, expects you to get him off. Just make sure no one at any step in this process violates his rights. Make sure when he dons those prison blues that he's satisfied he was given every reasonable chance. That he can never get off on some stupid technicality."

"What about Jameson Harper's rights? I know Brady Young is going to give that kid every reasonable chance, but maybe *I* can't reconcile giving Barlow *any* chances." Andie's eyes burned with the effort of holding back tears.

"Come on, Andie. No one said this case is easy, but you need to square up your shoulders and do your job. You know part of the victim compensation money will be used to make sure that kid gets all the therapy he needs to move past this."

"And how fair is it that a thirteen-year-old boy has to spend part of every week laboring with a therapist to 'get past' something that never should have happened? How fair is it that every time he closes his eyes he sees the face of a twisted psychopath who forced him to the back of an SUV and took something that can never be restored? How fair is it that every time he sits in class, every time he crawls into bed, every time the noise of the rest of the world stops, he hears a gravelly voice telling him he's about to die? There's nothing fair about this. And there's not enough money in the victim compensation fund to make this right, because the worst parts of it can't be fixed with money."

Sloan breathed out a heavy sigh. "You're right, of course. None of it's fair. But it's what we signed up for when we chose this profession. We both knew we'd sometimes have to defend—help—people we were fairly certain were guilty. Even people we *knew* were guilty. Even monsters. You've done it before, and so have I. I like it a lot more when I'm on the prosecuting side, believe me—or when I get a real chance to help someone who is legitimately innocent."

Sloan paused, but when Andie didn't respond, he continued. "I'd much rather be in Brady Young's shoes right now, and I'm sure you would too. But everyone—even a creep like Brock Barlow—has the right to defense counsel and a fair trial heard by a jury of his peers. Unfortunately, Brock wants you. I can't change that fact. Neither can you. Even if Barlow continues to demand that you represent him, we *could* petition the judge to release you from the case based on the assault at the jail, and you might have a decent chance of that happening. But I'm going to ask that you do your utmost to follow this one through."

"How much did he pay, Sloan?" The question hung heavy in air already charged by more emotion than Andie had experienced since Beau's death. Sloan's eyes met hers. "How much, Sloan?"

"Fifty thousand. Cash."

"Up front?" Andie was shocked. "*A fifty-thousand-dollar retainer?* What on earth does this guy do?"

Sloan's laugh was bitter. "Oh, I'm pretty sure the money's dirty. I don't know...drugs, gambling, human slavery...the sky's the limit. Happily, it's not my job to ask him where the money came from."

Andie shook her head. "I feel like a prostitute, Sloan. Like a two-bit whore who was just plucked off the corner at the bottom of Main Street. Because I *really* don't want to do this. No one in his right mind would want to do this. But wave enough cash in front of the firm, and I'm forced to abandon all sense of reason and logic. I *hate* this. *Hate it.*"

Sloan's voice softened. "What's *really* going on here, Andie?"

"*Seriously?* I think I've been pretty clear about how I'm extending a helping hand to a guy who brutalized and terrorized a little boy—an innocent, relatively helpless little boy—and I don't like it."

"I don't think that's all of it, Andie." Sloan met her eyes, and she glimpsed something. Sympathy? Pity? "I think it's Beau. I think you see Beau in that boy whose innocence was ripped to shreds, and I think it hurts you at a level so deep you don't even realize it."

Suddenly her tough exterior ripped in half and the torrent broke loose. Andie turned away, covering her eyes with her trembling hand. The rawness of the emotion startled her. She clutched at the arm of her chair and sunk into it heavily. She was vaguely aware of Sloan's hand on her shoulder.

"I'm so sorry, Andie." His voice was almost a whisper.

"It *could have been* Beau—Beau, or someone just like him. And even though it wasn't Beau, I'm just like Ms. Harper—helpless to stop the carnage. Where was I that day...the day Beau looped that rope around the tree and soared beyond my grasp forever? Ms. Harper was home, probably fixing dinner, peeling potatoes or braising a chicken breast, totally unaware that her son was being kidnapped and raped and was in danger of his very life. Never a clue. And where was I? Here, without a clue that a piece of my heart was being snatched from my chest and cast off where I'd never find it. I was standing in a courtroom defending a criminal when my son drew in his last ragged breath. How do I live with *that?*"

ANDIE'S HEAD throbbed with a dull ache brought on by too much crying. Her raw eyes were swollen. Her nose dripped. How long ago had Sloan walked out of the office? How long had she been crying? How long had it been since she had faced the obvious—that she was a Ms. Harper, that Jameson was a Beau...only Jameson had somehow, by sheer force of will, escaped. Gotten away. Beau had gotten away too...his way. And Andie had been permanently and irrevocably left behind to wonder what on earth drove him to commit such violence against himself.

CHAPTER
6

*B*eau. How on earth could she have landed a case that brought Beau into every corner of her thoughts?

Her mind moved across the miles and the years—as easily as a long yawn—to a shabby two-bedroom apartment in Omaha. She was five months pregnant, poring over university texts between classes during the day and waiting tables at a busy truck stop four evenings a week. It was the only job she could find that let her work around her class schedule. Her feet and ankles were already swollen and her back constantly ached. Truckers who noticed her budding belly beneath the tacky brown uniform were generous with tips. Maybe they felt sorry for her, having to be on her feet through a six-hour shift. Or maybe she reminded them of the wives and children who remained at home, faces pressed against the window in the rhythm of waiting.

She and Colin Harrison had been married not quite a year. By the book, that meant they were still newlyweds. Honeymooners. Colin was finishing his degree and juggling an internship at an accounting firm. He worked hard. He played even harder. Sometimes he surprised her in those first few months with flowers for no reason at all. Now and then they dropped everything for a spontaneous weekend road trip. He was handsome. Romantic. Someone to grow old with.

Not quite half a year—half a carefree, delicious year—into their marriage, Andie learned she was pregnant. She was elated. He seemed the same. It was definitely sooner than they had planned, but they had talked about children. They would simply need to make adjustments and modify plans.

Andie found herself daydreaming about names. Searching baby shops for furniture and clothing.

Colin seemed to be daydreaming, too. And then he became a little distant—not as interested in her, in how she felt, in what she thought, in how things were going at work. Andie couldn't quite put her finger on it, but she vowed to figure it out after. After the baby came.

One night, almost into her sixth month of pregnancy, Andie's back was so sore and tight that dispensing plates of hash browns and scrambled eggs and balancing steaming mugs of coffee became sheer agony. Even after she gobbled a few Tylenol, the deep ache didn't let up. Just two hours into her shift she punched out, tossed her soiled apron in the hamper, and limped out to her car at the edge of the well-lit parking lot. Maybe she and Colin could just relax. Talk. Maybe even laugh. Start to warm up the cold spot between them.

She quietly let herself into the darkened living room, where she had expected to see Colin situated at the desk, studying. A groan drifted from the bedroom. Was he sick? Andie rushed down the hall and to the bedroom to find Colin in bed with a dark-haired woman from his study group. A woman with glistening, ebony eyes. Andie remembered the first time she had seen the woman on campus— remembered thinking how beautiful she was.

She stood paralyzed at the threshold of the bedroom, her heart pounding in her throat. Finally catching a glimpse of her, Colin pushed his friend—Jenny, was it?—away and clutched the dusky rose sheets with both fists, tucking them firmly against his chin. His friend let out a moan and buried her face in the pillow. Her rounded buttocks were exposed by Colin's frenetic efforts to cover himself.

"Uh, look, Andie," Colin started.

"Don't. Don't say another word, you son of a bitch," she said, amazed at her ability to utter a single sound. Amazed at her own spare, emotionless tone. "I want you out. Tonight. Gone. Don't come back here. Ever again. I mean it." She placed one hand in the hollow of her back, pressing against the aching muscles. She ran the other over her swollen belly, caressing the life inside. "We will be just *fine*."

She stood like that—one hand pressed into her aching back, the other comforting the baby she didn't yet know—until the silence became suffocating.

"Look, Andie, can we just talk about this?" Colin was sitting up now but kept himself swathed in sheets. The woman in the bed inched toward Colin, trying to cover herself.

"No. I have nothing to say," Andie said. "And I don't want to listen to anything *you* have to say. I think you've said it all."

The woman in the bed cursed repeatedly into the pillow, making it hard to tell who her words were aimed at. The only thing visible now was the back of her head, her hair tousled. "And you," Andie directed to the tousled hair, "I don't want to ever see *you* again, either. Please put on your clothes and get out of here. Get out of my bed. Now."

Colin suddenly narrowed his eyes. "Are you just going to *stand* there?" he shouted. "At least go back in the living room so she can get dressed!"

Andie spun around in the doorway, the rubber sole of her waitress shoe squeaking against the threshold. "I'll be back in an hour," she said. "I want you both gone when I get back. And take all your stuff with you because you're not welcome to come back. Not ever. I mean it."

Grabbing her purse, she lunged through the front door and into the cold air. She started the car, jammed it into reverse, and stomped on the gas pedal. The squealing of the tires unleashed her pain.

She drove the few blocks to the highway, then eased into the slow lane. They had only one car. What would Colin do? Her chest heaved and her lungs burned from the screams that erupted from her raw throat. *Stop caring about Colin! He certainly doesn't care about you.*

Her head pounded. Where would she go? She knew she

couldn't sleep in that bed again. How many times had Colin lay there, sucked into a whirlpool of passion with someone other than her? She despaired of ever searing the image from her mind. She couldn't go back to the shabby two-bedroom apartment on West Dodge Road—couldn't risk a chance encounter with even the smell of him. That left only one place to go. She stopped at a gas station, topped off the tank, and headed for Minden, a stone's throw from Kearney and halfway to the Colorado border. To her mother's white clapboard house, situated on a lonesome road surrounded by grain fields.

Thirty-five miles down the road, she stopped at another gas station. Pumping quarters into the pay phone, she punched in her mother's number. Four ring tones drifted through the mild crackle of static that mimicked the chaos in her mind.

"Hello?" Her mother sounded somehow older. Somehow sadder. Somehow more beat up from keeping up all the pretenses she created to look good to *everyone*.

"Mom, it's me." Suddenly the tears started. "Something awful has happened. I'm on my way there. I need to stay with you for a while."

"This might not be the best time, Andrea," her mother drawled. "Lillian's boy was just injured in a silo accident, and she needs me to help her right now. We were just having pie."

Andie's throat felt like it was closing off, and she started to hiccup. "Mom, I'm sorry about Lillian, but *I* need you, too. I walked in on Colin in bed with someone. He betrayed me in the worst possible way. I can't stay there anymore."

Andie could almost hear the palpable silence that followed a muffled gasp—could see in her mind's eye her mother grabbing for a chair as her legs collapsed beneath her. Could see the startled expression on Lillian's face as she forked another piece of jumbleberry pie, wondering what was happening. Andie heard her voice. "Nora," Lillian ventured in the background, a bite of pie probably staining the corner of her mouth, "whatever is the matter?"

"Oh, dear," her mother whispered into the phone. "I think it's best that we not say anything about this to anyone. It's no one's business but ours."

Still concerned about appearances. Still smarting, no doubt, from her own failed marriage.

Back in the car, Andie cranked up the radio to fend off exhaustion and contemplated taking another couple of Tylenol. Instead, she thought about Colin. About her father. She'd seen all the television talk shows in which women were berated for choosing men who were just like their own dysfunctional fathers. The thought made Andie laugh out loud—the first time that night she had found humor in her situation. *That's certainly not the case here,* Andie thought.

My father left before I turned two. Went to buy a pack of smokes. Never came back. Just drifted out across the Nebraska plains, like a hapless tumbleweed. Never to be heard from again. I don't even know *what he was like.*

Suddenly her laughter turned bitter. *What was he like? What did he look like? Why couldn't I have known him? Why couldn't he have been part of my life—read me stories, pushed me on the swing, let me ride with him on a tractor? What* happened *to him? How does someone just disappear?* A filament of disjointed thoughts flooded her mind. He was gone, but it was as though he had never been there. No more than a gossamer strand drifting on the breeze.

Andie gently caressed her belly again, thinking about the baby who floated warm and serene, innocent in a cushion of amniotic fluid, unaware of the world just inches outside his safe cocoon. *I grew up without a father, and now you will, too.* The thought generated a stabbing pain. It was not what she had planned—not for her, and not for this baby. Before the day he disappeared across the Nebraska plains, had her father held her? Rocked her? Sung to her? Nestled her into his lap while he read the paper or watched a football game?

After her husband vanished like blowing dust across the plains, Nora stayed in the white clapboard house on the lonesome road in Minden, trying to act nonchalant. Years later Andie would catch her lingering near the big picture window in the living room, gazing vacantly down the road. She was a survivor—Andie had to hand that much to her. She had taken in sewing, cleaned houses, found several waitress jobs in Kearney—had even done child care for a while. She had worked for years at a sewing factory. As a child, Andie had found peculiar comfort in picking stray threads off her mother's clothes, the threads Nora had missed as she left the factory each day. Nora had never remarried. Somehow, she had managed.

So would Andie.

The divorce was a breeze. Colin didn't contest it. In fact, Colin did exactly what Andie had asked: he disappeared. Andie still had a network of friends who would certainly know where he was, but she didn't want to know. The betrayal was too raw. Too fierce.

A few weeks after she arrived in Minden, Andie and Nora borrowed a pickup truck from a neighbor around the bend and went back to Omaha to collect Andie's things. There wasn't much. She asked a friend to sell the bed for her. She hauled the worn sofa out to the curb and tacked a sign to it that read *Free to a good home*. She gathered up dishes, pots and pans, and her clothing. There was just enough room in the back of the truck for the kitchen table and chairs and the sturdy wooden desk. Two men in the upstairs apartment helped wrestle it into the truck. She didn't remember ever having talked to them. She was glad they didn't ask about Colin. They probably already knew.

With efficient dispatch, Andie gathered a few things Colin had left behind into a plastic garbage bag and deposited them in the dumpster out back. After settling with her landlord and arranging to take the final exams for her classes at the university's satellite campus in Kearney, she and Nora hit the road. Andie never looked back.

Andie kept her clothes in the house, but she hauled the cardboard boxes filled with the rest of her things into the ramshackle garage behind the house. She was actually surprised it still stood— and she figured a stiff wind could take it out any day. Using a rusty shovel to clear away a tangle of cobwebs, she stacked her boxes against the wall. Her contribution to the building's structural integrity. They were the last vestiges of a life she left behind in Omaha.

A life she left behind forever.

Nora was a woman of ferocious routine. Monday mornings, laundry—hung on the line with wooden clothespins—left to flap in the stiff breeze when weather permitted. Every Thursday, a trip in to Kearney with Alta King and Carole James: lunch at the Souper Salad Buffet, and Bingo at the local church. Every other afternoon, her favorite daytime soap operas—Nora in her brown nubby recliner sporting a stack of sugar cookies with a tall glass of diet cola, complete with a brightly colored straw, the kind that bent. Having someone else in the house, *especially* someone about to give birth, disrupted the routines. Nora was nervous.

Living in her mother's house, sleeping in the sagging single bed of her childhood, Andie waited. The days dragged. With each passing day, she imagined herself growing a little larger, her lips becoming a little fuller, her hair a little thicker. All the while she tried to stay out of her mother's way. Whenever a friend or neighbor dropped by, Nora fluttered, fanning herself with anxiety—and Andie hauled herself up the stairs, flopping onto the bed and switching on the archaic metal fan. Most of the time the racket made by the fan drowned out any conversation from downstairs. Undoubtedly a blessing.

Every few days, Nora tried to get Andie to see the error of her ways. Her lectures always began the same way, as though someone had deposited a quarter and wound her up.

"I had to raise you without a father," she would always begin, bleating ever so slightly as though to stir up sympathy. "It wasn't easy, Andrea. In fact, it was awful. I didn't have a minute to myself. When I think of the hours I spent at those industrial machines, putting in zippers for *other* little girls, I just want to cry. I don't know how I did it." *And did you ever stop to think how* I *did it?* Andie wondered.

Here there would be a pause for dramatic effect. Nora would

shake her head slowly, dabbing at the corners of her eyes with a tissue or a paper napkin, or, lacking anything better, the collar or bodice of whatever she was wearing. After the first few times, Andie entertained herself by watching for the anticipated moves—listening to the well-worn phrases.

"Now, I know Colin betrayed you," Nora continued, shaking her head a little more vehemently. "And I know you think you're better off without him. That's just...why, that's just ridiculous, Andrea." More dabbing of the eyes. "I just think you ought to consider long and hard before you take on the responsibility of raising a child by yourself. I know the divorce is final, but it's never too late to go back. To change your mind. To get *him* back. You'll see. And Lord knows *I'm* too old to start raising babies again."

About that point, Nora would usually run out of steam.

And about that point, Andie would just look at her mother—searching her face for any sign of common sense. Not finding any, Andie would generally drift out the back door and sit in the shade in the old turquoise metal lawn chair she remembered from her childhood. Closing her eyes, she would focus on the chirping of crickets and the throaty song of a blackbird and the humming engine of a tractor two fields over.

On a sweltering July afternoon four months after she arrived at Nora's house, Andie heard the first wails of the boy-child that was lifted from her incised abdomen. "Oh, this one's going to make a dandy beau for some lucky lady," the aging nurse cooed as she laid the squirming, red-faced infant on Andie's chest. *Beau.* That was it. His lips suckled, and his fists waved frantically. Aimlessly.

As she gazed deeply into his eyes—the color of the sky just before a summer storm—an intense love overwhelmed her. Stroking his damp hair, she whispered to him. "We're going to be just fine, Beau. Just fine."

Minutes later, the nurse took him to be bathed. Andie glanced around the room. "Could someone please find my mother?"

After Beau's birth, Andie decided to take a little time to get her feet under her again. "A little time" became a few years. Without ever admitting it, Nora seemed to love the little boy with his thick mop of dark auburn hair. Andie once caught her laughing as she poked at the stubborn cowlicks that danced across his crown. But if Andie's presence had made Nora nervous, the arrival of an infant—who grew into a toddler—seemed to send her into apoplexy.

Beau's toys obstructed Nora's usual pathways through the house. There was so much *laundry*. The neighbor's dog, catching a whiff of the soiled diapers in the large metal garbage can out back, tipped the can over and spread shreds of disgust all over the lawn one impossibly hot day. The safety gate Andie put at the bottom of the stairs left marks on the wall. And there always seemed to be dirty bottles on the kitchen counter, small traces of curdled milk lingering in the bottom.

As Beau celebrated his second birthday under the sizzling sun at the Minden Fourth of July bash, Andie decided it was time. Time to resume her life. Time to get on with things. Time to let Nora return to the peace of her blessed routines.

Andie hoped for the slightest word of protest—regret, maybe—from Nora. None came. Nora left a box of plastic garbage bags outside Andie's door on her way in to Kearney with Alta and Carole to play Bingo.

So Andie enrolled at the University of Nebraska at Kearney, garnering a scholarship and working with determination toward her history degree. Three years later she enrolled at the University of Nebraska Law School in Lincoln, where she graduated with honors. She settled into her first day of law school an hour after dropping Beau off at his first day of kindergarten. He was surrounded by fat crayons, wide-lined paper, and white paste in the red brick school building—while she juggled thick textbooks and complex legal briefs in the law school corridors. Andie posted colorful finger paintings on the refrigerator door the same afternoon she published her first article in the law school review.

She might have stayed in Nebraska forever.

But she didn't.

And that—next to marrying Colin—may have been her biggest mistake.

CHAPTER 7

Inexplicably, it seemed that Brock Barlow's case was almost jettisoned. The prosecution filed an unprecedented number of requests for discovery, even though there was no way they could fail to nail Barlow to the wall. Andie focused on making sure that all of Barlow's rights were protected. With a few days before she was needed again, Andie took a break.

She took a week off—drove with Grace to Jackson Hole, where she settled on a bench and gazed at the rugged Tetons for hours at a time, wrapped in a scratchy Indian blanket. Once back home, she bought the biggest caramel apple in the glass case at Rocky Mountain Chocolate Factory—the one drizzled with chocolate and studded with walnuts—and savored it with her favorite video. She baked two loaves of moist pumpkin bread, which she nibbled on instead of cooking real meals. And she repainted Beau's room a light, creamy color. The box springs and mattress stood stark and bare in the center of the room, stripped of all bedding—but all this time later, she still hadn't packed up his things.

Then, too soon, it was time to go back to work.

At the end of the morning briefing, Sloan stood. The associates scattered. Phones started ringing. Andie picked up her briefcase and moved toward the door. The thought of picking up Brock Barlow's case again sickened her. Before she reached the door, her eyes met Sloan's.

"You're going to be fine," Sloan said, patting her on the shoulder. "You'll handle this. When I asked you to come and work with me in Park City after our association in Omaha, I knew I was getting one hell of a great attorney. I have all the faith in the world in you."

"I know that, and I appreciate it, Sloan. I know I can handle it. No question. I just wish I wasn't filled with such horror over what happened to the victim."

Before she went to her office, she stopped halfway down the hall, leaning against the doorframe of Jack's office. Unaware of her, he stood with his back to the door, tucking files into a yawning drawer with practiced efficiency. Mumbling under his breath, he dispensed each folder. Not until he slammed the drawer shut and spun around did he see Andie, looking somehow smaller. A smile washed easily across his face.

"Hey."

"Hey, yourself. I'm so glad you're back. And I know you're dying to find out what happened to the grocery store bandit."

"Actually, that's *exactly* why I'm here. I want *that* case back right now. It's just—uh, disturbing enough in a really comical way to get me jump-started again before I face Mr. Barlow. Yup. Me and the grocery store bandit. We're thick as...thieves." They both laughed.

Jack opened the drawer, fished out the file, and passed it to Andie. "I guess you'll be happy to know that yours truly did nothing at all on it while you were gone."

Smiling as she nodded, Andie tucked the file under her arm. "I still don't understand how someone gets all dressed up in a three-piece suit, *with Italian leather loafers, for crying out loud,* fills his basket to overflowing with groceries, tucks it all away in his own personal stash of plastic bags, and then calmly walks out of the store to load it all into his SUV. What goes on in some people's minds?" She laughed despite herself.

"Yeah, I don't care what you say—there's a definite blush on the bloom of public defender work."

"Indeed there is." Andie turned to leave, but Jack gently caught her arm.

"Listen, Andie, I know this Barlow case is testing you to the limits. A lot of people would have run the other direction. And if you ever need a distraction, my offer still stands. Maybe now more than ever."

The corners of Andie's mouth turned upward, almost imperceptibly. "You know I haven't changed my mind," she said quietly. "I don't date anyone here. Never have. Never will. It was the first thing they taught us in Lincoln—never mix business and pleasure. So, although your offer is certainly tempting, I'm afraid I simply can't take you up on it."

Jack squeezed her arm gently before releasing his hold. "Andie, it doesn't have to be a *date*. If you just ever need someone to talk to... I'll even let you pay for your own drinks. Look at me as one of the great clichés—a listening ear. A shoulder to cry on. No strings attached. I promise."

His face was a pleasant surprise, just like the splash of wildflowers in the meadows beyond town. Unexpected. There, just around the bend. Tucked in among the tall, unremarkable grasses. A spot of glad respite in an otherwise uneven landscape. He was handsome, no denying it. In another place, another lifetime... She smiled. "I know, Jack, and I appreciate it. I do. It's just—"

Jack pressed an index finger against his lips. "Don't," he whispered. "It's okay. Enough said."

Oh, but it wasn't, she thought as she rounded the corner to her office. Instead of turning on the light, she tilted the wooden slats of the blinds to let in the morning light, then collapsed into her chair. The buttery soft leather felt good against her bare arms, and she ran her fingers across the dark polished surface of her desk. What she couldn't tell Jack—what she could scarcely tell herself—was that every time she considered getting out there, the vision of Colin bobbing around under her grandmother's patchwork quilt with the delicate-featured woman from his study group seared through her thoughts with distorting speed. *Trust issues,* Nora called them.

Of course, Nora hadn't been there that night, perched on the threshold of the bedroom they shared, watching her marriage shatter and fall in shards around her feet. Nora hadn't stood there in the paralyzing seconds before being discovered. Nora hadn't remained in the doorway, wanting to flee yet riveted by the scene before her—like staring at a fatal collision, noticing the small rivulets of blood from the crash victims.

Nora's threshold scene with her husband had been worlds away. Perhaps the sky had been overcast that day—a typical late spring morning in Nebraska, corn not yet planted in the neighboring fields, but furrows set nonetheless. Perhaps an intermittent breeze from the east had playfully tugged on the shirts Nora had pinned to the clothesline at the side of the house. She might have looked up long enough to study his back as he sauntered down the road for the last time, but just as likely she was consumed with scrubbing the kitchen floor for the third time that week. Chapped hands were a small toll to exact for the gleam of freshly waxed linoleum.

She must have wondered when he didn't come back. Had her wondering crept in slowly over a few hours? Or had it startled her against the waning light of the afternoon? Whenever it had happened, it had been solitary. Nora had been alone except for a dark-haired girl whose halting steps had kept her far away from the threshold, worlds removed from the drama that swirled against the horizon.

THE SHARP SLAP of a file against the polished desktop startled Andie away from the long-ago threshold in the Omaha apartment. "I've gotta tell you, Andie, this public defender gig is going to be the death of me," moaned Thom Andrews. Running his fingers through his hair, he continued, "You should see the collection of derelicts I've got to defend in the next month. I honestly did not know there were this many, uh...*misfits* in Summit County."

Most of the people in Park City who required the services of a public defender—the ones who couldn't pay for legal representation—came from the cluster of dilapidated mine houses, paint peeling from the old wood siding, thick bubbled glass in the windows, asphalt shingles patched with thick tarpaper. The original miners were long gone—most of their descendants, too. The remnants of their houses, many sagging on their foundations, changed hands frequently as twenty-somethings tired of full-time skiing and moved on to find their fortunes elsewhere.

Almost all the others who needed public defenders came from the tiny towns dotting the landscape of Summit County, not much more than wide spots in the road tucked into the canyons along the highway. Something about the sheltered hamlets seemed to attract an unrelenting stream of people who, for one reason or another, had gradually become unhinged. They were peppered among the solid old-timers who had coaxed veins of ore out of the hills and who had run the general stores.

They were the sorts who stockpiled munitions against the impending Armageddon, but who, because they were too suspicious to work for someone else, were driven to shoplift the basic necessities of life. Some, fearing Armageddon had already begun, wove down the narrow walkways of town every once in a while, brandishing a weapon and babbling incoherently. Uniformed sheriffs flipped coins for the chance to bring them in.

And running like a twisted thread among them all were the drug dealers who thought they'd never get caught "up in the hills" and the drunks who careened down the canyon roads after staying for the very last set in one of the bars on Main Street.

It was thankless work. A dozen firms in Park City took turns, dedicating part of their time serving as public defenders. A few weeks before Beau was found dangling from a tree, the assignment had fallen to Sloan Tate and his team of polished associates. Every attorney at the firm had to keep up with regular clients while taking on a handful of public defender cases; the state paid the firm a modest fee in return. But it was only for twelve months—and as Sloan always said, "You can *crawl* that far."

"So, what do you have there?" Andie asked, gesturing toward the pair of folders Thom had flung onto the desk.

"You're not gonna believe it, Andie, I promise you," he smiled, shaking his head.

"Try me."

"Close your eyes," Thom teased. "Now, picture it: tall, light brown skin, thick black hair..."

"Go on."

"Cream-colored suit, silk tie, Italian leather loafers..."

Andie's eyes flashed open. "You have *got* to be kidding!" she cried. "What's he done now?"

"Same thing, different places, upscale merchandise," Thom smirked. "Filled up a fancy shopping bag with electronics over at the outlet mall, then strutted right out of the store and into the parking lot. But get this: a week after he was bailed out of jail by a minister, he went into an art store on Main Street, swaddled a sculpture in bubble wrap while the proprietor was helping some tourists, and strolled out the front door like he didn't have a care in the world. He's got two new charges—but since he's your boy, Tate wants you to handle the whole thing. Kinda like a package deal, I guess."

"Unbelievable," Andie muttered. "I guess groceries got boring."

"Yeah, well, he's cooling his heels in jail," Thom replied. "Apparently the minister decided he wasn't a very good risk the third time around. At least he didn't skip town."

"That's what I like about you: always finding something positive in every situation."

"Hey, that's *church* money we're talking about," Thom chuckled. "Anyway, he's down at the jail, so he's a captive audience. He can meet with you just about any time. And the stuff he lifted is in the evidence vault at the sheriff's office. But look on the bright side: this time, none of it is perishable."

Andie wrinkled her nose. "I don't think the sheriff will *ever* forget the ungodly stench that slapped him in the face when he rolled in to work that Monday morning," she said, laughing. "Nineteen bags of groceries—including a respectable collection of meat—swathed in plastic and fermenting in the heat of the evidence room all weekend had to rival the roadkill he's always complaining about. I bet it virtually peeled paint."

"Yeah, I heard he tried to bribe the hazmat team to come and dispose of it." Thom grinned. "They didn't want anything to do with it. Then he called over here—demanded that we come and pick up the evidence so we could determine our strategy. I thought Tate was gonna burst a blood vessel laughing. He told the sheriff that the *prosecuting* team needed the evidence, not the *defense* team. Rumor has it he paid a couple of teenagers to get rid of the foulest bags—the ones that were slimy or foaming—and made them put the bags in a dumpster clear across town."

Thom shook his head as he stood and moved toward the door. "Anyway, Andie, he's all yours. Oughta be a riot."

A SHUDDER SKITTERED up Andie's spine as the interior door of the Summit County Jail clanged shut behind her. This was her least favorite part of her job: meeting with clients who were incarcerated, penned up in a world whose walls were splashed beige and whose concrete floors were spattered with unidentifiable stains. Following the guard through the first block of cells, Andie kept her head down as one inmate after another shouted obscene catcalls.

"I'm sorry, Ms. Harrison," the uniformed guard mumbled.

"It's not your fault," Andie responded. "I just hate being the entertainment *du jour* for these guys."

The young guard, still in his twenties, unlocked the door of the interview room and gestured toward a beige metal table surrounded by four beige metal chairs. An overhead light shone directly over the table. "Take a seat," he instructed. "I'll go get Mr. Hernandez."

As Andie walked toward the table, the guard shut and locked the door, then disappeared around the corner. As much as she detested being locked in, she was grateful for the impenetrable barrier of steel mesh that stood between her and the jail population. Andie opened her briefcase, pulled out the three files, and put them on the table next to her laptop. Just as she finished, the guard was back with David Hernandez.

"You've got an hour," he said, pulling the door closed behind the inmate. "There's someone in the hallway just outside if you need anything." The key turned in the lock.

Andie stood, smiled, and offered her hand to the man clad in the orange jumpsuit. "I'm Andrea Harrison, and the county has retained me as your defense attorney." Mr. Hernandez was slow to take her hand, but finally offered a reluctant handshake. Andie gestured toward one of the chairs, and they both sat down. Mr. Hernandez hung his head and kept his hands in his lap.

"Mr. Hernandez, it looks like there are three separate charges against you," Andie began, picking up the three files. "Since all three are for retail theft, the judge has agreed to hear all three charges at the same time. That's not the usual way they do things, but we petitioned him, and he agreed. Doing it this way will save a lot of time and a lot of hassle."

"And a lot of money," Mr. Hernandez muttered, without looking up.

"That, too," Andie acknowledged, "but the important thing is making sure that you get the fairest trial possible. My colleagues and I believe that having all the charges heard in the same session will be less damaging to you than having three separate trials. You'll get a single sentencing and only one fine, which will almost certainly be better for you than if you got three separate sentences and three separate fines. Are you okay with that?"

Mr. Hernandez shifted uncomfortably in his chair but continued staring at his hands. "Uh, yeah, I guess."

"Look, Mr. Hernandez, I'm here to help you," Andie said. "I can't do that effectively unless you'll talk to me. I need to know what happened, and—just as important—*why* it happened. Unless you help by talking to me, I can't do a good job defending you. And with the situation you're in, I'm your only advocate right now."

Slowly looking up, he finally made eye contact with her. "You can call me Dave," he said quietly. "I'm...I don't know what to say."

"Okay, Dave," Andie smiled. "Let's start out with some basics. It says here that you live in Marion—is that right?"

"Yeah, right now. We moved there from Kamas a couple of months ago."

"We? Do you have a family?"

"Yes. My wife, Miriam, and I have six children. The oldest is eleven; the youngest was born in January."

Andie tried to keep the surprise from registering on her face. She realized she had regarded this man as a bizarre loner, someone who wandered from one retail establishment to another, bagging up goods and sweeping out the door without paying for any of his purchases. It had never occurred to her that he was a husband—a father.

"So you say you just moved to Marion from Kamas," she said. "How long did you live in Kamas?"

"Just a few months," he said. Andie noticed the muscles in his taut cheeks ripple as he clenched his jaw. "We came to Kamas from New Mexico. Had a job offer from a rancher up there. Got here, and moved into a little place near his ranch, then found out he was a cheat. Didn't want to hire me after all."

"Had you signed anything?" Andie asked. "Did he give you any written offer of employment?"

The man's head dropped again. He hesitated a minute before answering. "No. My brother told me I was a fool. Told me I shouldn't come. Said I was an idiot to drag my wife and kids up here for something like this. But I didn't know what else to do. I had been cleaning up some tailings from a mine in New Mexico, and we were done. A bunch of us got laid off. I couldn't find anything else. I took a chance. It turned out my brother was right after all."

"What happened then?"

"I looked around for something else but couldn't find anything. We couldn't pay the rent on the house where we were in Kamas. A guy we met right after we came here has been really good to us. He offered to let us stay in his mother's old place in Marion. It's small— two bedrooms—and run-down, but I've been making some repairs on it in exchange for rent, and we're grateful for a place to stay."

"So you're not working now?"

"I have a part-time job at a gas station here in Park City. It barely covers the gas it takes to get here from home. I'm still looking for something full-time, but haven't been able to find anything."

Andie realized she had been absentmindedly tapping a pencil against the cold metal of the table. This wasn't at all what she had expected to find. She remembered all the laughs she and her colleagues had enjoyed at this man's expense—assuming he was one of the oddities who often inhabited the solitary hills.

"Dave, I'm so sorry you're in this kind of situation," Andie said sincerely. "I think I can figure out what happened at the grocery store."

He nodded slowly. "We didn't meet all the requirements for food stamps," he explained. "They said if Miriam left me, and it was just her and the kids, they'd qualify. But with me in the family, we couldn't get any kind of help. We've relied on the kindness of others far too long. It just got to be too much. After work one night, I just couldn't take it anymore. I got dressed up to look respectable. I went in one store and got a bunch of grocery bags—nobody asked me why. Then I went in Albertson's and got the groceries. But my family didn't even get them. I got arrested, and came here, and I guess they took the groceries back to the store."

Andie's heart sank. *No, they didn't. They logged the groceries into evidence and stacked the bags up in the evidence room all weekend, where the fresh meat and vegetables proceeded to spoil. The whole slimy mess ended up in a dumpster at the far end of town.* Six innocent children never got their fill.

"I'm sure you know it doesn't matter *why* you stole the food—what you did was still against the law," Andie explained. "And you don't strike me as being stupid. You know that. But I want to find a way to help the court understand the circumstances and see if there might be some lenience in the situation.

"So, I understand the food," she continued. "Your family was hungry. But—what about the electronics? And the sculpture? What happened there?"

Down went the head again. "We have expenses," Dave explained quietly. "Two of our children need to see a doctor. I didn't have the nerve to rob a bank. I figured I could sell the electronics."

"Okay, that makes some sense," Andie said. "But what about the sculpture? Surely you weren't planning on selling *that*."

"No. It was my mother's birthday. I couldn't let her know what's happened to us—how bad everything is. She loves Native American art. I just wanted to surprise her for her birthday."

Andie's eyes locked on to those of David Hernandez. "Dave, you've got a bail hearing Thursday morning. To be honest, I'm not sure how good your chances are. You were released on your own recognizance after the grocery store situation, but then you offended again. I understand that a minister in Park City posted your bail after the electronics store theft, but then you offended a third time. He's not willing to put up any more money, and let's just say the court is feeling fairly skeptical about your willingness to stay out of trouble."

For the first time, the man took his hands out of his lap and placed them on the table, fingers interlocked, almost in a posture of prayer. "What do you think will happen, then?"

"I'm betting the court is going to impose the maximum bail it can for this kind of offense. But I'm going to argue to have you released on your own recognizance again. If you can guarantee you'll stay out of trouble, I'm going to argue that your family needs you working—

bringing in an income, regardless of how small it is. I'm also going to ask that you be assigned a counselor from the county who can help you and your family get qualified for whatever aid you're entitled to. I know the county has programs that can help. Let's see what we can line up."

"Yeah?" he asked, the expression on his face brightening. "Oh, ma'am, that would mean so much to us."

"Just until you get back on your feet," cautioned Andie. "And it won't be an easy sell. You've got to do your part. The judge has to believe that you acted out of desperation because you were down on your luck, and that normally you are a model, law-abiding citizen— and that you *want* to go back to that kind of life."

"I am. I do!"

"All right. Your bail hearing is scheduled Thursday morning at eleven. I'll present your situation and plead for leniency. You make sure you can give some solid guarantees to the judge."

"I will," he smiled. "And, ma'am, thank you. Thank you very much."

CHAPTER 8

Back at her office, Andie had barely settled into her chair before Jack catapulted, wide-eyed, through the door.

"Oh, man, Andie!" He seemed to skid to a stop as he made eye contact with her. "Is this a bad time?"

"No, it's okay. I've just finished interviewing the grocery store bandit and am trying to work up the nerve to tackle the horror of Brock Barlow—of defending a really awful man."

"You don't know the half of it! The exculpatory information I just received will blow you away. And you will *not* believe what happened. Damn!"

Jack had her full attention. Her senses were acute. "Try me."

Jack slapped a sheaf of faxed pages on the desk. "Our man Barlow has been a busy boy—and let's just say he gets around. They printed him when they booked him the other day, of course—just like they do everyone who checks into the gray-bar hotel. Well, once his fingerprints were in the system—attached to a *name,* that is—all hell broke loose."

Andie snatched the papers off the desk. The top page was a cover fax from a sheriff in North Carolina who had matched Barlow's recent fingerprints to a stone-cold case almost a decade old. A rash of cases, actually. The perpetrator had left behind fingerprints at some of the crime scenes—along with a variety of DNA evidence in every case—but without any existing prints or DNA in the system, the detectives investigating the cases had nowhere to go. And so the cardboard boxes of evidence and the dog-eared files had ended up in a storage room in the basement, stacked precariously on the shelves with the other unsolved cases. Until now. Until Brock Barlow's fingerprints got put into the system.

Andie stared, slack-jawed, at Jack.

"So Brady called this sheriff the minute the fax arrived. Seems the sheriff has had some personal interest in the cases there, and he routinely searches more than 70 million prints in IAFIS on the second Tuesday of every month. It was the same every time. Nothing. No match to any known set of fingerprints. No name. Then this morning, jackpot! One of the prints in the criminal database was Barlow's, and it was a perfect match to the ones the perpetrator left behind in North Carolina."

Andie's thoughts raced as she took in shallow breaths. Ragged, uneven breaths. "Do I even dare ask what happens now?"

"The sheriff in North Carolina, who has now filed charges against Barlow, wants DNA samples and wants to get them into CODIS. In a handful of this guy's cases, there were no prints, but plenty of DNA—hair, saliva, semen. If the sheriff can match the prints where they exist and the DNA evidence in all the cases, especially the ones without prints, he wants to extradite Barlow to North Carolina to stand trial for various degrees of assault and sodomy against about a dozen kids. Oh, and two murders."

"What about the blood on the end of the skateboard?" Andie asked. "There should have been plenty of that to get a sample."

"Unfortunately, it was compromised—contaminated. It was all mixed up with soil and contaminants from the snow, and even junk that was on the concrete where it fell to the ground at the gas station. And by the time they tried to get a semen sample from Brock's victim, he had vomited and had a bowel movement at the hospital. Any possible DNA sample was so compromised that Brady figures it wouldn't hold up in court."

Andie's heart felt like it might stop. "So I'm assuming someone is down at the jail collecting DNA."

"Barlow is screaming bloody murder, claiming the collection of DNA evidence violates his rights, since no one has made any *mention* of DNA evidence in our case here and since we don't really need it with all the witnesses they have. He's determined he shouldn't have to cooperate. Obviously, he realizes he left behind plenty of evidence in North Carolina that no one has yet been able to match it to him—and the minute his cheek is swabbed, he loses that precious anonymity. And, quite frankly, he'll be hosed. Jameson Harper and the drama down at the Sinclair will be the very least of a whole lot of really gnarly problems for him."

Andie leafed through the rest of the pages attached to the sheriff's cover letter.

"Those are the details of the cases," Jack explained. "You can read them if you want to, but I wouldn't if I were you. Lots of nightmares in that little stack of faxes. In fact, if I were you, I'd pray my heart out that the DNA evidence gets entered right away, because that means the sheriff will extradite Barlow as quickly as he can manage. You can wash your hands of the whole thing and go back to defending minor thugs and small-time drug dealers and careless thieves. You'll never have to give Barlow another thought—big fat retainer and all."

"Oh, that I should be so lucky."

A red-headed clerk from the front office appeared in the doorway. "Andie, you're wanted down at the jail. Some guys from the forensics lab are there trying to swab Brock Barlow, and he says it's a violation of his rights. Won't let them near him until his attorney is present. Even threatened to bite one of them. He's pretty agitated, and they're almost ready to sedate him. Someone at the jail asked if you could get down there right away—and right on the heels of that call, Brady Young called and asked the same thing."

Andie met Jack's gaze. "Can you please go? I can't face him yet—not after my interview with Jameson Harper."

"I'll go *with* you, Andie, but I can't go *instead of* you. There's a huge retainer on the line demanding that *you* show up. This time and every time. Every time Brock Barlow wants you—even if it's just to see what you're wearing—you have to go. I know there's no rule about that, but with the size of retainer he paid, it's reasonable for him to expect *your* attention and services—not mine—whenever he wants them. It sucks, I know."

"No, I don't think you do."

"Why don't you let me drive you over? You look like you could use a break."

"That would be nice. I don't ever want to be alone with him again."

"You wouldn't be alone. There are guards and the forensics guys and Brady and—"

"But I'm the one there to make sure he's getting a fair shake. And I just don't want to be alone with *that*. I can't stand it, Jack. I know this goes against everything I learned for three years in Lincoln and everything I've stood for ever since, but if it were up to me, I'd lock him up and throw away the key. To hell with a trial. And I felt that way *before* I found out about North Carolina. North Carolina just makes the whole thing that much worse."

Jack approached the desk and held out his hand to help Andie out of her chair. "You know I've got your back here. I'll move mountains to make sure you're never alone with him."

Andie slipped her hand into his and stood before gathering the faxed papers into a neat pile and tucking them into the top drawer. Her eyes met his before they left the office. He was right—he *always* had her back. It was something she had taken for granted far too often.

ANDIE AND JACK heard Brock well before they saw him. It was clear he wasn't alone—the voices of at least three or four other men punctuated the air between Brock's wild rants.

The interrogation room looked like the scene of a disaster. Brock was restrained in a metal chair, his feet manacled to the legs of the chair and his hands cuffed to its arms. Cloth restraints—they looked oddly like her mother's dish towels—had been tied at his elbows to more securely tether his arms to the chair. Sometime before Andie got there, he had thrown his weight against the back of the chair so it tipped up on two legs against the wall. The chair looked like it might tip over.

There was a small metal table between Brock and two uniformed officers from the forensics team; they had likely pushed the table against him in an effort to protect themselves. One was rubbing his forearm distractedly—Brock had probably grabbed him. Maybe bitten him. The contents of a couple of DNA kits were strewn across the table, and what looked like a third was scattered on the floor.

Two jail guards stood near the uniformed forensics men, and it looked like a third was crouching too close to Brock for his comfort. And in the corner—the far corner—Brady Young shifted his weight nervously from one foot to another. Most of the color had drained out of his face. As soon as he saw Andie, he slipped his cell phone into his pocket and crossed to the door.

"Thanks for coming," he said. "Your client doesn't think he should have to provide his DNA and has refused to cooperate without his attorney present."

"Damn right!" Barlow screamed. Ropelike blood vessels stood out on his neck, his face deep red and his eyes filled with rage. The front of his orange jumpsuit was wet. Blood seeped through the bandages on his nose from his injury at the Sinclair. "This is a violation of my rights! I don't *have* to provide my DNA to you or anyone else!"

"I'm afraid you do, Mr. Barlow." Brady stayed next to Andie and spoke in a firm but controlled voice. "We received a subpoena, and we are required to comply. By law, you must give us a sample of your DNA. No one is going to hurt you; we don't need to draw any blood. We simply swab a Q-tip along the inside of your cheek. It's simple and fast and completely painless."

"And it violates my rights!" Barlow exploded.

"No, Mr. Barlow, that's incorrect. You still have certain rights, among them the right to a fair trial, but we have rights as a prosecution team as well. And one of those rights is to gather the evidence we need to conduct that trial, just as your attorney has the right to examine what we gather."

"Shut up!" Barlow thrust himself forward as much as he was able against the restraints. The chair skidded away from the wall, and Barlow tried scooting it forward with only his weight. His teeth were clenched. The guard who was nearest Barlow immediately stood up and squeezed Barlow's shoulder.

"Easy there," the guard commanded. "You've been warned. Like it or not, you've got to cooperate."

"Or *what?*"

"Or I'll call for medical staff, and they'll sedate you," the guard continued evenly. "So you've got a choice—you can let these guys swipe your cheek, or you can let someone plunge a needle into your neck. I promise, it'll hurt. Bad. Either way, they're gonna get what they came for. So you can do it the easy way, or you can do it the hard way. Up to you."

For just a glimmer of a moment, Barlow actually looked scared—but the vulnerability vanished as quickly as it appeared. "Fine. But I want to talk to my attorney first. Alone."

The forensics team stepped back, and Andie searched Jack's face. "I'm afraid that won't be possible, Mr. Barlow." Jack took a step toward Brock. "The last time you were in this room with Ms. Harrison, you assaulted her."

Barlow snorted. "Yeah—like I can even *move* right now." He tugged his arms against the restraints in a caricatured demonstration.

"He got a little abusive with Maxwell," one of the guards explained, pointing at the forensics officer who had been rubbing his arm, "so we upped the restraints. He won't be touching anyone."

"Do you feel okay about this?" Jack asked quietly. "Because if you don't, I'll tell him the only way he talks to you is if I'm in here with you."

"I'm not deaf," Barlow snarled. "Don't talk about me like I'm not here. She'll let me talk to her. She's not afraid of me."

"You're right, Mr. Barlow. I'm *not* afraid of you. But I don't like some of the choices you've been making. And I don't like that some of those choices affect me. So if you calm down and conduct yourself appropriately, then yes, you can talk to me alone."

"*Fine.*" Brock's voice seethed with belligerence, but he was out of options.

One of the forensics officers gathered up pieces of the DNA kits from the table and floor while the others in the room made their way into the hallway. Jack was the last to leave, just behind Brady. "Look, Andie, I'll be right outside—"

"*She's fine.*"

"I'm fine. I'll let you know when we've finished talking."

The door to the interrogation room clicked shut. Andie kept her distance, leaning against the wall opposite Brock Barlow. "You know, Mr. Barlow, I'm not very happy about the subpoena. I know we haven't had a chance to start working on your defense, and you and I haven't really had a chance to talk in much detail, but you can imagine I was blindsided to find out you have previously engaged in criminal conduct."

Barlow sat perfectly still. Head bowed, he stared at the floor. Silence filled the room. Through the metal door, Andie could hear Jack's muffled voice. Still Barlow sat quietly, head hung.

"Look—you wanted to talk to me. If you don't have anything to say, I'll invite the officers back in, and you can let them swab your cheek."

"Are they right? Do I *have* to give the sample?"

"I just got here, Mr. Barlow, so I haven't actually seen the subpoena from North Carolina. I will examine it carefully before I allow them to take the sample. But if they do indeed have a subpoena and if it has been properly signed and issued, then yes, you must provide the sample. It's required by law."

"North Carolina?"

"Apparently so. It seems the sheriff there believes, based on fingerprints, that you were involved in the sexual assaults of some boys in his jurisdiction. In fact, he believes you are the person who murdered two of them. He's got quite a collection of DNA evidence that was left behind by the perpetrator in those cases, and he's eager to find out if that's you. So what's the story, Mr. Barlow? *Was* it you?"

"I'm not saying it was, but what happens if it was me? What happens if I tell you it was me?"

"I'm your attorney, Mr. Barlow, and anything you tell me falls into the category of *privileged information.* That means I can't tell anyone. I can't tell Mr. Young and I can't tell the judge. Even though I can't share that information, it's critical for me to know so I can determine how to proceed in defending you. And I'll be honest, Mr. Barlow—it won't be an easy defense. I've already got an almost impossible job, considering the circumstances. Add to that a string of related offenses in another state that can be linked to you with fingerprints and DNA, and I have to be straightforward with you—I don't think you've got a prayer of avoiding prison time."

"So what would happen...if I told you it was me?" Barlow's voice grew smaller, and Andie thought she saw a glimmer of fear flicker in his eyes again.

"You need to understand something. Regardless of whether you tell me anything about your activities in North Carolina, Mr. Young is already aware of that possibility and is already fully cooperating with efforts to collect the necessary evidence. The sheriff there has pressed charges against you and has alerted Mr. Young, and he can move forward with or without any information you might provide. You need to understand, too, that if the DNA evidence is a match, you will be extradited to North Carolina to stand trial there."

"Does my retainer cover that?"

"Excuse me?"

"Will you be able to represent me in North Carolina?"

"No. I'm not licensed to practice law in the state of North Carolina. And even if I were, it would be impractical for me to do that. I know you paid a substantial retainer to secure me, but I'm sure my firm would refund part of that money to you so you could secure an attorney in North Carolina." Andie swallowed hard. That was *exactly* what she hoped would happen. With any luck, Brock Barlow, decked out in an orange jumpsuit, would be loaded on a plane with a couple of burly guards and she'd never see him again.

Barlow was silent again, but the vulnerability had vanished from his expression, leaving a hard edge of bitterness and hatred. His eyes locked on hers.

"Well, Mr. Barlow? Was it you?"

"I plead the Fifth."

Andie honestly couldn't blame him. He was backed into a corner —he'd unwittingly left pieces of himself tucked here and there along a horrifying trail of depravity in a state all the way across the country. And that was okay, as long as officials had no way of connecting those pieces to a living, breathing person. As long as the evidence remained nameless, he was safe. But with a simple swab of the cheek, all that was likely about to end. His admitting involvement to her really didn't make any difference at all in her ability to defend him, because there really wasn't any possibility of defense.

It startled Andie to realize she almost felt sorry for him. And it shamed her just a little to realize that she wanted his confession not because she wanted to better help him, but because she wanted to hear it from his own mouth. She wanted to hear him *admit* how despicable he was. And she wanted him *gone*. Extradited to another state, another defense attorney's nightmare. Off her radar forever.

Andie asked a guard to open the door. She pulled the door closed behind her before she spoke. Andie reached for Brady's clipboard, and he handed it over. The subpoena seemed to be in order. She looked up at Brady. "He's ready. He's not happy about it, but he finally realizes he doesn't have a choice. I don't think he's going to cause any more problems."

"Hey, I'm sorry I had to have you come down here, Andie. You have to know the DNA is going to sew this thing up. I don't think you're going to be able to do anything toward his defense if any kind of DNA match is made."

"Brady, let me make something completely clear here. I sat in the Harper living room and listened to Jameson Harper describe what happened to him that night at the hands of Brock Barlow. I'm here because Mr. Barlow threw an obscene amount of money at my firm as a retainer to secure my services, apparently because he's familiar with my work. I'm not happy to be here. Just so we're clear."

A faint smile crept across Brady Young's face. "I can't say that I blame you. I'd probably feel the same way myself."

"My sole objective is to make sure that Brock Barlow receives what is constitutionally due him. Period. I don't want any glimmer of a chance that he'll be let off down the road on some technicality. That's my only goal. I have explained to Mr. Barlow what the DNA sample means and what will likely happen once it is entered into CODIS. I'm satisfied that he understands the implications. I'm sure the forensics team would like to get back to work."

One of the guards stepped forward and unlocked the door. The group that had been huddling in the hall hesitantly entered the room and one of the forensics officers approached Barlow cautiously. A cotton swab protruded from the vial in his hand. "Sir, I need you to open your mouth as wide as you comfortably can. I'm going to wipe this swab against the inside of your cheek, which will gather saliva and some of the microscopic cells from the lining of your mouth. It shouldn't hurt at all."

Barlow narrowed his eyes and glared at the officer before finally opening his mouth. Throughout the procedure—which lasted only a few seconds—he glowered at Andie. There was no trace of the fleeting vulnerability she had glimpsed just minutes earlier. Barlow was once again steeped in arrogance and defiance.

The forensics officer snapped a cover over the swab and hastily scribbled Barlow's name on its label. Tucking the vial in his jacket pocket, he smiled briefly at Andie and nodded his thanks on his way out of the room. His partner followed close on his heels.

One of the guards untied the cloth restraints binding Barlow to the chair while the other unlocked the manacles and cuffs.

Apparently resigned to his circumstances, Barlow slowly stretched before allowing a guard to lead him quietly out of the room. As he passed Andie, he sneered.

Brady glanced at Andie, and she was sure she detected in him a feeling of real sympathy. "Thanks again for coming over. I think he just panicked, and I really didn't want them to have to sedate him. He wasn't expecting this, and obviously it's a major blow. Within the next week his DNA report is going to be in the hands of the sheriff in North Carolina, and I think your client is going to be facing some very serious charges."

"Obviously. Thanks for calling me; I think the sedation just would have messed up his mental state even more. I think you're right; I think he panicked. If he *is* their perpetrator, he's been out and about for almost a decade with no one able to link him to the crimes. I'm sure he was pretty secure about having beat the rap. This has to have been a big shock for him. And you know what shocks *me*? I almost feel a little sorry for him."

"Don't be shocked. I often feel just a little sorry for the people I prosecute. You have to wonder what happens to people. How does someone go from designer jeans and the latest in cell phones to an orange jumpsuit and a pair of handcuffs?"

IT WAS AFTER TWO A.M., but Andie couldn't shake Brady's question. *What had happened to Brock Barlow?* Burrowed under two patchwork quilts, Andie stared at the ceiling, trying to imagine Brock as a six-year-old boy, learning to ride his first bike; who pushed from behind, eventually letting go and cheering as Brock navigated the narrow sidewalk in North Carolina? She tried to envision an eight-year-old boy carefully making a Mother's Day card, using purple and yellow and green crayons to create a field of flowers across heavy construction paper. She tried to see him as a ten-year-old, tapping his pencil on the edge of his desk and watching his teacher write math problems on a dusty chalkboard. She tried to imagine him as a fourteen-year-old, already tall and lean, stealing his first kiss from the blue-eyed girl next door.

Where had it all gone wrong? And, even more terrifying, why had it picked Brock Barlow and not Beau or Brady Young or Sloan—or Andie herself? How unwittingly close to the edge were they? Were they all dancing perilously close to whatever evil had snatched Brock Barlow and turned him into a monster?

Andie's last thoughts as sleep overtook her—this night, as all other nights—were of Beau. She wasn't so sure about everyone else, including herself. Maybe it *would* grab them...maybe there was a reason depravity struck like it did, or maybe it just randomly selected its victims. Maybe it slithered along behind you most of your life and then struck, just like that, sinking in its poisonous fangs before you even saw it coming. But Beau...it would never get Beau. For the first time since the stooped birdwatcher saw Beau dangling from a tree that early spring afternoon, Andie felt a powerful sense of relief wash over her.

Beau was safe.

For the first time, she felt the unimaginable.

She was glad he was no longer subject to the trials and pain of this life, no longer vulnerable to whatever evil lurked nearby.

CHAPTER 9

For what seemed like the millionth time, Andie's mind took her back to that day almost a year ago. The day Beau left.

No one could determine the exact time of death.

He had talked to two girls at school that morning. He had been late. Agitated.

Sometime before school let out, he was spotted through binoculars by a geriatric birdwatcher. He hung limp from a tree at the fringe of a vacant lot. The rope he had looped around his neck—not much wider than wire—had cut into his neck, severing both the carotid artery and the jugular vein. As his body had plunged toward the damp earth, a brittle branch had pierced his chest.

His red t-shirt, boldly emblazoned with the single word *brave*, was soaked. Even his shoes were filled with blood.

That's what took him. Loss of blood. Not the hangman's noose.

Paramedics responding to the scene erected a ladder...cut the tangle of line that tethered him to the tree. He hadn't even tied it. It was thrown helter-skelter, skirting around the thickest limb, looped around his neck. Perhaps he thought he would fall all the way down, impeded only slightly by the thin black rope. As it was, his feet dangled only inches off the ground.

They tucked him into a black body bag and carried him away just before the throng of elementary school children came along the edge of that same vacant lot, clutching colorful backpacks, scurrying toward home and warm chocolate chip cookies.

It was the first day of spring. His mother's birthday.

AT THE MORTUARY the next day, Andrea Harrison sat, stunned and disbelieving, choosing a casket for her only child like she was perusing the pages of a Nordstrom catalog. There was something said about the funeral cortege. Mention of insurance. Queries about a cemetery lot. She hesitantly placed what she had written for the obituary on the glossy surface of the mahogany table, her fingers lingering at its edge, as though surrendering it signaled *her* final surrender. She slid it toward the funeral director.

A door opened, and someone wheeled in the table. Perched on its shiny metal surface, cold and still and partially covered by a white sheet, Beau looked peaceful. Eyes closed. Andie approached slowly, her gaze riveted on the deep wound that encircled his neck. The edges of flesh gaped wide, but no blood dribbled out. It was gone. Not as the result of the embalmer's art but spilled onto the ground beneath a towering tree whose bare branches scratched a cloudy gray sky.

She stared. Time stopped. She finally moved, slow as the opening of the intrepid sunflowers that once lined the fence of her childhood home in Nebraska. Her fingers fluttered against Beau's chest, circling the wound where the errant branch had impaled him. His flesh was cold, unyielding. Firm, like wax. She shuddered—partly from the cold that seeped into her own fingertips, partly from the horror of seeing the depth of rage that a person could exact upon himself. A person no older than thirteen.

The funeral director's hand rested softly on her shoulder. She turned, barely able to wrench her eyes away from the table. He clutched a large paper grocery sack, the top folded neatly over.

"His...effects," he said quietly, holding the bag out to her.

She took it. Opened it. Gazed mutely into its rank interior.

There was the red t-shirt. A braided leather belt. Levi jeans. A thin wallet a friend had given him. His white shoes. All soaked with blood. Dried now, and brown, rendering the fabric stiff and unyielding.

The bile rose in her throat, bitter...burning. She thrust the bag back at the funeral director.

"Do you cremate here?"

He nodded, folding the top of the paper sack back down.

"Please...the next time you...can you please just burn this?"

He nodded again, moving away, the sack held tightly against his side.

Her feet felt like lead and her knees threatened to buckle, but somehow, she bolted through the door into the crisp air outside. She stumbled toward her car and, leaning heavily against it, vomited onto the asphalt.

Returning from the mortuary, Andie eased slowly into her assigned parking space in the garage beneath her condo. Turning off the engine, she sat rigid in the seat, her hand clutching her set of keys. It was dusk, and the garage was dim and cool. She had spent the last hour—or had it been longer?—driving up and down the steep, narrow streets of Park City, alternating between stunned silence and heaving sobs. The ski resorts were still open, and moneyed tourists in Norwegian sweaters clogged the sidewalks, ducking in and out of the gift shops and specialty restaurants that lined both sides of the streets.

Momentarily stopped in a line of cars trapped behind a delivery truck, Andie had stared out the window in a state of disbelief. In the previous twenty-four hours, her heart had broken into a thousand pieces, like brittle clay under a potter's mallet. Her precious son—the one who just last week had mastered a grinding slalom course and who had come in second in the district geography contest—lay on a cold metal table, pale. Bloodless. Lifeless. Forever gone.

Just feet from her idling Honda, people went about their business as usual. A couple in front of the coffee house held hands, fingers laced; he laughed, tossing his head so that his shoulder-length brown hair caught pieces of sunlight. A trio of women emerged from an art studio, carrying small, framed pieces swaddled in bubble wrap. The mailman, a dark canvas bag slung over his shoulder, shouted a cheerful greeting to a man who stood on the corner, sipping steaming coffee from a narrow brown disposable cup.

The people became distorted, viewed through pools of tears that spilled onto Andie's cheeks. The traffic started to move, and she thrust the gear shift into second. Betrayed possibilities tumbled down, burying the pieces of her heart.

Beau would never cut high school classes to feel the wind in his hair as he crested a hill, his boots strapped to his snowboard.

He would never hold hands with his first love, fingers laced, laughter carried on the breeze.

He would never spend a carefree Saturday afternoon with friends, teetering on the edge of the steep curb along Main Street.

He would never hold the mittened hand of his chubby toddler or skillfully direct a surgeon's scalpel.

He would forever be in the seventh grade. Just discovering girls. Begging for a ride to the ski resort. Bargaining for privileges despite a riotously messy room. Eating too many French fries. Flashing that broad smile, punctuated with metal, as he rushed out the door.

He would forever be there, entombed beneath a simple granite marker in the stretch of cemetery along the highway that led to Park City's commercial district.

SHE WANTED to sit forever in her car that day, silent and anonymous in the darkened garage. But with dusk brought the bone-chilling cold that still fell over the mountains, even on the second day of spring. She shivered. Her toes, though insulated by woolen socks, ached from the cold. She glanced into the rearview mirror and was shocked by the red-rimmed eyes that gazed back at her, haunted.

The key slid effortlessly into the lock, and Andie involuntarily shuddered at the cold. Or was it the silence? She flipped on the light and adjusted the thermostat. The furnace growled, and warm air coursed from the vents. Plopped on the middle of the kitchen table was a collection of still-wrapped, beribboned boxes, intended for a birthday she hadn't felt like celebrating. Maybe she never would.

She ran a hot bath and sunk into the tub, the soothing water lapping at her chin. She desperately wanted to think of something else. *Anything* else. But the image of Beau's violated body, stretched out on that cold, metal table, was etched on the inside of her eyelids. Open or closed, it was the only vision that filled her mind.

Tomorrow, she was due back at the funeral home—this time, to dress the body. She was "lucky," the funeral director had whispered. Because the cause of death was obvious—suicide by hanging—there was no need for an autopsy. Beau's body would not be mutilated by the medical examiner's knife, not rippled and puckered by rows of metal staples, so she could dress him herself. Prepare him for burial. *This* was luck?

The phone rang. She heard it jangling on the rustic table beside her bed. She was too exhausted to pull herself out of the warmth of the tub. Four rings. Five. Six. She had turned off her answering machine late last night, right after calling her mother. *That* had gone well. Nora Carlson, afraid to fly, would need to check the train schedule. *It might take longer, but it would be safe. Safer than catapulting through the air in a rickety plane. After all, trains are solid. Dependable. How many times do you read about hundreds of people being killed in a train crash?*

Andie's attention had drifted from her mother's droning partway through the great transportation debate. She needed her mother. Now. Not three days from now. But, as always, it was all about Nora. Finally muttering her agreement, Andie had hung up. Had her mother even remembered to wish her a happy birthday?

Beau. What had happened? She had always thought Beau was

happy. Relatively carefree. Looking forward to a medical career. A family.

Maybe the transition to a new school had been too traumatic. Maybe they should have stayed in Nebraska. Maybe, despite his seemingly cheerful façade, he had longed too much for the windswept prairies and the slower pace of home. For the sunflowers that bloomed with wild abandon. For the tumble of friends who surrounded him there.

Maybe, despite his love of skiing, he had felt crowded by the towering mountain peaks. Crushed. Trapped.

Soaking in the warmth of the tub, she considered with swelling panic that perhaps she had made a mistake. A serious, irreversible mistake. Maybe more than one.

The water in the tub had cooled, and Andie realized she was actually chilled. Too many memories were crowded into three-plus decades of life. She grabbed a plush bath sheet and wrapped it almost twice around her tall, willowy frame. Out of habit, she found herself straining to hear whether Beau was playing a video game in his room.

The tears started so suddenly they startled her. Beau's room...she would eventually have to go in there. Sort through his things. Decide what to keep. Decide what to give away. The image of plowing through the things he would never again need filled her with a rising sense of panic.

It would have to wait.

She couldn't do it. Not now.

Pulling on a pair of pajamas, Andie filled a glass and washed down a sleeping pill her doctor had prescribed months earlier during a particularly tough time at work. She slipped between the sheets and turned off the lamp on her bedside table.

Despite the sleeping pill, a cacophony of thoughts crowded her head. Who would handle her cases at the law firm for the next week...weeks? What details did she need to jot down? She didn't know what kind of flowers to order for the funeral. What if no one came? Should she track down Colin? No. She hadn't heard from him since that night in Omaha. Beau was his son in every biological sense of the word but in none of the important ways. Sleep finally overtook her as she realized Colin didn't even know he had a son. No need to tell him now about a senseless death at the end of a thin black cord.

Andie slowly crawled out of sleep the next morning like a swimmer in the deep end, struggling to reach the surface. In the second before she could put a name on it, she frantically pushed away the dread of something having gone terribly wrong. It coursed through her like ragged lightning, striking first at her heart and then at her brain.

Beau.

Beau was dead.

Cold. Waxy. Antiseptic. Unfeeling.

And today, she needed to dress him for his funeral.

She pulled herself from bed and padded down the hall to his room. She stopped with one tentative foot inside his door. Her head throbbed. She quickly moved her foot back and clung to the door frame for support.

His blinds hadn't been closed since he had left for school that morning—the morning of the tree in the vacant lot. Shafts of bright sunlight danced across his floor, leaping over his bed and cascading across his dresser. Andie gazed intently, taking in the sight of the room in the same intense, deep way that she would inhale a profuse array of lilac blooms. Slowly. Completely. Nothing taken for granted. Nothing left to chance. Breathing it in as though it were her last chance—as though at the end of the breath, it would all vaporize. Forever.

A smile emerged through her throbbing head, and she saw Beau clutching a bucket and scampering across the sandy beach of Sanibel Island. It had been her reward to herself for passing the bar exam. Beau had been almost ten. He had been fascinated by the hundreds of alligators in the wildlife refuge and displayed no aversion to the beady eyes and prehistoric scales. But he had been even more excited about combing the beaches for shells.

The travel brochures hailed Sanibel as the best shelling in this half of the world. It had delivered on the promise. Beau had scored several handfuls of perfect smaller specimens, but they paled in comparison to a pair of pearly pink conch shells, each as big as the palm of his hand.

He had been landlocked all his life, but that wild week—tasting the salt in the air, dumping sand out of his shoes—had infused him with a love of the sea.

He was gone—maybe off to a sea of his own?—but that love still seeped from the very walls of his room.

Model ships were perched on the shelves among his books. An antique ship lantern, its brass now tarnished, dangled over his computer. On the dresser, in a place of honor, was a delicate sailboat in a bottle. Scattered around it were the shells he had gathered at Sanibel Island, carefully washed and buffed until they gleamed.

Just a month ago, between bites of cereal, Beau had considered his career. If his plans to be a surgeon fell through, he had told Andie, he would seriously consider being a ship's captain.

In his plunge from the tree, had Beau yearned to be like the sea? Powerful? Free? Carving out his own course, undeterred by mere branches?

Andie stepped into his room. She was surrounded by his treasures. The things he valued most. Yet none of them mattered to him now. Wherever he was, he had taken none of them with him. He had left them all behind, castoffs in a life he had also cast off.

Swallowing her sadness, she opened the closet and lifted his black suit into the daylight. It was tired. Worn. Not altogether unlike the way she felt. The hems on the pants were slightly frayed. The fabric at one elbow was becoming thin. A button on the jacket was missing. Slipping her hand into the pocket, its lining starting to ravel, she felt the round hardness of the missing button.

Where on earth had he worn it so often? She hadn't noticed its quiet descent toward shabbiness.

She couldn't bury Beau in this suit.

CHAPTER 10

Once Grace arrived, the two of them held Beau's suit, turning it over, surveying it from all angles.

"I think if you take it to the cleaners, it will look just fine," Grace said. "It's an expense you don't need right now. The funeral cost will be bad enough."

Andie knew Grace meant well, but maybe she hadn't noticed exactly how bad things were. "The hems are frayed."

"Andie, no one will *see* the hems. Only the top half of the casket will be open."

"And the elbows—look at how the wool is wearing thin on this one."

"Oh, Andie, no one will see the elbows, either."

"I can't, Gracie," Andie whispered. "I can't bury him in this suit. That might not make sense to you, but...I just can't."

"If it makes sense to you, it makes sense to me," Grace sighed, running her fingertips lightly over the lapel. "That's what best friends are for." After a brief pause, Grace spoke quietly. "Right now, I wish I had a child—just so I could know your pain."

Andie wished so too.

THE DRIVE down the canyon to Salt Lake City passed in a muffled daze. It was as though Andie pushed her way through the deep end of the pool, straining to see the filtered light that hovered above the surface. Grace had insisted on coming with Andie to buy the new suit, nearly forcing her way into the car. But Andie wanted to be alone. If she was quiet enough, she reasoned, there was a chance she might hear the echoes of Beau's laughter bursting out of the dark corners of her memory. It was a sound she wanted to grasp and cling to while she could still appreciate every nuance.

THE NORDSTROM SALESMAN was politely efficient, leading Andie to a rack of suits in Beau's size. He held up three or four suits for her approval. She returned only blank stares. He squeezed the suits back onto the crowded rod and turned to face her.

"Well, let's see," he said. "What's your son's coloring?"

"His hair is deep auburn," Andie replied, "and his eyes are dark gray-blue...the color of the sky when serious storm clouds are gathering. And...he has braces on his teeth."

The salesman smiled. "That's a good start," he assured her. "What's the suit going to be used for? Church? Or more formal occasions?"

Andie's heart plummeted. "Um...more formal occasions."

"Were you looking for something solid, or would you like some kind of pattern in the fabric?"

Andie swallowed hard, battling the emotions that rose precipitously. "I don't think it really matters," she said quietly.

The salesman pulled two suits from the rack—both black, one with a subtle pinstripe. "Do you think one of these would work?"

Andie looked at the two suits, picturing them on the cold, waxy form that used to be her son. She reached for the pinstriped suit. "This," she said, simply.

The salesman—Chase, his nametag said—laid the suit out over a display of folded shirts, smoothing the slacks. "This is one of our nicest suits," he boasted. "I'm sure your son will love it!"

He pulled a stiff, yellow tag out of his pocket. "Do you happen to know your son's inseam and sleeve length?"

"Oh...I, uh, don't."

"Hmm," the salesman said, his voice edged with the slightest tinge of frustration. "You'll have to bring him in, then. We'll have him try on the suit, and one of our tailors will chalk the measurements. We want to make sure it hangs properly."

Hangs. Just like Beau.

Andie stared for what seemed like an eternity. Stared—first at the suit, then at the salesman.

"Look, my son died day before yesterday," Andie finally blurted out, struggling to stay even. "I'm sorry. I didn't want to mention that. It's hard for me to say it. I'm here to buy a suit to bury him in. Maybe the inseam doesn't matter that much."

The salesman visibly blanched. "Oh...oh...I'm so sorry," he stammered.

Andie felt the cold tears slide down her cheeks. "Thank you," she said. "Can you just have the pants hemmed to...whatever? He was five foot six. And I need to come back and get it in an hour. I need it today."

"We can make it work," he assured her. He awkwardly grabbed the suit and hurried toward the cash register. Following him, Andie plucked a sage-green tie from a display rack and set it on the counter next to the suit. She realized later the salesman didn't charge her for the tie.

Andie sat in her car outside the funeral home. The new suit dangled from the hook above the back door. Next to her on the front seat was a small duffel bag filled with a new white shirt, still in the package, along with the sage-green tie, underwear, socks, and black oxford shoes.

It was all there.

All but Beau.

She trembled. *Don't lose it now. Not now. You've got a receiving line day after tomorrow, and the funeral the day after that. Then you'll have all the time in the world to lose it.* Her hand gripped the door handle.

The sky had grown overcast. She started the engine and kicked the heater up a notch against the familiar early-spring chill. Easing the car into gear, she drove slowly around the block. Twice. Three times. Pulling back into the parking lot, she turned the engine off and leaned forward, resting her forehead against the steering wheel.

This was it. The last time she'd be able to do anything for Beau. The last time they'd be together—just the two of them.

"We'll put on his underwear for you," the funeral director nearly purred, "and then we'll invite you into the room to dress him in the rest of his clothing." He took the duffel bag and the suit from Andie. "You take a seat out here," he said, gesturing to a small waiting area, "and I'll be out in a minute."

Andie lowered herself into an overstuffed love seat. The air was thick with the heavy fragrance of flowers. Two employees scuttled by, carrying wreaths and sprays into the next room, where a casket stood ready for a viewing. One glanced at her and smiled. The French doors opened, and the funeral director motioned to her.

"We're ready for you in here," he said.

Andie hesitantly walked into the room. This time there was no sheet partially covering Beau's body. He lay, clad only in the boxer shorts she had brought, atop the wheeled, metal table. So cold. So still. She knew this time that it would be there, but her eyes still riveted on the gaping wound that circled his neck.

"We haven't applied any of the makeup yet," the funeral director explained. "We don't want it to get smeared while he is being dressed. We'll take care of that later today. I think we'll be able to cover most of the blotches where blood vessels broke beneath the skin of his face from...the pressure...and he'll look very natural when you see him tomorrow night."

Natural?

This wasn't *natural.* This wasn't Beau, who never stopped moving. Never stopped smiling. Never stopped cracking a joke or asking her to quiz him on his geography questions.

The funeral director left the room, leaving just Andie and Beau. Andie stood and stared at his body. A tsunami of love pounded through her, threatening to slam her to the ground. The tears welled up and streamed down her cheeks with such force that it startled her. She reached into the duffel bag and pulled out the black socks, suddenly wanting this to be over.

She gathered up the sock and tried to slip it over the toes of his right foot. They were stiff and unyielding. His skin was even colder, waxier than she had remembered it from the day before. She shuddered as she pulled the sock on over his foot and ankle. A wave of nausea swept through her as she struggled to put on the other sock.

Taking the shirt out of its package, she unbuttoned it and reached for Beau's hand. His arm was stiff. Unbending.

She didn't want this to be her last memory of Beau.

She didn't want to wrestle with a rigid, cold shell of a boy just to dress it for a funeral.

Dropping the shirt on the polished floor next to the wheeled table, she fled out into the hallway. The funeral director approached immediately. He had obviously been lingering. Waiting.

"Is something wrong?" he asked. "Do you need help?"

"No. I don't need help. I just need *you* to do it."

He gave Andie the same smile he had undoubtedly given countless others—countless others who could not bear to touch the once-supple skin they had so often gathered into their arms. "We can take care of it, Ms. Harrison," he said.

As she went for the door, he reminded her, "Please be here half an hour early Friday evening. Just in case there are any last-minute details."

ANDIE STOPPED AT A CROWDED INTERSECTION. Nora Carlson stared vacantly out the car window. The sky had turned gray. A cold wind whipped and scattered the litter that had been carelessly dropped outside the train station. Nora clucked her tongue, barely audible above the sounds of the rush-hour traffic, and shook her head. Andie knew exactly what she was thinking. *Big cities. They are all the same.*

Lost in her own thoughts, Andie let out a little cry as a wad of grief tugged at her throat. Clutching her purse tightly with one hand, Nora reached over and patted Andie's leg, again and again, like it was a mound of yeasty bread dough. "I don't suppose that friend of yours —Grace, is it?—has been over to help?"

"Yes, Mom," Andie sighed. "She has. Quite a bit, actually."

"Then I guess there's nothing for *me* to do." Nora pursed her lips and stared out the window again.

What do you say about a suicide?

Driving across the city toward the mouth of the canyon, Andie wearied of the suffocating silence. "So, Mom, how was the train?"

"I should have gotten a sleeping berth," Nora complained. "It was twice the cost, but you know I can't sleep sitting up. Especially not with all those people. There was a woman with two children behind me," she grumbled. "I don't think she brought enough diapers. One of them, a little girl with tangled hair, kept kicking the back of my seat. Every time I dozed off, she did it again. Ragged clothes. Snotty noses. Smelled like they needed a bath."

Andie felt sorry for the woman. Traveling on a train with two small children, one in diapers...and Nora sitting in front of them. Not an enviable prospect.

"Trains used to have such nice dining cars," Nora continued, as though her only grandson had not just been found dangling from a tree. "Tablecloths. White. Nice silverware. Good food. Worth getting up out of your seat for. Not anymore! I felt like I was eating at the

Sno King Drive-In. They gave us *plastic utensils* at breakfast." The tone of disgust was unmistakable. "I didn't even go down for lunch. Just ate the granola bars I had in my purse."

"That was smart—taking granola bars in your purse."

"How much farther is it to your place? A condo, is it? I'm starving."

Andie remembered with a slight start that Nora had never visited her in Utah. Had never seen her home. Had never ridden through the steep canyon peppered heavily with evergreens. Had never driven to the top of the narrowest street in Park City, the curve where the old miners' houses still clung precariously to the side of the mountain.

"We can stop somewhere here in the city if you're hungry," Andie offered. "There are lots of good places."

"No fast food," Nora spat. "And nothing fancy. I just want some plain good cooking. Homestyle."

It was going to be a long three days.

It was dark by the time they pulled into the parking garage. Andie was weary from forced conversation about everything but Beau. How long will it be, she wondered, before Nora broaches *that* delicate topic?

Nora struggled out of the passenger side of the car while Andie wrestled her suitcase from the trunk. Nora had insisted that it be put in the trunk. "You never can trust people in big cities...someone might see it in the car and smash the windows out to get to it," she had babbled. *Not this suitcase,* Andie had thought. *This suitcase must have been flung from an aircraft carrier at the end of World War II. It must have stopped bouncing somewhere on the road to Minden. And that's where you must have picked it up, dusted it off, emptied it out, and carried it home.* It smelled like mothballs.

Nora clutched her purse tightly to her chest and glanced around at the lights in the garage. "I don't know how you dare park down here!" she whispered hoarsely, her eyes wide. "So poorly lighted! You could get attacked, Andrea! Robbed! Or worse."

Andie pointed to the tiny security camera just above them. "It's really very safe, Mom. There's a full-time security guard on the premises. He watches for any unusual activity. No one has ever had a problem."

"Well, you can't be too safe!" she hissed.

They climbed the stairs, Nora in the lead. Andie pulled the mothball-scented, tattered suitcase behind her. For all its hulking silhouette, the bag was deceptively light. Nora liked to pack light. Seeing her mother for the first time since coming to Utah, Andie realized she looked older than her fifty-eight years. Her gray hair was thinning. She hauled herself up the stairs breathlessly, pausing for a second on each one. Rounded and soft, she filled out the floral dress amply. She wore sensible shoes—always, sensible shoes.

Finally reaching the landing, she dramatically gripped the railing. "Good gravy!" she said, trying to catch her breath. "Don't they have an *elevator?*"

"They do, Mom. It's clear at the other end of the garage. I thought it would be faster and easier just to climb the stairs." When had her mother lost her balance and fallen down the slippery slope into old age? Puffing melodramatically and slapping her hand against her heaving chest, Nora leaned heavily into the railing.

Andie slipped her arm through her mother's and urged her forward. "Hang on, Mom; we're almost there."

ANDIE FLIPPED the lights on and checked the thermostat. She eased the lever up a few notches. Nora tended to get chilled.

"What on earth are these?" Nora asked, waving at the still-wrapped gifts on the kitchen table.

Unbelievable.

"Mom, Beau died on my birthday. I didn't feel like opening gifts."

"That was three days ago, Andrea," she sniffed. "You can't let clutter get out of control. Especially not in a place *this* small."

Andie swept up the boxes in one fluid motion and deposited them on the shelf in the coat closet. "There," she said. "No clutter."

Nora narrowed her eyes. "Don't you get smart with me, young lady," she said, setting her jaw. "I manage a spotless house. Something I see didn't rub off on you."

Anger slapped Andie with brutal force. It was the first time in three days she had felt anything other than profound sorrow. It almost felt good—a one-way ticket out of the sodden deep end of grief where she had become exhausted trying to claw her way to the surface.

What seemed like a million thoughts raced counterpoint through her weary mind. Nora's house was spotless because Nora herself was spotless—too afraid to get any smudges on the flat veneer she splashed onto her walls and her soul. Andie's house was just fine. Plenty big, and plenty clean. What Nora saw as *clutter* were interesting pieces of an interesting life, tokens of trips and people and places that Andie could hold in her hand. To remember. Nora had scarcely strayed out of the tight little radius around Minden, Nebraska. She didn't *have* anything to remember. No need for souvenirs.

Despite Andie's silent self-assurances, the sarcasm cut into her soul like salt being rubbed into an open wound. But Andie couldn't yell at Nora. She couldn't even *talk* to Nora—not about the important things, anyway. It wouldn't do any good. Nora had shut off her heart and locked up her soul that day thirty-five years ago...the day her husband left for a pack of smokes and never came back. Nora couldn't bring him back. And Andie *certainly* couldn't bring him back.

Nor could she change Nora.

Oh, if she could, she would fashion a mother who would scoop her up in her arms and ease away the hurt. Wipe away the tears.

Apply a Band-Aid to the worst of it. Instead, she had Nora. Nora, who—Andie had to admit—loved her in her own way.

Maybe Nora needed that same thing, something she had never gotten from her stern Methodist mother, a woman who had turned her back on Nora the day she married Drew Carlson. Had that severe, unsmiling woman seen something in Drew Carlson that Nora hadn't? Had she known that one day, only a couple of years into Nora's marriage, Drew would drift off across the barren Nebraska plains like so much windswept debris?

Nora had learned how to mother from Elizabeth Gray—not one given to mothering. Nora had grown up in Iowa in the shadow of a dashing, talented brother...until one early summer day, when, at the age of fifteen, he and two friends had dived into the rushing currents of an irrigation culvert. He had been pulled, bloated and lifeless, from a grate four miles downstream. At that very moment Elizabeth had withdrawn from life and had ensconced herself behind a solemn, unyielding face that rarely rippled. She and Nora, living under the same roof, had lost touch that day.

When Drew Carlson vanished, Nora was utterly alone. Her austere mother stayed in Iowa. Her distant father, Jonathan, faithfully tended after his Methodist flock but ignored his own daughter. As Andie rehearsed it all in her mind, she realized exactly why Nora felt pressed to make sarcastic comments. Why she was so dour. Why, as they stood at the table, now bereft of birthday gifts, she refused to deal with the obvious. *Beau was gone.*

Andie hurt. She wanted her mother to comfort her. But Andie couldn't battle generations of icy indifference. And so it was she determined simply to make it through the next three days—Nora and all.

Instead of engaging in combat, Andie ignored the remarks and set about preparing a simple meal and setting two places at the table.

The meal complete, she said simply, "Come on, Mom, it's getting late. Let's get to bed. We've got a tiring day tomorrow."

Andie led the way down the hall to Beau's room, where she had put clean sheets on the bed and a box of tissues on the bedside table next to a vintage pitcher brimming with daffodils. She had bought a few magazines she thought her mother would enjoy. They were fanned out on the bedside table as well. She had cleared out a dresser drawer and had pushed Beau's clothes to the end of the closet rod. In their place were half a dozen scented, padded hangers Andie had bought at a boutique on Main Street.

Andie walked quickly into the room, carrying her mother's suitcase. Nora remained behind, suddenly surveying the room and noticing the ships, the shells, the navy-blue border.

"Oh, no!" Nora exclaimed forcefully, staying in the hall like a mule that had dug in its hooves. The sudden outburst caught Andie off-guard. "I won't be sleeping in *there.*"

"Mom, I fixed it all up for you," Andie coaxed. "I know it's just a single bed, but I think you'll be very comfortable. And the bathroom is right next door."

"It's not *that,*" Nora said. "It's just that this is...I'm not going to sleep in..."

Andie set the suitcase down next to the bed and stared at her mother.

"I can't..." she stammered. Andie continued to stare.

"You know what I mean!" Nora snapped.

"What, Mom?" Andie ventured. "This is Beau's room, and Beau is dead, and you don't want to sleep in a dead person's room?"

"Oh, Andrea, that's not necessary!" she said. "Please don't talk like that! I just...don't think I'd be comfortable in here, that's all."

"Fine, Mom," Andie sighed. "You take *my* room, and I'll sleep in here. Wait a few minutes while I change the sheets for you."

Nora brusquely slammed the bathroom door, and within a minute Andie could hear the water running. She could visualize Nora, bent over the sink, scrubbing the dingy vestiges of the train trip from her face—then patting it dry and smoothing it with the pungent white Noxzema cream she had used for decades. Andie smiled. Every midnight crisis of her life—nightmares about monsters in the corn field, bad reactions to Tetanus shots, the frightening sound of bare tree branches scratching her window, stomach aches from eating green apples—had been infused with the drifting scent of Noxzema.

Andie stripped the jersey knit sheets from her bed and tucked the cotton rosebud ones around the corners of the mattress. Nora seemed unwilling to even form the words. Of giving rise to the horrible truth. *Beau was dead*—and it was the proverbial pink elephant in the room. Was the topic too sad? Too threatening? Too reminiscent of Drew Carlson vanishing without a trace? Maybe *he* was dead, too. Maybe he hadn't slipped away to assume another life with another woman and child. Maybe that day he lay rotting in the Nebraska sun in a ditch at the side of the road, clutching his smokes tightly in his rigid hand. Maybe that's why Nora pretended.

Andie set clean towels on the edge of the tub in the master bath, then tried to make space in her closet for Nora's things. She set the suitcase on the bed and grabbed her flannel pajamas from the dresser drawer. Walking past the bathroom in the hall—where the water was still running—she called through the door, "Okay, Mom, the bedroom's all ready for you. Sleep tight."

"I hope there are enough blankets on the bed," Nora shot back, turning off the water. "I'm freezing."

"There are two more on the shelf in the closet," Andie replied. "Help yourself." She left the light on in the hall and quietly shut Beau's door. Stepping slowly to the bed, she eased between the sheets. She could smell him. Without warning, the sobs propelled up her throat; she muffled her face in the pillow, not wanting to alarm Nora.

Oh, Beau. My beautiful boy.

CHAPTER 11

Beau's viewing was nice. The associates from the firm came, as did lots of kids from Beau's school. They seemed fearful. Confused. Several leaned shyly into a parent. Andie was amazed at their courage: many stood stiffly at the casket, tackling the situation head-on, surveying every inch of Beau's face. *For what? They're probably trying to figure out what happened. Why he sunk into this terrible choice. Just like I am still trying to figure it out.*

A few skirted by quickly, darting cautious glances from the corners of their eyes. A few others clung to friends, moving awkwardly in a group like clusters of grapes.

Some, like Nora, drifted around the perimeter of the room, avoiding the casket altogether.

The next morning, just before the funeral director closed the lid of the casket, Andie leaned over and kissed Beau on the forehead. Then she tucked the two pearly pink conch shells next to his arm and pressed his ratty old rabbit's foot between the fingers of his right hand. The talisman was soiled and the soft gray fur was starting to disintegrate. He'd had it since he was four, and he rarely went anywhere without it. He'd want it wherever he was going now.

Andie's fears about the funeral were unfounded. People *did* come, filling the chapel to capacity. She sat numbly through the program, vaguely aware of wet sniffles and muffled sobs echoing through the room. The casket was adorned with massive yellow sunflowers, their blooms as large as a dinner plate, mixed with purple irises and red roses. Curly willow branches jutted out of the arrangement like the tendrils of fireworks soaring skyward. *Soaring like Beau.*

As the funeral ended, the plaintive sound of a bagpipe punctuated the air outside the chapel doors. The notes seemed to hang there, mournfully suspended. Andie watched helplessly as eight of Beau's friends clutched the grips on the sides of the polished oak casket. Nora turned away and walked down the aisle, wringing her hands. Andie thought—imagined?—she saw a solitary tear dribbling down her mother's cheek.

THE NEXT DAY, Andie delivered Nora back to the train station in Salt Lake. Aside from a tantrum about not being able to get her favorite brand of sugar cookies, things had gone pretty smoothly— until they got into the car to drive to the train station.

The sound of Nora clearing her throat pinched the nerves in Andie's already throbbing head. "Now, I know I've tried to talk to you about this before, Andrea, and you just haven't listened. You're so *stubborn*. But now that you're...alone—"

"Mom," Andrea said, cutting Nora off abruptly. It was the well-practiced shtick again. Deposit the quarter, wind her up. "I won't start dating just because Beau died. I'll be just fine. I'm not afraid of being alone."

"I just think you should reconsider, Andrea. You're not getting any younger, and it's just going to get harder to find someone."

"Mom, do you *honestly* think that finding a man would fill the hole that Beau has left in my heart? That a man would *replace* Beau? Because he wouldn't. No one will. And that's an amazingly stupid reason to start dating. Actually, I think I *need* to be alone for a while."

"No, you don't, Andrea." Nora shifted under the confinement of the seat belt. "Nothing is easier alone."

Andie tightened her grip on the steering wheel.

"Did you try to find someone after my father left?" It was

desperately raw, something they had never talked about before. Andie realized they had never really talked about her father at all, how things were before *or* after he left. She deeply regretted that now. The silence was deafening. Andie saw from the corner of her eye that Nora stared out the window. Motionless.

"Well, did you?"

Still staring out the window, Nora mumbled so quietly Andie almost couldn't hear her. "That's none of your concern."

"It's every bit as much my concern as my dating is—"

"No, Andrea, it's not." The anger flared in Nora's voice, piercing through the silence like the quills of a porcupine poised to attack. "That was different. You have no right to talk about something you know nothing about."

"That's just it, Mom!" Andie cried in frustration. "I *don't* know anything about it! I was there. I may have been a baby—a child—but I was there. I lived it. You and I were under the same roof for two decades, and you *never once* took enough notice of me to even explain what was going on!"

"And I'm not going to now."

Andie's cheeks burned. Was she feeling rage? Confusion? Pain? She waited until she felt a hint of composure before she spoke again. Her voice was even, controlled.

"Mom, you got burned by my father. I don't care how you look at it—the fact is, you got burned. And you chose to stay single. I don't know why you did. Frankly, I don't really care any more. And I'm not saying I blame you. But can't you see that the same thing happened to *me?* No matter how you cut it, I got burned by Colin. I knew him for years. I thought I knew every single piece of him, inside out. Turns out, I didn't know him at all."

"Oh," Nora snapped. "So that's it. You have trust issues."

"Yes, Mom, I think I do. But *I'm* the one I don't trust. I don't know that I can make a decision that important again. But here's the bigger issue: I'm happy. Obviously, I'm sad beyond belief that my son died. And I'm sure I'll feel that way for a very long time. But I have an interesting life. A job that challenges me. Friends that provide diversity. I just don't feel that I need to be dating or married to have—"

"I don't believe it," Nora fairly snorted. "I do not believe that you can be happy all alone. You are fooling yourself, Andrea, and that's a dangerous thing to do."

"So, what are you saying, Mom? The whole time I was growing up—all the years since then—were you unhappy? Because from where I see things, you didn't get out there and try to get married again. I know there were rough spots here and there, but I always thought we were pretty happy."

"If you're saying you thought you filled my life, Andrea, you didn't." The words were a sharp slap across Andie's face. Nora pressed her lips tightly together, holding back years of...what? Resentment? Fury?

This time, it was Andie who stared out the window. A few minutes later, she turned on the radio. They rode the rest of the way in silence.

A few blocks from the train station, Nora insisted that Andie not park the car. She wanted out at the curb.

"Goodbye, Andrea," Nora said sharply as she pulled her suitcase from the back seat. "I hope you're not going back to work too soon. Those people at that law office can certainly get along without you for a few days." Then she slammed the car door.

Andie sat at the curb, her car idling, watching Nora lug the suitcase through the massive glass doors leading in to the train station. Walking with rigid determination, Nora never looked back.

"Goodbye, Mom," Andie said, quietly. "I love you."

ANDIE HAD BEREAVEMENT LEAVE, and she took some time away from the office—but one day she knew it was time to go back.

She was nervous. She wasn't sure she wouldn't wither under the piercing scrutiny of sympathy. Andie didn't know which was worse: the people who said nothing, acting like business as usual, or the ones who looked at her through thinly veiled pity, tears ready to spill. There would be both, she knew. Just thinking about it caused a thin bead of cold sweat to break out across her forehead.

It was a Tuesday. The day associates met to discuss the status of cases. She sat in her car behind the office building, looking at herself in the rearview mirror. Her stomach fluttered. Despite the makeup, she looked a little pale. Not distraught—just pale. Maybe a little fragile. Reapplying her lipstick, she pinched her cheeks hard, ran her fingers through her short-cropped hair, and grabbed her briefcase.

Just like the first time she finally pushed away from the terrifying high-dive at the city pool, Andie sliced through the air and catapulted with dizzying speed toward the surface of the associates' meeting. And now, just as then, she didn't drown. There were a few moments she thought she might, swirling through the chilly water, getting oriented, feeling just a few seconds of panic. But before she knew it, she'd found the surface again, filled her aching lungs with air, and known she could conquer anything.

CHAPTER 12

Andie remembered that feeling—the conviction she could conquer anything. Now, squared up against Brock Barlow, she wasn't sure. She shifted her weight to the other leg and leaned heavily against the wall outside Sloan's office. He'd left a quickly scribbled note on her desk asking her to come to his office, and now he was on the phone. Waiting, she realized how exhausted she was—how utterly worn to the bone. It struck her that she couldn't remember the last time she had eaten. Had it been lunch yesterday?

She couldn't remember the last time she had really slept, either... had enjoyed quenching, deep, renewing sleep instead of just tossing around on the bed. How was it possible to be so *exhausted* but not *sleepy?* As soon as she turned off the light and burrowed under the patchwork quilts each night it all started up with relentless force. Like a whirlwind gathering intensity and scooping up every small bit of debris in its path, her mind became a vortex that sucked up endless details in a set of arduous mental aerobics—Jameson Harper's battle-weary voice, Brock Barlow's cold eyes, DNA kits scattered across the room.

But that wasn't the worst of it. Those sounds and images sucked her mind into scenes she'd never even witnessed—a teenaged boy brutalized and battered and thrown into a heavily wooded area in North Carolina. Beau dangling from a tree. And from there her thoughts bridged the chasm of years and miles to her bedroom on West Dodge Road and her last glimpse of Colin. How tenaciously and nimbly the mind translated one set of horrors into another.

Sloan pulled his door open and gestured for Andie to sit down at the small conference table near the window. Sitting across from her, he slid a bottle of cold water toward her.

"Obviously, Brock Barlow has a significant problem. And that means *we* have a significant problem too."

"You mean North Carolina? Actually, I feel pretty relieved."

"Relieved?"

"If North Carolina succeeds in extraditing him, he's off my radar screen. I no longer have the repulsion of doing anything to help a man who has perpetrated the kind of horror for which he is responsible. He should be on a plane soon, and with any luck, I'll eventually forget the absolute mire he has dragged me through. I can stop having nightmares about him grabbing me and about what he did to Jameson Harper."

"Not so fast, Andie. I don't think it's going to work like that."

"Why not? Apparently, the DNA from the crime scenes in North Carolina was a match to Brock Barlow, and Brady Young told me the sheriff there is working on getting the motions in order to extradite Brock as soon as he can."

"What you're forgetting, Andie, is that as his counsel you need to do everything you can to delay or prevent his extradition."

"Wait! You told me just a few days ago that I didn't have to try to get Brock off! The only thing that has enabled me to endure this situation is your promise that I simply had to make sure his rights were protected."

"And working to delay or prevent his extradition is helping to protect his rights."

"How? They've got a pretty airtight case in North Carolina, and it's not because someone is trying to frame Brock or someone treated him unfairly. It's because he allegedly committed a series of heinous crimes, and while he has not yet been found guilty of those crimes, he left behind a trail of DNA that has now been matched to him in CODIS. I'm not understanding why he has a *right* to escape the consequences of that behavior. And I sure as hell don't understand why I have to help him do that."

"Andie, the minute Brock Barlow gets on a plane headed for North Carolina, we lose all control over him as our client and all ability to steer the direction of his defense. It's not really a case of you protecting him against consequences; it's more a matter of us maintaining the upper hand in what happens with the case here."

Andie felt the heat creep into her cheeks. "The retainer? Is that what's at stake here? Are you worried Brock will be sent off to North Carolina, and you'll have to refund a sizable portion of the retainer he paid you for my services?"

A palpable expression of anger washed over Sloan's face, leaving redness in its wake. "I resent that, Andie. I really do. You know that the firm desperately needed it, but this has nothing to do with money."

"Then what, Sloan? Because I'm having a hard time believing you are any more eager than I am to help a monster who not only sodomized and raped an innocent boy on the outskirts of Park City, but who apparently did the same thing in North Carolina—and succeeded in killing two of his victims."

"You know better than this, Andie. Doing your very best as an attorney doesn't hinge on your client's guilt or innocence. It means making every effort to the fullest extent allowed by law to give your client every fighting chance."

Andie sighed. "I know that, Sloan; thanks for the reminder."

"Don't you think Brock Barlow will fare better if he stands trial in Utah for sodomy and attempted homicide than if he is shipped off to North Carolina, where he will stand trial on two counts of murder?" Sloan asked. "I'm not talking about trying to get him off. I'm talking about doing what's best for him under the circumstances."

Andie took a slow breath and felt a measure of calm return. "Obviously. Of course."

"Then don't lose sight of that in your personal and very justified revulsion toward Brock Barlow. Look, I didn't get grabbed in an interrogation room by an unstable client. I didn't have to interview his victim and hear the remnants of terror in his voice. That's got to have been hideously difficult for you. And I can only imagine how it has haunted you. It will probably always haunt you. And it's easy to understand how the North Carolina revelations have only added fuel to the fire. I stand by my initial instruction: You don't have to get a jury of his peers to find Brock Barlow innocent. Just make sure that every protection under the law is afforded him—and keeping him in the state of Utah to face trial here on lesser charges is one of those protections afforded by law."

Andie lowered her head and stared at her hands in her lap. Her voice became quiet, emptied of its previous indignation. "I don't know if I can, Sloan. I mean, I know *how* to do it, but I just don't think I *can.*"

"You can, Andie. I had a few I didn't think I could face, and somehow you learn how to manage it. I've told you about the Miller case. That's the one that haunts me to this day."

Andie remembered it vividly, as clearly as if she herself had been the defense attorney instead of being a student sitting in a stuffy classroom in Lincoln. Sloan had shared the details, the various aspects of the defense, in several of his classes. Evidence had piled up against a man who was never convicted of killing his missing wife, and he became desperate when it looked like he might lose custody of his three children. He killed them and himself in a murder-suicide. The details never got easier to hear, and Sloan wasn't the only one who had trouble forgetting.

"You did tell us about it, Sloan, in a couple of our classes at Lincoln. I'll never forget it. I wasn't even there, yet it gnaws at the pit of my stomach. How were you ever able to come to terms with it?"

"It was tough, Andie. The defendant in that case was never arrested in Nebraska in large part because of my determined efforts to make sure things were done right—to make sure he wasn't arrested for a murder when there was no body. Yes, his so-called alibi was pretty flimsy—downright fantastic—but the fact remained that his wife's body was never found. And without a body, he should not have been arrested for murder. Because who knows? Maybe she *did* have a lover, like he claimed, and maybe they *did* take off for Portugal, which he also claimed. Or maybe she got sick of his controlling and abusive behavior and managed to get away. It was my job as his counsel to make sure things were done by the book. So he was never incarcerated, thanks to me. And thanks in part to my efforts, he was free to move to Missouri and blow up his three innocent children after taking an ax to their necks. It's hard to move past something like that."

"That's where I'm left reeling, Sloan. You were all over that man's rights—the *system* was all over his rights. But it seems that no one was very determined to watch out for his children's rights. Sure, a caseworker finally came in at the end when custody was in question, but even that was a case of too little, too late. Obviously, even she couldn't protect them."

"Don't think I haven't spent my share of sleepless nights over it. To know that your well-intentioned efforts resulted in the death of an innocent human being, or in this case *three or four* innocent human beings, is a tough pill to swallow. But even with all the anguish and the second-guessing that hounded me the first few years after he killed himself and those kids, I still have to ask: Do I fail to protect every client I might suspect is guilty because one guy did an absolutely atrocious thing? Do I use him as a benchmark and constantly wait for the other shoe to fall with every client I take on? Or do I recognize him for what he was—the rare exception to the rule, the truly disturbed psychopath?"

"You have a point."

"You know Brady Young had a similar case, don't you?"

"No—he's never said anything to me about it."

"I don't think he says a lot about it, but it really shook him up. In fact, it determined the course of his career. He used to be a public defender—one of the best in Salt Lake County. He worked like a dog to help out a kid who had been arrested on drug charges not long after he turned eighteen. Brady felt like the kid had made a stupid mistake in a moment of irrational reasoning, so he pulled out all the stops to keep the kid from serving any jail time. He didn't want to see a kid's life permanently ruined over what he saw as a simple bad decision. Maybe a fleeting one. Brady did a great job; the kid got little more than a slap on the wrist."

"And?"

"And three or four weeks later, the same kid drove to St. George with a couple of his friends, robbed a convenience store, and put a bullet through the head of the clerk."

Andie clapped her hand over her mouth. "I had no idea."

"That would have been tragic enough under *any* circumstance, but it turns out the clerk had been born with a disfiguring birth defect that resulted in a misshapen face. A *grossly* misshapen face. In the year or so preceding his murder, a beautiful young woman had recognized his generosity and kindness and sense of humor. They were engaged and were planning a life together. Our eighteen-year-old drug abuser ended all that on an oppressively hot night in a convenience store.

"It devastated Brady. He felt responsible. He quit as a public defender the next day and vowed he'd never again work on the side of the accused. It took him a couple of months, but he landed his current job in the prosecuting attorney's office. His eventual goal is to become a judge—and to make sure that when someone is convicted, the sentence matches the seriousness of the crime."

"Well, I guess there's enough evidence against Brock that he won't be the source of *my* nightmares...probably won't ever taste freedom again."

"Not if you do your job, Andie. Not if you make sure that he's afforded every chance and given every right due him by law. Not if you make sure your case is practically flawless, so he can't get off down the road on a technicality. If you do all those things, I'm pretty sure they'll lock Brock Barlow up for a long, long time—maybe for the rest of his life. And you will sleep well at night because you were careful enough to make sure that happened. *That's* how I know you can do your job with Brock Barlow. *That's* how you survive this case."

"So my first step is to delay or stop the extradition to North Carolina."

"Yes. And this won't even go to court if you can persuade him to plead guilty. You're going to have to move quickly. Maybe you can work with Brady to come up with a somewhat reduced prison term if Barlow will agree to save the state the cost of a trial. You might even work to prevent the North Carolina cases from being introduced in court, which would garner a prison term based only on the crime he committed in the state of Utah."

"But if the North Carolina crimes were committed almost a decade before the crime he committed here, is there any way to delay extradition? Isn't North Carolina guaranteed the right to extradite under those circumstances?"

"No. Extradition isn't based solely on the date the crime was committed, if at all. Sometimes it's based on the severity of the crime, but not always. Once we've sentenced him here, North Carolina can extradite him, even if he hasn't yet served his sentence here. And they will, so fast your head will spin. But they can't extradite while a sentencing hearing is scheduled. Your job now is to get him in front of a judge, get him to plead guilty, and get a sentencing hearing on the books before North Carolina actually finishes the process to extradite. We *want* him sentenced here. And do it fast, Andie. You're up against the clock."

CHAPTER
13

As if she didn't have enough on her plate, Andie realized she was also up against the clock on David Hernandez. Situated back in her office, Andie filled out the necessary forms and made three copies of each, one for each of the Hernandez files. It *was* going to be a hard sell—no doubt about it. She had already asked for, and gotten, an exception by having all the charges heard as part of the same trial. Now she was asking for what the judge might consider an outrageous request. Hernandez had become somewhat of a laughingstock at the firm, and she couldn't imagine it was much different among court personnel. But even as she considered that, she could hear David's soft voice in her head, a voice tinged with embarrassment and defeat. Another of the old adages they taught in law school popped into her mind: things are rarely as they seem at first glance.

There's always more to the story.

Even as she rehearsed the sad facts surrounding the Hernandez history—even as it seemed she could see in her mind's eye a family of small children, hungry, crowded into a few ramshackle rooms, a husband and father swindled by a wealthy rancher—she couldn't get something else off her mind: his hands.

Eager to get her interview started, she hadn't noticed anything during that first handshake. But now, having heard his background, Andie realized his hands were oddly out of character. Closing her eyes, she tried to visualize them again, resting against the metal table, the fingers interlocked. They were smooth, soft—the color of coffee heavy with rich cream. There was not a callous on them, not a nick or a scrape, not even old scars. The cuticles were trimmed and pushed back, the nails short but filed neatly, with rounded edges. These weren't hands that cleaned up mine tailings. They certainly weren't hands that made repairs on an old house that had been neglected for decades.

She picked up the top file, opened to Mr. Hernandez's address, and scrawled it quickly on a Post-It note. Grabbing her briefcase, she headed out through the reception area.

"I'm following up on a hunch," Andie told the secretary. "I'll probably be gone a couple of hours, maybe longer. I don't expect any calls, but if one comes in, just take a message. See you."

Hurrying to her car, she bumped into Grace. "Hey, where are you going in such a hurry?"

"Gracie, remember that construction manager you dated for a while?" Grace nodded absently. "What were his hands like?"

"A mess!" Grace laughed. "The crazy thing is, he didn't do that much of the work, but he always had wounds. Cuts, scrapes, slivers, bruises—you name it. I'm not sure I ever saw him without at least one bandage on his hands. And they always felt like sandpaper! It was awful. I always made him use some of my lotion before I let him hold my hand."

"Thanks! That's just what I needed to hear!"

"So where are you going?" Grace called after her.

"Just checking something out—something a client's hands told me."

MARION WAS A SMALL, unincorporated town nestled among the towering pines and clusters of quaking aspens that made up the surrounding Wasatch-Cache National Forest. The only real traffic it got were cars on Highway 32 headed for Kamas or the remote camping areas of the Uinta Mountains. Andie turned down the volume of the CD and slowed to negotiate the turn onto Upper Loop

Road, just past the Kamas Valley Co-Op. Tucked against the narrow asphalt road was a sprawling cemetery dotted with a few pine trees, its crumbling tombstones peeking out of tall, yellowed grass. Half a mile ahead was 2100 North; she plucked the Post-It note off the visor of her Honda and checked the address again: 439 East 2100 North.

These homes were scarcely the run-down bungalows David Hernandez had described. Most were newly constructed log cabins or timber frame homes on one- or two-acre lots; Andie recognized the loop as a trendy area where people built recreational homes to escape the pressure-cooker atmosphere of the crowded cities along the Wasatch Front. It provided a relaxing, forested place where people could get away without investing hours in the journey.

Andie slowed to a crawl, craning her neck so she could see the house numbers. These were far too high. Had she missed it? She turned around on Lower Loop Road and drove the stretch of 2100 North again. She eased the car to a stop in the loose gravel on the shoulder of the road. There was no 439. Nothing even close.

David Hernandez had provided a false address.

Pulling back onto Highway 32, she drove the fifteen minutes to Kamas, parked outside the first corner store she saw, and pushed open the tinted glass door of The Grocery Girls. Leaning against the counter near the cash register was a woman about Andie's age wearing a dark-green tunic and a name badge.

"Hi, Karie," Andie smiled. "My name is Andrea Harrison; I'm an attorney in Park City, representing a client from this area. I'm wondering if you know of any large ranches in town."

"Sure. You're probably looking for the Blue Moon Ranch—they breed and raise alpacas up there. It's the only ranch in Kamas."

"You're positive it's the only one?" Andie asked. "My client mentioned he had a job lined up with a rancher here in Kamas."

"I'm positive. It's got to be Ed Heiner. He's been here since the late seventies. I don't know of any other ranchers who are still running active operations."

ANDIE EASED to a stop in the parking area adjacent to a large barn with *Blue Moon Ranch* painted in an arch above the double doors. Across a massive spread of what would be rolling lawns when summer arrived was a spacious log cabin; a small stream wound lazily through the grounds. Tucked against the foothills to the north were fenced pastures boasting several herds of gentle alpacas.

The barn seemed to be the center of operations, and Andie stepped through the large doorway. A friendly woman in a buffalo-checked shirt approached and offered her hand. "How may I help you? Are you in the market for an alpaca?"

"No," Andie smiled. "I'm Andrea Harrison, an attorney from Park City. I'm trying to verify some details provided to me by one of my clients. Is Ed Heiner around?"

"He's not here right now, but I'm his wife, Laurel. I run the ranch with him, so I can probably answer any of your questions. Who's your client?"

"David Hernandez," Andie said. "He claims he moved here from New Mexico on the promise of a job at a ranch in Kamas, but that the rancher refused to hire him once he got here."

Laurel Heiner looked genuinely puzzled. "I actually do all the paperwork for employees," she explained, "and I don't recall ever hearing that name. We're a small community—only about twelve hundred people—and we've got the only ranch around these parts. He'd have to be referring to us, but..."

"Is it possible your husband offered to hire him, but then changed his mind?"

"I can't imagine that," the woman said. "We've had the same three ranch hands for almost five years now, and we haven't considered expanding our operations. The only other people we hire are seasonal workers, and they're mostly kids from the high school. Ed has never mentioned someone from New Mexico. Was it recently?"

"Within the last three or four months," Andie answered.

"I'm certain it wasn't us, then. We do all our hiring for spring during the previous September. Then we have a couple of training sessions and give folks a chance to be around alpacas—you know, get comfortable—before the real work begins the end of March."

Andie shook her head slowly. "Thanks so much for your time," she said, shaking Laurel's hand again. "I'm afraid this gentleman has given us some inaccurate information."

Back at her office, Andie called a friend in the police department. Things were not looking good for David Hernandez.

THE NEXT MORNING Andie paced next to the same metal table in the same cramped interview room. As the inmate approached the door, Andie heard him grumble, "My court date isn't until tomorrow, so what's *she* doing here? I was winning an important card game."

As the guard ushered him through the door, Andie extended her hand, pumping it up and down in a firm handshake as she said, "Good morning, Mr. Martinez. Sorry to interrupt your card game, but it's truth or consequences time."

He jerked his hand out of hers, the color draining from his face; his eyes were wide, and his slackened jaw hung open. "I...don't know what you're talking about," he stammered.

"Have a seat, Miguel. Here are the things I know: your name isn't David Hernandez; it's Miguel Martinez. You don't live in Marion; in fact, you haven't had an address on record for the last year and a half. Seems you're somewhat of a drifter. You don't have a wife named Miriam, and you don't have six children—at least not the six children that you claim." The man grimaced slightly. "You didn't come to Utah from New Mexico, at least not to work on a ranch in Kamas. You see, the people at the Blue Moon Ranch have never heard of you."

"They're liars!" Martinez cried. "I told you. Liars and cheats.

They offered me a job, and when I got here, they refused to make good on the offer."

"Really?" Andie asked. "What's the name of the man who offered you the job?"

"Um, I don't remember right now."

"Well, then, what did they say they were hiring you to do?" Andie persisted.

"Cattle hand. Help herd cattle. That's what I did before I worked at the mine in New Mexico."

"I'm going to stop you now, because I don't want you to embarrass yourself any further. The man who owns the ranch is named Ed. And there isn't a cow on the place; they breed and raise alpacas."

Martinez fell silent.

"So, that's the truth. Now for the consequences. We entered your fingerprints in the system, and it seems you have quite a record. Quite a few aliases, too. It looks like you've done this same kind of thing in—let's see—was it four, or five other states? Only when you got caught there, you simply jumped bail and vanished. How come you hung around Park City for a second and third arrest? You liked the scenery too much to leave?"

Andie took a seat across the table from Martinez. He remained silent, so she did, too. Finally he looked at her. "If it makes you feel any better, you're not the first one who fell for the wife and kids story," he said with a sneer.

"Thanks," Andie said sarcastically. "Actually, what makes me feel good is that I *didn't* fall for it—not for long, anyway."

"What gave me away?"

Andie chuckled. "Your hands," she said. "A guy who cleans up mine tailings and works on ranches and repairs old, dilapidated houses doesn't have hands that look like they just emerged from a salon. My hands haven't looked that good since I left high school."

"Hmmm," he shot back. "Maybe you should think about taking

better care of them. I know a good manicurist right here in Park City."

Andie glowered at the man sitting across the table—a man whose demeanor had completely changed since the day before. "Well, despite the fact that I've uncovered your deception, I'm still your defense attorney. And that leaves both of us in a very difficult position."

"What did you do?" he cried. "Did you tell the county attorney?"

"No. I didn't have to. The police did. When we ran your fingerprints through the system, a dozen warrants for your arrest popped up. By law, the police were duty-bound to tell the county attorney that he had a wanted felon in custody. But that's not all, Miguel—they also reported your whereabouts to the agencies that issued the warrants. And with your experience in the criminal system, I'm sure you know what that means. People should be landing in Salt Lake City within a few hours, and they're very anxious to talk to you."

"So what are we going to do?"

"Simple," said Andie. "At your bail hearing tomorrow, the county attorney is going to waive his right to prosecute you in Summit County. Effectively, he's turning you over to one of the agencies that has existing warrants for your arrest. They'll fight it out to see who gets the first shot at you. You'll be extradited—because Utah *does* extradite—and you'll stand trial in one of those states. Your crimes here, at least the ones we *know* about, were just crimes against property. I'm guessing you'll be extradited to face either the assault charges or the attempted rape charge...Texas, wasn't it?"

"You're my attorney," Martinez growled. "Can't you do something to stop them?"

"I can't," Andie said in return. "I'll be there at your bail hearing. I'll make sure you are treated within the bounds the law has established and that no one takes unfair advantage of you. Other than that, Mr. Martinez, I'm afraid there isn't much I *can* do."

"Guard!" Martinez shouted. The key slid into the lock, and the uniformed guard took Martinez by the arm. "Get me outta here," he demanded.

"See you tomorrow," Andie called after him.

The guard who escorted her out of the secure part of the jail looked at Andie with concern. "I guess that didn't go too well, huh?"

"Oh, on the contrary," Andie smiled. "It went *very* well. Mr. Martinez is in for a rude awakening."

"Martinez?" the guard asked. "I thought his name was Hernandez."

"It's a long story."

In the months following Beau's death—those months that had dragged by with agonizing slowness—Andie often felt sluggish, as though she were swimming upstream, pushing against a powerful current. She had lost spring—hadn't noticed the first crocus pushing up through the snow, couldn't begin to imagine where the forsythia and violets had gone. Andie had drifted through summer, floated through autumn, and was slogging her way through winter when it finally occurred to her.

I need something to distract me. Something other than the horror of Brock Barlow. Something other than a string of atrocities in North Carolina.

She didn't necessarily have anything in mind. Couldn't really wrap her arms around a distraction big enough to do the trick.

And then the phone rang.

CHAPTER 14

Andie had just polished off a piece of vegetarian pizza and had settled in to watch a documentary Sloan recommended. One ring. Two. Andie pulled the quilt up to her chin to chase away the winter chill before reaching for the phone.

"Andrea?" The voice was unfamiliar, a little muffled through the slightest crackle of static.

"Yes?"

"This is Carole James, dear—your mother's friend."

"Oh, yes, Carole; I remember you. Is there something I can do for you?" Andie glanced at the clock; it was after ten in Nebraska.

"Andrea, I'm...so sorry. Your mother has passed away."

The next few seconds pounded recklessly against Andie's chest, knocking the wind out of her. "What? When?"

"Apparently sometime this morning, probably early." Carole sounded slightly uncertain. "Alta King and I stopped by to pick her up. We were going to Kearney to play Bingo. She was expecting us. When she didn't answer the door..." Carole's voice trailed off.

Andie struggled to catch her breath; it seemed like every cell in her body was trembling, misfiring, out of control. When Andie didn't respond, Carole tried to continue the account, putting one faltering word after another.

"Alta went around to the back door...and..." There was an odd hiccup.

"And?"

"Nora was in a heap on the floor by the kitchen table. We called paramedics, and they forced the door open. Your mother was already gone. Had probably been gone for several hours, they told us. I'm so sorry."

"What happened?" Panic swelled in Andie's chest until she felt it would burst, followed by waves of shock grabbing mercilessly at her mind. "Does anyone know what happened?"

"No one knows yet. The paramedics said it was probably a heart attack. It looks like she hit her head when she went down, though, and that may have been part of it, too. They've taken her to the medical examiner's office. They'll be doing an autopsy in the next day or two."

Autopsy. Beau hadn't needed one, which had made it possible for Andie to dress him for burial. But she had bailed out. The image of Beau laying on a cold metal table in his boxer shorts was still carved into her mind.

It was too late for her and Beau, and now it was too late for her and Nora, too. *No question, Nora was difficult.* Arduous. *But I could have made my way through that a lot more often than I did. Been there more for her. That wouldn't have killed me...but now it's gone. Forever. And there's no way to retrieve it.*

Andie's silence seemed to make Carole James uncomfortable.

"I would have called earlier...but we couldn't find your number."

Hadn't her mother written it down somewhere? Printed it precisely on a slip of paper and taped it to the phone? She rarely called, but where did *she* go for the number?

"The police finally got it for us. We told them your name and told them where you lived. They found it."

The number was unlisted. Had to be, considering her job. Carole couldn't have found it on the internet or through directory assistance.

"Um...thank you for calling, Carole. I'm sorry about the hassle with my number. And I'm sorry...you and Alta had to be the ones to find her. That must have been an awful experience."

"There's nothing to apologize for, dear. I'm just sorry we couldn't let you know earlier. And we didn't know of any other family members."

"No, there aren't any," Andie sighed. "I appreciate your help. I'll get there as soon as I can arrange a flight."

"Oh, and don't worry, Andrea—the police have already secured the back door."

Andie pressed the speed dial and waited for Grace's voice. Grace was barely through *hello* when Andie interrupted, "My mother died."

"What? When did this happen?"

"I guess sometime this morning. One of her friends just called me. When they went over to pick her up for Bingo, she was already gone."

"Oh, I'm so sorry, Andie."

"I don't know yet *how* I feel, to be honest. I've only known a few minutes...but you remember how she acted when Beau died. That was classic Nora. She's just always been...I don't know...*difficult*. I never felt we were connected—not in the important ways. We rarely even talked. Scarcely saw each other. To be truthful, Grace, I don't know that it'll matter that much to me that she is dead."

"I know you feel that way now, Andie, and you might still feel that way a year from now. But, still, it's your *mother*."

"You're absolutely right. I love her, and I think part of what I'm feeling right now is a lot of regret—about things I wish had been different. I could have done so much more to build some kind of relationship between us. I could have helped her be not so alone. And that's not all—I'm dreading having to go to Nebraska to settle her estate and tie up the loose ends, but there's no one else to do it. And here's the sort of creepy part: I'm all alone now, Grace. Nora may not have been the most nurturing soul, but with her death, I now have no parents. But that's not all. I have no siblings. No spouse. No children. I'm it. There's just me. The last pole in the fence, as they say."

The next call was to Jack. "How on earth am I supposed to do this?" she asked. "Sloan just put me on the hot seat to delay Barlow's extradition to North Carolina. He's totally determined that we can't let Brock get on a plane. Sloan wants him sentenced first in Utah.

And I've got only a matter of days to get that accomplished. How am I supposed to hop on a plane to Nebraska and spend God knows how long getting my mother buried and her stuff taken care of?"

With a suddenness that shocked even her, Andie cried.

"Hey, hey," Jack almost cooed. "You have co-counsel, remember? Good grief, Andie—you're not taking off on a cruise to the Caribbean. *Your mother died.* You *have* to go. Meet me at the office at seven and brief me on what's got to happen. I'm familiar with the case, and I'll step in for you. Grace and I can handle it."

The tears streamed down Andie's cheeks and dripped off her chin. "Jack—"

"No use even *trying* to object. You're overruled."

ANDIE EASED the rental car to the shoulder of Garfield Street and onto the driveway that ran alongside the house to the garage. It was obvious there had been a storm within the last few days, but someone had steered a tractor with a snow blade down the wide concrete driveway to clear it for Andie. Still, there was thick ice in the tire tracks where Nora had driven back and forth in her reliable blue Pontiac for the last few weeks. Andie crawled to a stop. The Pontiac stood like a silent sentinel in front of her, just outside the garage, buried in at least a foot of snow.

The sky was gray. The prairies to the west were windblown with snow drifting against fences; dead stalks poked randomly through stretches of farmland that the wind had swept almost clean. Though it was just past three in the afternoon, it looked like dusk. While Nora's house looked eerily deserted, lights shone through the windows of the houses on either side.

Andie turned off the ignition just as a yellow school bus rumbled to a stop on Garfield. The door swung open, and the bus belched out a tumble of elementary school children clad in heavy coats and an assortment of hats and mittens. Andie smiled, watching them stomp in the piles of snow left by the county plows. A couple of boys scooped up mittens full of snow and launched snowballs at the girls, who squealed in mock terror and ran down the street to the south. She wiped the back of her hand across her damp eyes: the last she remembered, Beau had been the one pitching the icy missiles.

Tramping through the snow between the rental car and the house, Andie found the old metal washtub, pulled it out of the drifted snow, and carried it to the kitchen window. Though it had been more than a decade, she knew the routine so well it was almost automatic: she turned the washtub over, situated it solidly on the ground beneath the window, and stood on top of it. Pulling off a glove, she ran her fingers slowly and carefully over the ledge above the window; the paint was starting to peel, and two or three times she thought she had found it. Finally she felt the icy metal of the key against her fingertips.

Putting the washtub back in its place, she jammed the key into the back-door lock and turned it. The lock turned easily, but the door wasn't budging. *That's right. The paramedics had to force the door. And the police had to secure it.* Andie palmed the key and walked down the driveway, around to the front of the house.

The first thing that hit her when she stepped inside the door was the smell. The house *smelled* like Nora. Tears stung Andie's eyes. How was it that paint and wallpaper and curtains and carpeting so thoroughly absorbed the presence of their owner? It wasn't any one thing—not a signature cologne, not the laundry soap she always used, not the lemon-scented cleaner she used to scrub the linoleum. It was *Nora*. It was her hair, her hands, her cheeks, her sensible shoes.

The house was tidy, picked up, just like Nora would have wanted it for company. Andie walked slowly through the living room, noticing details she'd never bothered to see before. The small, rounded window closest to the kitchen was lined with glass shelves; had they always been there? Queued up in neat precision on the shelves were various sculpted hummingbirds. Andie picked up the largest one, turning it in the shaft of light that beamed through the pane. It boasted various jeweled colors and its long, needle-like beak penetrated the heart of a delicately veined red blossom. It was beautiful. *When had Nora started this collection?* Andie didn't know that Nora loved hummingbirds.

What else don't I know? A sudden sorrow pulled at Andie's heart. *I wanted to know.*

Andie ground to a halt in the doorway leading to the kitchen. She was reluctant to cross the threshold into the room that had served as Nora's initial grave. Her eyes darted frantically over the floor around the kitchen table, fearful that there was still some hint of where Nora had fallen, had sucked in her last breath, had lain crumpled in a heap until her Bingo buddies happened upon her.

How long had she lain there before life had slipped away? Had she been in pain? Was there a crushing pressure in her chest? Did she black out when she struck her head—had it been on the floor, or against the unforgiving edge of the table?—or did she lay for minutes, hours, with a blinding headache? Worst of all, did she feel a jolting sense of panic as she realized her life was ending, or did she go quietly, accepting—or even embracing—her sudden ability to slip from the tethers that had bound her to mortality?

Andie realized she was holding her breath, and she exhaled a long, slow torrent of relief as she saw no hint of Nora's demise on the floor. She envisioned Carole and Alta scuttling around the kitchen, picking up random debris left by the paramedics, sponging up any dried fluids that might have leaked from the shell that had been Nora. Her eyes brimmed with tears as Andie—bereft of logic—regretted not being here for Nora, being states away, dealing with hundreds of cases on the public defender docket.

If she had been here, living in this house, sleeping on the sagging single bed of her childhood, would she have heard Nora collapse? Could she have saved her?

When did my work become so important?

ANDIE CARRIED her luggage up the stairs and into Nora's room.

Typical.

The bed was made, the peach floral bedspread smoothed into place. Her dark-blue bathrobe hung on the hook inside the closet door. Nothing was out of place—not one thing. Andie flung her larger suitcase onto the bed. It just made sense to stay in this room instead of her old room; the bed was bigger and firmer, the room was larger, and there was a phone on the bedside table. After all, no one else was using it. *Then why do I feel like such an interloper?*

Andie slowly opened the closet door. The closet was full. Andie scooped almost half of the items off the rod and into her arms, then walked down the hall to her old room. A patchwork quilt was draped over Andie's old single bed, but it didn't look like there were sheets on the mattress. Andie dropped the load of clothes on the bed and opened the closet door.

A worn cardboard box was pushed into the corner; a thick film of dust covered the rest of the hardwood floor. A pile of old yearbooks Andie didn't recognize sat on the shelf. Other than that, the closet was empty.

Andie hung the pile of clothes on the rod before going to get the rest of the things from Nora's closet. Just as she was about to close the door, the cardboard box on the floor caught her eye again. She bent to lift it and found it surprisingly light. Collapsing onto the foot of the bed, Andie pried open the flaps.

Baby blankets?

Confusion washed over Andie as she lifted the blankets from the box. The blankets appeared to be brand-new, totally unused. Two were crocheted—one blue, one yellow and green with nubby blue accents. One was a crib-sized patchwork quilt with a profusion of blue floral patches dancing across its surface. Someone had hand-embroidered decorative accents along the sides of each patch, much like the "crazy quilts" Andie had admired in the pioneer museum in Salt Lake City. And two were sweet blue and yellow flannel receiving blankets with multicolored, crocheted edges.

As she lifted the last of the blankets from the box, Andie felt as though she had been slapped in the face. There, nestled in the bottom of the musty cardboard box, were four pairs of Beau's baby shoes. One was the pair he had learned to walk in. The laces were tattered, the toes scuffed. Andie picked them up and pressed them against her chest, heaving with sobs.

ANDIE FORCED HER EYES OPEN. It was dark outside, and the room was shrouded with blackness. She still held Beau's shoes against her chest. She relaxed her grip and stretched her sore fingers. At what point had she leaned sideways into the sagging mattress, and how long had she slept? She realized she was cold and pulled the edge of the patchwork quilt over her shoulders. She realized, too, that her eyes stung and felt swollen. *Is it possible to keep crying after sleep anesthetizes you?*

She finally stood and flipped on the light. It was almost seven. She stared again at the pile of baby blankets, strewn at the foot of the bed. What had happened? Who had made them? Who were they for? How long had they been cocooned in the worn cardboard box on the floor of Andie's closet?

The same dread that had clawed at her earlier sunk in its talons again. She struggled against the only conclusion that made sense, not wanting to believe it. *No. Nora couldn't have made these blankets— not for Beau.*

Then why were they stashed away with Beau's shoes—shoes that had been secretly plucked from view and hidden in the two years Andie lived at home?

Why had they been pushed into a corner in Andie's closet?

And why had the blankets never been given to Beau?

ANDIE PUT Beau's shoes on the night table next to Nora's bed. She went into the bathroom, rinsed out a peach-colored washcloth in cold water, and held it against her puffy eyes as she lay down. The coolness felt good.

She grabbed her cell phone and dialed Jack's number. He didn't answer; Andie prayed he wasn't being held captive by Brock Barlow at the jail. Jack had told her not to call—not to worry. She felt responsible for how things were going but decided to set it aside. At least for tonight.

Next, she dialed Grace's number. She'd be home by now, picking over the remnants of leftovers as she read her new *People* magazine. Grace sounded relieved.

"Hey, where have you been? I've been worried about you!"

"I fell asleep—pretty much as a result of shock," Andie explained.

"What happened? Not worrying about Brock, I hope, because Jack and I have it under control."

"No, not Brock. I was moving my mother's things into the closet in my old room, and there was this dumpy old cardboard box on the floor of my closet," Andie started. "So after I got all my mother's things moved, I opened the cardboard box." Tears welled up again, and Andie pressed the cloth more firmly against her eyes.

"Don't tell me—it was a dead animal!"

Andie chuckled, relieved at the comic aside. "No. I'm *still* not sure what it was."

Grace's voice fell quiet. "Um, what do you mean, you're not sure what it was?"

"Okay, Grace, maybe I'm overreacting..."

"Andie, you're the most level-headed person I know. *What was it?*"

"Five baby blankets. Brand-new. Never been used."

"Uh, I'm not sure I get it. Why is that so odd?"

"Because, Grace, they were in the box on top of four pairs of Beau's baby shoes."

The gasp was audible. "Okay, Andie, that's just plain...weird."

"It's weird on so many levels!" Andie cried. "First of all, I never *gave* my mother those shoes. I saved them so I could give them to Beau someday. I figured they'd been lost in the move when I packed up my things and went to school in Lincoln. *She had to have taken them from me.* Intentionally taken them, hidden them. And—"

"She has to have made those blankets for Beau, Andie. Why else would she have put them in a box with his shoes?" Grace sounded as unnerved as Andie felt.

"Okay. So far, your logic has gone along the same lines mine did. But if she made five beautiful baby blankets for Beau, *why didn't she give them to him?*"

"You've got me there. I honestly don't know."

"Well, here's the other thing, Grace—I *lived* with my mother during the last half of my pregnancy. I hardly left the house. She hardly did either, for that matter—just once a week to play Bingo. I never saw her working on any blankets. Never saw any traces of any kind of handwork. That means she either had to make them for him *before* I moved in with her, or..."

"I don't know how you're doing this, because I feel sick, and I'm not even there."

"Yeah, I don't think she made them before I moved in, either. I didn't know I was having a boy—and all the blankets are blue."

CHAPTER 15

Surprisingly, Nora had a will. The day after she arrived, Andie received a phone call from Douglas Nelson, a soft-spoken attorney with Nelson & Brown in Minden. The details of the will were fairly simple. Her hummingbird collection went to Alta King and Carole James, and they were to decide who got which ones. A few thousand dollars from Nora's modest savings account went to the Catholic Church in Kearney that sponsored the Bingo games, and a few thousand went to Best Friends, a sanctuary for abused and abandoned animals in Kanab, Utah; the donation was sizable enough to designate her a "Guardian Angel."

The rest—the house, the furnishings, the car, some stock in Hormel Foods and Swift & Company—went to Andie.

Nora's will specified that she be cremated. Andie hated the idea of cremation. Hated the idea of her mother's body being tucked inside a corrugated cardboard box and slid into an oven called a *retort*. But that's what Nora wanted—what she carefully spelled out in her will—so Andie reported to the Laycock Funeral Home precisely at ten to supervise her mother's incineration at 1,800 degrees. They had done a quick once-over of Nora's body before Andie got there and had removed her watch and two rings; these were in a zip-lock plastic bag that James Laycock thrust into Andie's hand.

The box that contained Nora—a sturdy white cardboard container with the word *Head* in large letters at one end—was perched on a motorized trolley when Andie arrived. "Do you want to see your mother?" James Laycock asked in a voice that provided very little persuasion.

Andie hadn't thought about that. By the time she saw Beau, the mortuary had embalmed him—had replaced the blood that had coursed through his veins with a preservative that would keep him fresh, lifelike, for months. Maybe years. Destined for cremation, Nora might have already started the steady process of decomposition.

"No, I don't think so," Andie said quietly.

"Most don't," Laycock said with swift dispatch. Motioning to an upholstered chair, he invited Andie to take a seat. "The incineration takes about two hours. That, and about an hour to pulverize the bone fragments."

Incineration. Pulverize. Bone fragments. Andie felt faint. She lowered herself into the chair and watched as James Laycock moved the motorized trolley up to the door of the retort, which was already heated to two thousand degrees. The door opened quickly, and the bearings on the trolley rolled the large white cardboard container into the oven smoothly and quickly to avoid too much heat loss. Laycock rapidly latched the door and pushed a series of buttons on a computerized control panel.

"If you need anything, I'll be in the next room," he said.

Andie was alone with a bulging oven that would incinerate Nora. Flames would flash through the cardboard container in seconds and would begin to burn the remains of her mother. Her flesh and fat and organs would, Laycock had explained, vaporize in the heat; the resulting vapors would be swept away through the exhaust system. The material that would be left, what most people referred to as "ashes," weren't ashes at all, he told Andie. They were bone fragments that hadn't completely burned. Some, like the ball joints of the hip, would still be intact. All of it would be pulverized, he assured her, into a substance that looked like fine grains of sand, the so-called "ashes." The remains would be sifted through a sieve to remove dental fillings, any missed jewelry, and any surgical implants. The remaining pure cremains, he told her, would be hers to keep.

Andie studied the door of the retort. A small window, about ten inches wide and surrounded by thick rubber insulation, was roughly at eye level. Should she look? Would she see pieces of Nora, fat crackling, skin shriveled and black?

She walked hesitantly toward the door and peered through the window. She sighed with relief: all she could see were bright flashes of intense flame, leaping and licking everything in its path.

Andie sat back down, pushing into the soft upholstery. Nora had not kept vigil at the most important moments of Andie's life—at the discovery of Colin wrestling under the sheets. At the birth of Beau (why hadn't she been in the room?). At her admission to, or graduation from, law school. At the death of Beau. But Nora *had* silently hovered in the background during the first two years of Beau's life, smoothing his cowlicks, sweeping him up and away from the foot of the stairs, wandering beside him as he took his first barefooted walk in the grass of the back yard. In exchange for that dogged determination, Andie felt the need to keep vigil now, as all but the last few fragments of her mother vaporized and disappeared forever into a finely engineered exhaust system.

Two hours later, James Laycock pronounced the cremation complete and busied himself scooping the ashy remains into a grinding mechanism that would pulverize the chunky, blackened pieces of bone. An hour later, he presented Andie with a rectangular, plastic container tucked inside a black, velvet bag with a drawstring top.

It was finished.

Andie tucked the pieces of her mother securely under her arm and stepped outside into a late winter snowstorm. The flakes drifted lazily to earth, and a chill bit Andie's exposed cheeks. Now the caretaker of all that was left of Nora, Andie put the five-pound bundle on the front passenger seat of the car. As she started the ignition, she glanced at the bag.

"Oh, Mom," Andie said, sighing as tears dribbled down her cheeks. "I wish we could have been friends. I would have changed whatever it was I did wrong...whatever it was that kept you away. I wish you would have known me—and that I could have known *you*. I wish I could have said goodbye."

THE MEMORIAL SERVICE OVER, Andie needed to dispose of her mother's property. Douglas Nelson had arranged for transfer of the designated funds to the Catholic Church in Kearney and the animal sanctuary in Utah, but there were still the furnishings, household goods, house, and car to be dealt with.

But they could wait.

There was something more pressing for Andie to accomplish while she was in Nebraska. She wanted to find out what had happened between Nora and Drew Carlson—what had caused her father to drift away across the lonely Nebraska plains, and what had caused her mother to pretend as though it had never happened.

She figured she had a couple of weeks; things were still on the front burner with Brock Barlow, but regular check-ins with Jack and Grace assured her that all was on track.

Andie knew how to ferret out even the most stubborn information—she'd been doing it for years as an attorney. She also had friends in the Omaha law firm where she and Sloan had worked before leaving the windswept plains of Nebraska for the snow-packed peaks of Utah.

It was time to button down some answers about Drew and Nora.

ANDIE KICKED the toe of her boots against the concrete foundation as she leaned on the doorbell a second time. She knew they were home—they were expecting her, and she thought she could hear muffled voices somewhere on the other side of the door. At last the door swung open, and Florence Anderson gathered Andie into her arms, pulling her into the sunlit living room. "Quick, before we let out too much heat!" she smiled, pushing the door firmly shut behind Andie and motioning toward a sturdy sofa upholstered in tightly looped nylon. "Let me take your coat, dear; here, sit down by Frank."

More than a dozen years older than his wife, Frank was settled in a recliner with a crocheted afghan draped across his lap; he wore a plaid, flannel shirt. He smiled and nodded, holding out his hand to Andie. It was large and weathered and peppered with age spots, a mute testament to a lifetime of coaxing crops from the land; the joints were gnarled by arthritis, and his clasp was not as strong as Andie would have expected from a man of his size. Rheumy gray eyes swam behind the thick lenses of his glasses. Andie was mildly alarmed to see how rapidly he had declined; he hadn't been at Nora's memorial service, so this was the first time she had seen him in years.

"It's so good to see you again, dear," Florence said, settling into an overstuffed chair next to her husband's recliner. "The memorial service was very nice. I think Nora would have been pleased." She dabbed at the corner of her eye with a wadded handkerchief, which she then tucked into the bodice of her blouse. *Just like Nora,* Andie thought—*never more than a few inches away from her trusty handkerchief.*

"Thanks, Mrs. Anderson," Andie said. "I appreciate your friendship with my mother over the years; I know she enjoyed the two of you."

"Nobody made a better key lime pie," Florence smiled. "I think it was Frank's favorite." At that, Frank chuckled. *Key lime pie?* There was a painful catch in Andie's throat. *Another thing I didn't know about my mother. How many more would come bubbling to the surface?*

Andie pulled her notebook and pen out of her bag and opened it on her lap. Suddenly she felt color creep into her cheeks as she met Florence's gaze. "Mrs. Anderson, this might seem kind of unusual, but...I don't know quite how to say this. I don't really know much about my mother's background. I know hardly anything about my father. I've wanted to know for a long time, but she just didn't like to talk about it. Now that she's gone, I want to know more than ever. And since she's not here, I didn't think it would hurt to get some information...now that it won't bother her, I mean."

The smile faded from Florence's face as she looked nervously at Frank. Both of them sat rigid, motionless.

The silence was suffocating.

Finally, Andie spoke again. "You two have known her the longest of anyone. She mentioned once that you lived in this home when she and my father moved here. If anyone knows what might have happened, you must."

"We enjoyed your mother very much, Andrea," Florence said evenly. "Your father wasn't—"

"Florence!" Frank said sharply, cutting off his wife's comment.

Andie turned and focused on Frank. "Please, Mr. Anderson...I can't even imagine what went on, and it is a source of great pain to me. I'm sure you know my son died about a year ago. Now that my mother is gone, I've lost my entire family. I *really need* to put the pieces together. I'm concerned that I won't be able to find any peace unless I can."

"I don't think you know what you're asking for, young lady." Andie was alarmed by the gruff tone in Frank's voice. She was even more startled when he added, "And maybe you should consider that this isn't just about *you*."

Florence grabbed his hand and squeezed hard. "What Frank's trying to say"—

"You'd better let me handle this," he spat, cutting her off again. "If your mother had wanted you to know, she'd have told you herself. Ain't our place to be discussing family business with you. Not ours, or anyone else's. Not even your mother's." He shook off his wife's handclasp and folded his hands resolutely in his lap on top of the afghan. "Now, I think you'd better go on back to your mother's house and be happy that you've got a good job and can support yourself over there in Utah." With that, he turned his head to avoid Andie's gaze.

Andie looked at Florence; she thought she saw an inkling of empathy in the woman's cornflower-blue eyes. Florence shrugged her shoulders and looked beyond Andie. "Let me walk you to the door, dear," she said quietly.

Andie tucked her notebook back into her bag, pulled on her coat, and walked toward the door. There *was* something—otherwise, these two wouldn't be so...were they *frightened?* Angry? Or just locked in resolution to protect Nora's secrets?

Florence put her arm around Andie's waist as she opened the door, nearly pushing her out onto the porch. The icy wind howled with such ferocity that Andie could barely hear the whisper against her ear.

"Come back on Thursday at two. Our son is taking Frank to the doctor. We can talk then." A second later, the door slammed. Andie stood riveted for a full minute before she dashed for the car. There *was* something. And in two days, she'd know what it was.

Andie nursed a cup of coffee and watched through the kitchen window for Bill's car. She didn't know him that well; he was the oldest of the Anderson boys, and he'd been in high school by the time she had begun playing with Teddy. She smiled at the memory of the two of them, running in the narrow spaces between rows of corn, the stalks soaring far overhead, arriving breathless at the end of the field in a contest of who was faster and stronger. She rubbed her arms briskly as she remembered the first—and only—time they had run through the sprinklers at the edge of the wheat field. The force of the water had felt like it was tearing off her skin.

The houses were scattered far and wide along the farm country back then, and there weren't any girls for miles. She and Teddy had been best friends. She had climbed trees with him, and he had fashioned hollyhock dolls with her—but only if she let him sail them down the ditch on a raft made out of Popsicle sticks.

At a quarter to two, Andie saw it—the deep red Nissan crunched over the gravel of the driveway and eased to a stop. Across the wide expanse of the side yard, Andie could see Florence, bundled in a coat, walk Frank out to the car; she watched eagerly as Bill helped get him settled in. The moment the Nissan backed out of the driveway and turned down the road, Andie grabbed her coat and hat.

She arrived at the Anderson house out of breath, gulping the painfully cold air. Florence must have been watching for her; before she could ring the bell, the door flew open. Still in her coat, Florence motioned Andie into the house.

"Let's sit at the kitchen table, dear," she said. "We don't have much time. They'll be back within the hour."

Andie smiled. "I am so grateful for anything you can give me," she said, taking off her coat and draping it over a kitchen chair. "This means so much to me."

Florence put a saucer of oatmeal cookies in the center of the table along with a bottle of milk. She handed a glass to Andie. "Help yourself, dear. Now let's get started."

Andie opened her notebook. "Thank you so much for agreeing to talk to me, Mrs. Anderson. Anything that will help me put together the pieces will be another step toward arriving at some peace."

Florence nodded. "Well, as I said the other day, Andrea, we loved your mother. She was easy to talk to at first and seemed to love being a wife. She worked so hard to keep a nice house, even when there wasn't much money. But your father..."

"What, Mrs. Anderson?" Andie fairly pleaded. "What about my father?"

"He seemed, I don't know, stand-offish. Didn't like to visit much. Didn't smile a lot. I can't say we got to know him very well."

Andie felt a stab of disappointment. For all the drama of the other afternoon, maybe the Andersons didn't know much after all.

"And then there was...well, dear, did you know that your mother was expecting you when they got married?"

Andie gasped before she could stop herself. "I didn't know that, Mrs. Anderson. Not that it matters."

"No, I suppose it doesn't. Especially nowadays. But, oh, this is very difficult." Florence sat quietly, wringing her hands.

"Please, Mrs. Anderson, go on," Andie urged.

"Well, one time—I guess you were just a few months old—we didn't know anything about it. Didn't know your mother was pregnant when they got married. Frank had gone over to help your father fix a tractor he had borrowed. And it was just like...it was like your father needed to let all the pain come flooding out of his heart. He needed to tell someone else what had happened and how he felt. Frank is a man who keeps secrets. He didn't tell me about their conversation until after your father was gone."

"Go on," Andie pleaded. "I would never ask you to betray that if any of the people involved were still alive—anyone other than your husband, that is."

"I guess your mother and father met over in Iowa. He was a hired hand who was working to bring in the corn. Your mother was friends with one of the girls who lived on the farm, and she spent quite a bit of time over there. Well, he caught her eye—and she caught his—and I guess the rest is obvious. Your grandparents were furious. They thought Drew was shiftless and meant nothing but trouble. So your mother and father ran away. Just left together. Eloped somewhere between here and there."

Andie scratched notes rapidly as the story unraveled. After they married in a cramped office of a justice of the peace, they stopped somewhere east of Omaha so they could make enough money to move on and get something permanent. They lived behind a farmer's house in a structure that had once been a chicken coop. Nora had shoveled out chicken manure a foot deep, stopping regularly to retch at the edge of a wheat field. It was no place for a pregnant woman, and Nora had been terrified that her parents would come looking and find her there. By the time Andie had been born, they had moved into the frame house on Garfield Street, and Drew had struck up a deal with the owner to turn over a percentage of his proceeds from the farm in exchange for buying the house.

"Your father held up his end of the bargain with the farm," Florence continued. "There wasn't a lot owing, and he managed to take care of it. We're not sure where he got the money, but he did. But it seems he told Frank he wasn't very happy. Hadn't really wanted to marry your mother. Did it because he felt obligated—you know, because she was carrying his child."

Andie stopped writing and put her pen down. A powerful wave of sadness washed over her. She was almost afraid to ask, but once it tumbled out, it was too late to take it back. "So, did he seem happier once I was born?"

Florence grabbed the handkerchief out of her bodice and dabbed at her eyes. "Oh, Andrea, dear, this just seems so cruel. Are you sure you want to know the rest?"

"I'm sure," Andie nodded. She felt her own eyes brimming unexpectedly with tears.

"Your father never wanted to be married to your mother. He just didn't love her. According to what he told Frank, he didn't even really like her. Had just gotten carried away that summer. They were so different. Different as two people can be. Seems to me that Nora could tell, too. The harder she tried, the harder his heart grew. You were born, and..." Florence's voice trailed off.

"What? What happened?" Andie swiped at the tears running down her cheeks.

"He...he never really wanted anything to do with you. I think you represented something he didn't want—a marriage he didn't want to be in. He didn't know what to do. Couldn't leave. Knew your mother would never make it by herself, knew he had a child he was responsible for, even though he didn't want to be there. He coped by just staying away from the house, working out in the fields until it was too dark to see his hand in front of his face.

"Then, when your mother got pregnant with your brother—"

"What? My mother got *pregnant* after I was born?"

Florence clapped her hand over her mouth.

"What?" Andie cried again.

"Oh, dear," Florence mumbled. "I...I thought you knew."

CHAPTER 16

Andie felt as though she had been slapped across the face. "Mrs. Anderson, I had no idea. Please, go on."

Florence slumped into the kitchen chair, shaking her head sullenly. She dabbed again at her eyes. "When you were only a few months old, your mother got pregnant again. Your father was *sure* it wasn't his baby—was sure your mother had been with someone else. Your mother insisted that absolutely no such thing had happened, and that he was the baby's father. His heart was so hard I'm surprised it didn't shatter like broken glass. After that, he got mean. Real mean. This was after he and Frank talked. We don't know this from being told, but just from what we heard. Summer nights, we could hear him screaming at her through the screened windows...could hear the slaps...could hear her crying. And you, too. You screamed whenever he beat your mother."

Andie wiped the tears with the back of her hand. "I did?"

Florence reached across the table and took Andie's hand in hers. "Yes, you did. It nearly broke our hearts to hear it. But back in those days, folks didn't interfere. Didn't call the police. Just turned over in bed and tried not to listen."

"So what happened to my brother?" Andie cried "Where is he?"

Florence choked on a tiny hiccup. "Your mother had a very difficult labor and delivery. Your brother, Matthew, had to stay in the hospital for almost two months. Your mother went to see him every day, and I watched you while she was gone. Your father never visited. Just worked night and day in that field like his heart and head were about to explode. In every spare minute, your mother made blankets

—three or four of them, I think—dreaming of the day she could bring that little boy home."

The blankets. They weren't for Beau at all. They were for Matthew. And they looked...unused. Brand-new.

"It never happened," Florence said, her tears flowing freely now. "I was watching you one afternoon, and your father was working at the far end of the field, and your mother came in the door—just sort of stumbled in, with a blank look on her face. Her eyes were red and swollen. Your baby brother had died. She gathered you up in her arms and just sobbed, holding your head against her neck. You started to cry, just breathing in all of your mother's sorrow. From that moment on, something inside her just sort of died. She was never the same. A few weeks later, your father left." Florence dropped her head into her hands.

Andie felt...was it shock, or was it profound sadness? What had happened when Nora had wandered to the end of the wheat field to tell Drew that their son had died? Andie knew that feeling—being alive and busy and then having your very life pulled out from under you at the news that your son, your light, was extinguished. Had Nora carried Andie to the far end of the field? Had Andie continued to breathe in the pain of all that had happened around her?

Andie put her hand on Florence's arm. "Oh, Mrs. Anderson, I can't imagine how hard it was for you to tell me that," she said. "But I am so glad you did. I never knew. I just never knew. Even with what little you've given me, there are things that make so much sense." *Like the blankets. Like the fact that Nora vanished just as Andie was about to give birth. Like the fact that Nora never held Beau...never pressed him against her heart, physically or emotionally.*

"I hope it was the right thing to do," Florence whispered.

Andie squeezed her hand. "It was! You have given me a gift, Mrs. Anderson. I can move on in a way I couldn't have before. One more thing—what happened when my father left? Did anybody see him? Or talk to him? Do you have *any* idea what happened to him?"

Florence sat still, numbed with the effort of what she had already divulged. "I'm afraid I'm just like all the others, dear. One day he was here, and the next he was gone. Your mother didn't even tell anyone he was gone for a couple of weeks—until people came around asking about him."

"Came around asking?" Andie said. "You mean like the sheriff? Was he in some kind of trouble?"

"No, no," Florence assured her. "I mean some of the other farmers in the area. Even Frank. Frank noticed not having seen him in quite some time. The tractor stood still. Everyone else was busy preparing their fields for planting, and your father's tractor stood still for a long time, kind of in the middle of the east field. It was strange. It was like...like he hadn't *planned* to leave, because he didn't take care of his equipment. Didn't bring it up to where it would be sheltered. It was like it just suddenly occurred to him, and he stopped the tractor where he was right that minute and just walked away."

"Did he say anything to my mother?"

"That was the most peculiar part," Florence sighed. "He walked in from where he had been on the tractor. Your mother was sitting in the corner of the front room, wrapped in a shawl. She had been crying. He didn't even come in the house to see if she was all right. He stuck his head in the door and said he was going for a package of cigarettes. Nora remembered later that she had never heard him start up the car. She remembered thinking it odd that he was *walking* to get cigarettes, because the nearest place that sold cigarettes was a good six or seven miles down the road back then. That's a long way to walk when there's work to do in the field and the sun sets early."

"Why didn't she go looking for him?"

"Oh, I think she did," Florence responded, "but not right away. I think she was still so buried in grief over your little brother that she just sat in that chair until all the light had gone out of the front room. As I remember her telling it, you were in your crib, and you had started to cry. She finally got up and went into your room and changed your diaper, and then it dawned on her slowly that your father had never come back. The keys to the car were still hanging on the hook by the back door, and the car had not been moved.

"As I recall, the next day she went to the service station and asked if anyone had seen him. Asked if he'd been in to buy cigarettes. It was such a small place back then, everyone knew everyone—and no one had seen your father. She later told us she drove home slowly along the highway, and she got out five or six times to look up and down the ditch. I guess she went out a few days later and tried to look in some of the fields. She never saw a trace of him."

"Did she call the police?" Andie asked.

"No, she didn't," Florence replied. "It was almost like she was embarrassed. Like the whole thing was her fault. Like if she reported it or told people, it somehow made it truer. Like if she kept quiet, he would suddenly come back, and they could go on as though nothing had happened. She was terrified that it would end up in the newspaper and she would have to face people.

"She went on like that for a long time...two years, maybe three. Kept telling people he was coming back. That first year, she let the fields go to weed. Nearly killed Frank to see it happen. She wouldn't let anyone help, because that meant he really wasn't going to reappear some morning and pull himself back onto the tractor. I truly don't know how she got by. By that winter, she was taking in sewing and babysitting and doing all kinds of things to make ends meet. The next spring, she leased out her land to Frank and some others who wanted to farm it. A few years later, she sold it."

"And she never said anything more about where he might have gone?"

Florence shook her head. "I don't think she had a clue. Frank and I tried to be good friends, tried to help wherever we could. But the more time slipped away, the more bitter she became. It pains me to say this, but it wasn't very easy to like your mother by then. She could be downright nasty sometimes." She burst into a fresh round of sobs. "I just don't believe in speaking evil of the dead! Please forgive me."

"Oh, Mrs. Anderson, there's nothing to forgive. I saw that

nastiness much of my life. One other thing—do you know where my father and mother were married? Or what date my brother was born? Or anything about my father's family?"

Florence shook her head. "I just know they were married somewhere east of Omaha—they were on their way from Iowa. Could have been in Iowa. Probably was. And, let's see, they were getting the fields ready to plant when your brother was born. Maybe April. The year after you were born." She paused to think for a minute. "No, I can't remember ever hearing anything about your father's family. I'm so sorry."

"Don't be sorry!" Andie exclaimed. "I'm so grateful for what you *have* given me. I think it's enough to go on." She pulled her coat on and tucked her notebook into her bag. She pulled Florence into a hug. "Thank you so, so much. I won't mention a word of it to Frank."

"Yes, dear," Florence said. "He'd be very unhappy with me if he knew."

Hurrying across the yard to her mother's house, Andie choked back emotions. The tears stung her eyes and burned her cheeks. She never had a chance with Nora. Andie had arrived in the eye of a storm. The black funnel of pain with its destructive torrents didn't pass until the day Nora fell in a heap on the kitchen floor, taking with her the secrets dashed into pieces by the wind.

THE SERGEANT at the grimy desk seemed like he was having a hard time keeping his eyes open as Andie lowered herself into the metal chair across from him. He cleared his throat, straightened up in his chair, and flashed a wan smile. Picking up a pen and a small notebook, he scrawled the date on the top line before looking up at Andie.

"What can I help you with today?" he asked, barely skirting around the edges of feigned enthusiasm.

"I want to report a missing person," Andie said, struggling to keep her emotions under control. The sergeant tugged at his sleeve, glanced at his watch, and jotted down the time next to the date in the notebook.

"Okay," he said, a little more interest in his voice. "How long has this person been missing?"

"About thirty-seven years," Andie said.

The officer dropped the pen as he cleared his throat with a deep, guttural growl. "What?! Thirty-seven *years?* Wow, what brought you racing over to the station this afternoon?" As if to emphasize his sarcasm, he wiped the corners of his mouth with his thumb and index finger.

"Look, I'm not some lunatic," Andie shot back. "I'm an attorney, licensed to practice law in the state of Nebraska and Utah. It's not a news flash that my father went missing about thirty-seven years ago. But what I *just found out today* is that my mother never pursued the case. Period. Never contacted authorities. Never looked into it at all. She's dead now, and I'm here now to settle her estate, and I would like to find out if anything can be done about looking into my father's disappearance."

Officer Gerald Oldroyd shifted in his chair nervously. "I'm sorry," he muttered. "I wasn't meaning to make light of a painful situation. You've just got to admit—"

"I know," Andie interrupted. "Thirty-seven years is a long time. I'm not here to pass judgment on what my mother decided to do—or, more aptly, *not* to do—back then. I'm just wondering if anything at all can be done after all this time to investigate what might have happened."

Oldroyd rubbed his chin thoughtfully. "There's probably not a lot," he conceded. "Damn, that's gonna be a crap shoot."

"I'd like to try," Andie said. "I was only a year old at the time, and I don't remember anything about him or about his disappearance. It never ran in the newspaper, so there are no news clippings. Like I said, she never called the sheriff back then. My mother wouldn't talk to me about it when she was alive. All I have to go on is the memory of a neighbor who lived next door at the time."

"Could we interview the neighbor?" Oldroyd asked.

"That would be difficult," Andie explained. "She told me details about my parents that her husband didn't want her to reveal. I had to sneak over there today while their son took him to a doctor's appointment. She doesn't want him to know that we talked."

"Hmmm," Oldroyd droned.

"There's more," Andie said. "I don't know his date of birth or the names of his parents. I don't know *where* he was born. I don't even know when or where my parents were married. It was about six months before I was born."

Oldroyd raised an eyebrow. "Your mom not the talkative type?"

"That's putting it mildly. I don't have any brothers or sisters, and my grandparents passed away years ago. There's no family to get any information from. I'm all alone here—but it means a lot to me."

Oldroyd let out a low whistle. "Do you think he might still be *alive?*"

"I've never really thought he is," Andie admitted. "I grew up believing he was dead. Maybe it was just wishful thinking—deciding in my own heart that if my father was alive, he would care about me and get in touch with me. We never moved from the house we lived in when he disappeared."

"Oh, yeah, and where's that?" Oldroyd asked.

"The Carlson place on Garfield Road. My mother was Nora Carlson."

The officer shook his head. "I'm familiar with Garfield Road. I know where the Carlson place is, because we had to send officers out there when they...uh, found your mother's body. This is a small town, and something like that stays on the radar for a bit. Beyond that, I don't know anything about the place—or your family."

"She kept to herself," Andie said. "Apparently she was so embarrassed when my father disappeared that she didn't want anyone to know. She never treated it like it was a crime, and maybe it wasn't at all, but it's like she never really wanted to know where he went or what happened to him. *I do*—assuming it's not too late."

"Well, like I said, it'll be a crap shoot. Let's start with what we know." He opened a drawer in the desk, fingered through some files, and pulled out a stapled missing person form. "I'm gonna have you take this home to fill out," he explained. "It's not like we're racing against the clock here...and maybe if you keep it for a few days, you'll remember some things you're not thinking about now. Fill out as much of it as you can and bring it back when you're finished." Oldroyd paper-clipped his business card to the upper left-hand corner.

Andie took the form and stood, shaking the officer's hand. "I'll be back," she said. "I have a couple weeks before I have to get back to my job in Utah, and I want to find out as much as I can while I'm here." *Here.* Here, where Drew Carlson wandered off into an April afternoon and never came back. Here, where Andie herself grew up in the stifling air of a house filled with pain and confusion and lament without even knowing it. Sailing between the rows of corn on the breeze of childhood, she had never known the dark secrets that had held court in the white clapboard house on Garfield Road.

CHAPTER
17

Andie took the stairs two at a time and collapsed onto her childhood bed. Sobbing, she scooped up the pristine blue baby blankets and squeezed them against her chest. One of Beau's baby shoes tumbled to the floor. Nora had gotten rid of every other vestige of that life, that time when Andie had been a baby. But she had kept these blankets, crocheted with such hope, and had plucked Beau's baby shoes from corners and boxes to keep with the blankets in a pathetic cardboard tomb. A wave of nausea tore at her stomach. What on earth had gone on? What had possessed Nora to tuck these emblems of Beau among the only things she had left of her own baby boy?

Gulping air to regain control, Andie folded each blanket carefully. Then she gathered up Beau's tiny shoes and took the entire bundle to Nora's bedroom, where she laid them on top of her suitcase. She picked up the phone to call Grace.

As dusk slipped effortlessly into the black of night, Andie sat at the kitchen table with the missing person form in front of her. It was creepy. Nora should have sat at this very same table, in this very same kitchen, thirty-seven years earlier with papers much like these. She should have inked in every last detail she knew, before time and distance and death came between her and the elements that might have located Drew. No cloud of embarrassment—no frantic effort to escape looking bad—should have kept her from looking for the father of her two children, even if one of those children had vanished as well.

It took a few minutes to write the details of the disappearance; she combined the sparse bits and pieces she had heard over the years with the account Florence Anderson had provided. Beyond that, there were few spaces Andie could fill in. She realized grimly that she couldn't even provide a physical description. What had her father looked like?

Looking out the kitchen window, she saw lights on at the Anderson house. Checking the list near the kitchen phone, she dialed their number. Florence answered.

"Mrs. Anderson, it's Andrea again. I know you can't talk right now, and all you have to say is 'yes' or 'no.' I went to the police, and I am issuing a missing person's report on my father. I need a few more pieces of information, like a physical description. Do you think you could help me again?"

The silence lasted so long that Andie feared Florence had hung up. At last she quietly said, "Yes."

"Do you think I could come back over there?"

"No."

"Mrs. Anderson, maybe you could come over here. There are a few things of my mother's that I thought you might want. This should only take a few minutes. Could you dash over here for a few minutes to look at those things?"

"Yes, I think that would be fine," Florence said cheerfully. "Would tomorrow at around ten work for you?"

"That would be perfect." Andie smiled.

THE NEXT MORNING, Andie folded a few quilts and blankets and stacked some towels that looked as though they had never been used on top. She tied the bundle with a ribbon and waited for Florence to arrive.

She came to the back door—a long-standing custom, she said—and sat at the kitchen table where Andie motioned to the police form. "I did what I could," Andie explained, "but this really shows how little I know about my father—even after talking to you."

Florence met her gaze with trepidation. "Andrea, dear, why are you doing this? Are you hoping your father is still alive? If he is, do you want to get to *know* him after all this time?"

Andie sunk into the kitchen chair next to Florence.

"I don't really know—on either of those counts," she answered. "As I told the police, I grew up assuming he was dead. I still do. And I don't know if I would want to know him if he *were* alive. I mean, he left us in the worst possible way. It seems to me a *divorce* would have been easier. A *lot* easier. To just walk away and leave everyone wondering seems really cruel. Maybe that's it—I just don't want to be left wondering any more. I want to *know*."

"I can understand that," Florence said. "We all did. Wondered, I mean. I don't think a one of us ever really stopped thinking about it. That's a lot of folks tied up in wondering about something they never found answers to."

Andie thought about another situation in which people were left wondering—a heinous murder she had heard about when she arrived in Utah. A surgeon and his wife were butchered in their sleep; between the two of them, there were more than a hundred stab wounds. The mattress was soaked entirely through with blood. When the police arrived, the couple's seven-year-old son sat dazed in the corner of the master bedroom. Clutched in his hands was the murder weapon.

He was catatonic. He was covered with blood himself. Through a dozen intensive investigations, nothing that could be catalogued as evidence was ever found. There were "probable" pieces of evidence, but one by one they were discounted. Despite a year of therapy, the little boy never spoke of the murder. Never spoke of his parents. Seemed strangely detached from an event of cataclysmic proportions that changed his life forever. At last, with family members and neighbors and friends and law enforcement still wondering, his uncle —his murdered father's brother—who lived in another state adopted the little boy. Under the loving care of his aunt and uncle, he did well. Got good grades in school. Played on a few teams and joined a few clubs. Did well in college. Still, they wondered...and would never *stop* wondering. Andie herself wondered if his adoptive parents ever stopped being afraid to fall asleep at night.

"What questions do you think I could help with?" Florence asked, snapping Andie's mind back to the kitchen in her mother's home.

"What did he look like?" Andie asked. "I don't even know what color his hair was."

"Brown—dark brown, with some red in it. Almost a chestnut color. A lot like yours," Florence said. "He had the most beautiful, dark-brown eyes. We used to laugh—they were the same color as Old Joe's eyes."

"Old Joe?"

"Frank's favorite horse," Florence smiled. "He was...oh, about six feet tall. Lean. Very lean. Muscular. Didn't wear a beard, but usually had a few days' growth at any given time. He did have a mustache once for a few months. He usually kept his hair a little longer...came down and rested on his collar. It sure made him stand out around here. He had high cheekbones, too—almost looked like they'd been sculpted. A strong, straight nose. And a bit of darkness in his skin... more than just from being out in the sun all day. Not really olive— more light brown. And a dimple in his chin. He was a handsome one!" Andie thought she saw Florence blush slightly.

Andie smiled sadly. *So that's where I got my height. And my brown hair. I could never figure out why I looked the way I did...nothing like Nora.*

"That's a lot!" Andie said. "It's obviously from almost four decades ago, but things like height and eye color and general body build don't change. You don't happen to know his birthday, do you?"

Florence shook her head. "I don't ever remember them

celebrating a birthday. Hers *or* his. As far as the year of birth...I think he was three years younger than your mother."

That was a surprise. Andie had always assumed he was older—always assumed that her grandparents objected because he was carrying their baby off into the sunset. Perhaps it was just the opposite: they objected because they thought he was too young, not equipped to take care of her. She smiled slightly at the thought of what would have happened had they found Nora shoveling chicken manure.

Nora had run off with not much more than a *teenager*. No wonder he had felt trapped.

"Okay, I can estimate the age," Andie said. "At least it's a place to start. Do you have *any* idea where he was born, or where he had been before he met my mother?"

Florence closed her eyes and rubbed her forehead. She took her time before answering. "Oh...I'm trying to think if he ever mentioned anything. Frank would probably know better...I just didn't talk to him that much. *Michigan.* That's right—he said if we thought *Nebraska* got cold, we should try *Michigan.* He said the wind whipped off the Great Lakes and cut to the bone."

"Great! Anything else?"

"He talked about Chicago once, now that I think about it. A ball game there. The Cubs. Was that it?" Florence's voice trailed off.

"Okay, that fills in some holes," Andie said. "Thank you so much, Mrs. Anderson. I've got a few things here that I thought you might like." Andie handed Florence the blankets and towels.

"Thank you, dear," Florence said, taking the bundle from Andie. "This is very kind of you. I'll treasure them."

As she led Florence to the back door, her thoughts focused on a mother's shattered dreams wrapped up in a handful of blue blankets and a father who vanished into thin air. She wanted to start over—to put the pieces together in some sort of logical order, to make sense of it all.

CHAPTER 18

Florence had been out the door only a few minutes when Andie's cell phone rang.

"I hope you're sitting down, Andie," Jack said then took a deep breath.

"It's okay, Jack; what's up?"

"This whole Barlow case...if it weren't so damned tragic, it might be one of those cases where you could roll up your sleeves and really have some fun in the chase. But for me it's more like a train wreck—sickening in its scope but keeping me riveted."

"I'll be honest—as you know, from the minute that fax arrived, I saw North Carolina as my ticket out of a really nasty situation," Andie said. "If he got extradited, I'd be off the case—because they're not going to go to the expense or hassle of extraditing him unless the prints and DNA evidence are pretty compelling. He'd never get off there, which means he'd never be back in Utah. As you also know, Sloan wants me to get him sentenced before North Carolina can process the extradition papers so we can at least delay the extradition. I appreciate you working with Grace on that while I've been in Nebraska."

"Andie, North Carolina is just the beginning."

Heat rushed into Andie's cheeks.

"I told you this case was getting convoluted, Andie. We got more papers last night."

Icy fingers squeezed her chest so tightly it felt like her heart would stop. Her breath came in short, ragged gulps. "What now?" she asked, wondering if she really wanted to know.

"Montana."

She listened to Jack as though she were in a trance as he explained the contents of the papers that arrived. Somewhere along a desolate road between Kalispell and Whitefish, tucked just below Glacier National Park, detectives searching for a missing thirteen-year-old boy had found his body—he'd been missing for only three days, and the soil over the shallow grave was still fresh. The palms of his hands had been singed—burned—possibly to remove fingerprints? He had been brutally sodomized, probably repeatedly. At least one of the assaults had been inflicted with an object. He was wearing only a pair of torn, stained underwear. Cause of death was strangulation.

Whoever assaulted Riley Marshall and stuffed his body into a hurriedly excavated grave had left behind a wealth of DNA. Brock Barlow's DNA.

The medical examiner reports were dated just five months earlier.

Next was another report from Montana—this one from Dillon, several hours to the south of Kalispell and along the western curve of the state. Another body in a hastily dug grave, this one in a stand of pines at the edge of a popular campsite; two campers, a father and his son, had stumbled across it while hiking. The uneven grave and haphazard position of fourteen-year-old Kevin Duncan's body bore mute evidence that his killer had feared getting caught at the gravesite. No effort had been made to scatter the leaves, pine needles, and bits of pinecones back over the freshly turned earth. Its very barrenness was what caught the attention of the hikers.

Montana officials working the case in Dillon had connected it to the Kalispell case fairly early in the investigation. There were several parallels—shallow graves, similar-aged victims, evidence of an object rape along with sodomy, strangulation. Most telling, however, were the burned palms of Kevin's hands, flesh singed to remove the ridges of identifying prints. That, and the DNA. Again, Brock Barlow's DNA.

Jack then described a pair of newspaper clippings attached to the file, perhaps as an afterthought. The depravity was spelled out in the vaguest possible terms in the slightly smudged newsprint. It was vague, yet clear at the same time. Clear enough to outline a pair of senseless murders. Clear enough to rattle Andie's already tenuous equilibrium.

"Horrific, isn't it?" Jack asked. "You swab a guy's cheek, enter the microscopic bits into a database, and all kinds of evil comes crawling out of dark and desperate places. When I got this stuff this morning, I couldn't stop reading. I read it over and over, maybe five or six times. It was like I hoped it would change if I read it enough, hoped it would all be a stupid mistake. Hoped it wouldn't really be Brock. Hell, even hoped those boys were still texting their friends and kicking a soccer ball."

Hot tears suddenly spilled onto Andie's cheeks. Her completely unexpected sobs sounded like suffocating hiccups. "The hands." Jack kept quiet during the minute it took Andie to gain enough control to finish a sentence. "The hands—it makes me sick. Please tell me he burned those hands after he had strangled the last breath out of those poor kids. Please tell me those poor boys were not alive to smell the acrid odor of their own burning flesh."

Jack's voice was solemn, almost hushed. "You're doing just what I did when I first read it. Focusing on some gruesome detail, almost missing the big picture—almost as if it's just too terrible to comprehend all at once. Face it, Andie. Even *if* the hands were burned postmortem, the sodomy was almost certainly exacted on a living, breathing boy."

"The hands—"

"Yes. The hands of the murder victims in North Carolina were burned too. He *didn't* burn the flesh of the boys he assaulted but allowed to live. But listen to this: He may not have burned their hands, but he used a cigarette lighter to singe the edges of their shirt cuffs. One of them said that he survived the sodomy intact, but he passed out from sheer terror over that cigarette lighter because he thought Barlow was going to set his shirt on fire and turn him into a human torch."

"So he was trying to erase the fingerprints of the boys who died—"

"But he left a myriad of other evidence, including his own DNA. It seems he's not nearly as sophisticated as we might have first assumed. Maybe his botched getaway here and his encounter with the end of the snowboard wasn't just dumb luck on Jameson Harper's part. Maybe instead it indicates a perpetrator who didn't have it all figured out."

"Here's what amazes me: Had he not been caught here, had the jail officials not fingerprinted him when they booked him, he might very well have permanently gotten away with it all. Until his prints and his DNA were in the national databases, there was no way to connect all that evidence with a suspect. Obviously, the investigators could use the DNA evidence to connect the cases, knew the same guy committed both crimes, but they had no way of knowing *who* the guy was. No wonder he went ballistic when the subpoena came in from North Carolina for his cheek swab. Imagine the total panic. He had to have known it was over."

Whatever happened now, Brock Barlow's case *was* over. Suddenly Andie no longer felt the need to return to Park City immediately. As quickly as possible, yes—but there were a few more things she needed to do in Nebraska—a few more things that would guarantee that the anguish she felt for her family was also over.

ANDIE CLOSED her eyes and pressed her fingers against her forehead, trying to massage out the soreness. For almost a week she had crawled her way east, stopping first in Lincoln and Omaha and then wandering through the postage-stamp-sized counties dotting Iowa, calling Jack and Grace to report at the end of each day. One of the associates in her old firm told her the best bet for finding a marriage record was in the archives of the county where the marriage had taken place. Should have been a breeze—except Andie had no idea in which county her teenaged parents had officially tied the knot.

And so the search began. Most of the county clerks she had talked to had tried to help; a few had eyed her with suspicion, as though she had no right to be snooping into records more than three decades old. A few others had dispatched her with efficiency, telling her to make a written request by mail and to expect a three- to four-week response time. The last one—a petite woman with large brown eyes and short white hair—had worked with Andie for several hours, combing painstakingly through the records of Guthrie County, Iowa, as if she had been searching for her own lost child.

When the records yielded nothing, she had placed her hand gently on Andie's arm. "You know, if I were you, I'd try the newspaper...in Des Moines," she had suggested. "The *Des Moines Register*. For quite a few years, it was really the only paper of any substance in the whole central part of the state. Who knows—you might find a wedding notice or some other news item that would give you a clue."

And now, sometime after two on a sleepy Thursday afternoon in a back room at the *Register* office, Andie closed her eyes and drew in a series of deep breaths, trying to ease the headache that pounded against her skull. She'd been at it since eleven, sitting in a lumpy office chair at a microfilm machine, methodically winding strips of film past a projector bulb, scanning what seemed like hundreds of issues of the *Register* for even a mention of a marriage between Drew Carlson and Nora Gray. Several times a week there were marriage and death notices—one-column, sterile listings of names, dates, ages. Andie had started with the films for newspapers nine months before she'd been born, just to be sure. And right before the headache took over, she was up to a few months before her birthday.

Stretching first her neck and then her back, Andie realized that the tedious, mind-numbing work reminded her of some of the research she'd had to do in law school. The print seemed miniscule, and some of the films were so dark they were almost impossible to read. Moving from one issue to another on the same piece of film often required adjusting the focus before a readable photograph of a newspaper emerged from a smattering of soft blur. Her head ached, her eyes burned...and, she realized suddenly, she was hungry. Really hungry.

The office manager directed Andie to a small diner just down the block. Andie wrapped a knit scarf around her neck and tugged on a pair of heavy woolen mittens against the biting cold as she walked the hundred yards to a fifties-style diner. It was well past the lunch-hour rush, and only a few customers sat at Formica tables. Music from a jukebox hummed in the background, and the air was warm with the aroma of apple cobbler. Daily specials were spelled out in chalk on a large blackboard; someone with a respectable measure of talent and a handful of colored chalk had punctuated the menu with a series of clever drawings. Tugging off her mittens, Andie decided to sit at the counter.

Before she could pile her coat and bag onto the stool next to her, a stout waitress with gray hair and a ruffled gingham apron slid a menu toward Andie, followed by a tall glass of ice water. "Welcome to Max's," she smiled. Andie did a quick double-take: at first glance, Maureen—or so her name tag said—looked remarkably like Nora. Andie stared helplessly, face-to-face with a vision of how Nora would have looked in ten years. Unexpected tears suddenly surfaced.

"Are you all right?" Maureen asked, clearly concerned.

Andie plucked a napkin from a metal dispenser and quickly dabbed at her eyes. "Yes," she smiled. "I'm so sorry. You remind me of my mother. She just died a few weeks ago."

Maureen clapped her hand over her mouth. "Oh, dear," she said quietly. "Did you come from out of town when she died? Because I don't remember ever seeing you here before. Des Moines is a sizable place, but we generally have our regulars."

"Actually, she died in Nebraska," Andie explained. "I'm just in Des Moines for the day, trying to find some information at the

Register. In fact, the office manager there is the one who recommended this place. She said it's first-rate."

"Oh, Bethany," Maureen said, smiling. "She comes in two or three times a week. I'm glad she sent you over."

"Well," Andie said, sliding the menu back toward Maureen, "I'm exhausted—and really hungry. What would you recommend?"

"That's easy!" Maureen laughed. "Do you like Reuben sandwiches?"

"Absolutely."

"Well, we nearly built this diner on the reputation of our Reuben on rye," Maureen said. "That, and our fresh, hand-cut fries. And, of course, our cherry Cokes."

"Sold," Andie said. Maureen passed the order back to the older man in the kitchen and kept up a pleasant chatter, explaining that she and her husband Max had come to Des Moines twenty years ago from Ames, thirty miles to the north, to be near grandchildren. Andie liked this warm woman with her winning smile and her talent for dribbling just the right amount of cherry syrup into a tall glass brimming with ice and Coke. Somewhere between the first half of the most delicious Reuben she had ever tasted and a thick wedge of fresh-cut fried potato, Andie explained exactly why she was in Des Moines.

"Oh, my," Maureen said, shaking her head. "That must be something like looking for a needle in a haystack."

"I'm starting to think so," Andie sighed. "I mean, I have their names, of course, but—as astonishing as this may seem to you—I'm not even sure exactly when my father was born. Or where. Or who his parents were. He disappeared when I was just a baby, and I guess it hurt my mother so badly that she just wouldn't talk about it. And, like I said, I don't know where they were married. Apparently, they met somewhere in Iowa while he was working in the corn fields, and they eloped—somewhere between that farm and somewhere east of Omaha."

Maureen let out a quiet whistle. "Do you know *about* how long ago they would have married?"

"My best guess is thirty-eight years ago," Andie explained. "But I've searched the county records everywhere from the state line through Guthrie County and found no trace of a Drew Carlson anywhere."

Maureen visibly stiffened. "Carlson?" she asked, her eyes widening.

"Yes. Drew Carlson. Why? Do you know someone by that name?"

Maureen braced herself against the counter, and her hands trembled slightly. Andie searched her face, trying to interpret the meaning of the change that had swept across the woman's features. "What, Maureen?" Andie asked. "What is it?"

"Probably not the same person," Maureen finally said.

"Maybe it is!" Andie found it difficult to contain her excitement. "Where is he? Does he live here in Des Moines?"

Maureen pulled a stool up to her side of the counter and sunk heavily onto it, her head and eyes lowered. After a few deep sighs, she finally met Andie's gaze. "Look, I probably shouldn't say anything. It's almost certainly not the same person. I would never want to get your hopes up, just to—"

"Please!" Andie begged, placing her hand on top of Maureen's. "If there's any possibility, I want to check it out. I mean, you're right—what are the chances? But what if it is? How do you know him? Does he live here?"

Maureen shook her head slowly. "No. I don't even really know him. There was a family in Ames—the Carlsons. They lived in our neighborhood. Had a tribe of kids. One of them was named Drew."

"Then I need to look there!" Andie said. "Do you know if they're still in Ames?"

"There was an accident. A terrible accident. A fire." Tears slid down the woman's cheeks. "Killed the whole family, if I'm remembering right. But that would have been...let me think...

probably forty-five years ago. The Drew in that family would have been not much more than a child. And," she wiped her eyes with the back of her hand, "he would not have survived to marry your mother, anyway." Her lower lip quivered. "It was cruel of me to even bring it up."

Andie's heart plunged. "No, it wasn't. And you're probably right about it not being the same family," she sighed. "But, just in case, I think I'll take a look. I have to be back in Utah in a few days at most, so I don't have a lot of time left. But I don't want to leave this stone unturned, just in case. Thank you for telling me." She drank the last of the cherry Coke and stood to put on her coat.

"Good luck," Maureen said, but something about her demeanor seemed less than sincere. "Try the newspaper there—the *Tribune*. A story like that for sure would have made the front page."

CHAPTER
19

The next morning Andie sat at a microfilm machine much like the one in Des Moines, except this one was at the *Tribune* office in Ames—a much smaller paper with a much more haggard staff. It had taken a lot of effort to persuade the man at the front desk to let her look at the films of past issues. *We usually do that only by appointment,* he had explained brusquely, *and only for people doing legitimate historical research.* Brandishing her legal credentials and explaining that she was only in the state for the day, Andie finally convinced him to let her examine the films. She started with the issues from forty-eight years earlier, not long after the paper launched its first issue.

Andie worked her way quickly through the old films. This time, she looked only at the front pages. Maureen was right—a story of that magnitude in a town this small would have been front-page news. After working her way through the first year of issues, she had to wait while the harried lifestyles editor replaced the film boxes in the filing cabinet and gathered the films for the next year, rebuffing Andie's offer to help.

Another year, and another wait for a new stack of boxes. The woman who retrieved the third year of issues made it clear to Andie that she was interrupting much more important work and that her presence was an intrusion.

Almost at the end of the film for the third year, Andie thrust the wheel forward to the next in a series of decades-old front pages. Suddenly her heart clutched raggedly in her chest. *Nine Members of Ames Family Perish in Fire* the headline read; a grainy black-and-white photo captured the blackened skeleton of what appeared to be a farm-style house, an outside end wall the only thing still standing in its entirety against the gray sky. Below the photo was the subhead: *Officials Believe Carlson Teen Started Fire That Wiped Out Family.*

Andie stared in horror.

Buried in the columns of newsprint that spelled out a tragedy from the heartland were a handful of other grainy black-and-white photos—these much smaller. In one, a lean man with narrow eyes and thick, dark hair was identified as *William Carlson* in a brief caption. His wife, *Nannette Carlson,* was situated just below him; she, too, had dark hair, but her eyes were wide, her cheekbones high and sculpted, slightly reminiscent of Native American ethnicity. A smattering of other pictures showed a variety of children, innocently at play. A few of the photos looked like school pictures, snapped by a shrouded photographer as children moved with military precision in a steady line through one end of the school cafeteria.

Andie's eyes darted back to the picture of the house. The charred remains of a bicycle leaned against the one standing wall. A towering tree—was it an elm?—still stood, blackened, its bark blistered. All along what would have been the foundation of the house was black debris skirted by copious ash. Far in the background, only partially in the frame of the picture, was what looked like a barn. It had escaped the firestorm. Andie thought she could see a horse, its hindquarters protruding from one side of the structure.

A wave of nausea washed over her. *Could these people be related to my father?* Looking at a picture of two little girls with a small wagon, Andie cried softly. One had light hair and chubby cheeks; clad in bib overalls and a tattered sweater, she sat happily in the wagon. Her sister had darker hair and the same high, sculpted cheekbones as her mother; wearing a ragged dress, a straw cowboy hat, and battered cowboy boots, she was laughing as she tried to pull the wagon. The caption below the photo read *Myrna and Ann Carlson.*

Andie was startled by the intensity of her emotion. It was an obvious tragedy—an entire family wiped out in a house fire. Little girls, so carefree and happy, gone in an instant. Perhaps that was the reason for her upset. Or maybe it was the evidence that this family had so little—starkly demonstrated by the tattered clothing, the rusted wagon, the sad look in almost every pair of eyes—before it was wiped out completely.

Reading the bleak headline again, Andie rested her chin in her palms, took a deep breath, and started to read the story.

Fire officials have determined that 13-year-old Drew Carlson started the fire that killed his parents and all seven of his brothers and sisters on November 8 in Ames.

Andie gasped, then coughed erratically. The lifestyles editor shot a disapproving glance at her, undoubtedly annoyed at the disturbance. Andie clapped her hand over her mouth to contain the sound that now became a sort of strangled yelp. Her face flushed; her eyes brimmed with hot tears. Maureen had been *a neighbor* —certainly she would have remembered that a boy named *Drew* had started the fire—and that he had *survived* the fire! Why hadn't she told everything she knew? What other secrets were spread around with the sudsy dishrag as Maureen polished the gleaming counter? Andie felt confused and panic-stricken as she continued to read.

The teenager remains in state custody but has not been able to tell officials what happened the night of the fire.

Andie's chest burned; she felt like she was going to vomit. She checked the date of the newspaper again. The math worked: her father, married at seventeen, just months before Andie was born, would have been thirteen the night the fire erupted in Ames, incinerating an entire family in the heat of its intensity. All but one, that is. All but Drew Carlson. It wasn't *proof,* of course. But it was unlikely a coincidence.

A spokesman from the Story County Sheriff's office said that while criminal charges may be filed at a later date after the investigation has been completed, the teen is in the custody of the state and is being cared for by state social services. No relatives could be located.

According to results of the fire department investigation, the fire apparently started in a room in the cellar, and an accelerant was involved. Hank Carlson, 14, was sleeping in another room in the cellar, and was likely overcome by fumes almost immediately.

Evidence indicates that the fire spread rapidly, engulfing the main floor where William Carlson, 39, and his wife Nannette Carlson, 34, were sleeping with 13-month-old Betty. A second bedroom on the main floor was occupied by 11-year-old Jennie and nine-year-old Clare. All of those on the main floor were likely consumed by flames before they had a chance to awaken.

Apparently a "chimney effect" drew the flames to the second floor, where three children sleeping in a small bedroom were likely overcome by gases before the flames reached them. Seven-year-old Myrna, six-year-old Ann, and three-year-old Teddy perished in that room.

Andie frantically wiped the tears from her cheeks and bit her lower lip. Myrna and Ann, the little girls playing with the wagon… asleep with their little brother, tucked beneath patchwork quilts against the November chill, probably clutching a doll. Raw grief clutched at Andie's heart. For a fleeting moment, she thought she could smell the toxic smoke curling toward sleeping children just minutes before the flames consumed them completely.

Because of the intensity and rapid spread of the fire, officials believe it was improbable that any of the family members would have awakened or could have escaped the blaze. They are still not certain how 13-year-old Drew, the only survivor of the fire, was able to get out, and why he was not able to alert any of the other family members.

Funeral arrangements have not been announced for the nine members of the Carlson family who died in the fire. Officials are still trying to locate relatives, who will be responsible for making those arrangements.

William Carlson was a welder and was employed at the Ames Municipal Electric Company for the past six years, since relocating to Ames from Detroit, Michigan. Nannette Carlson taught at Roosevelt School for two years but has been at home with her children for the past four years. They were members of the First Presbyterian Church, and Mrs. Carlson was a regular volunteer at the local branch of the Red Cross.

Michigan. What was it Mrs. Anderson had said? Andie could almost hear her voice carried on the aroma of oatmeal cookies through her small kitchen: *He said if we thought* Nebraska *got cold, we should try* Michigan. *He said the wind whipped off the Great Lakes and cut to the bone.* Drew would have been seven when they picked up the pieces of their lives and moved south to Ames, to the heartland, to a place where the corn grew as high as an elephant's eye. He would remember those piercing winds.

Everything in the room seemed to grind to a halt as Andie started at the beginning of the article, reading again for any wisp of information she may have missed the first time. Scanning the spread across the front page, she realized there was no picture of Drew. Of course not—he had started the fire. The day a salty reporter wrote this story, the day these newspapers landed on the porches of the good citizens of Ames, Drew was not a boy who tragically lost his entire family. He was a boy who spread some sort of accelerant and lighted a match and failed to save even one of the people he had eaten with and played with and worshipped with. He was a murderer.

Andie shuddered, remembering the bulging retort at the funeral home in Minden—remembering the thought of Nora stuffed into a cardboard container, being pushed head-first into an oven that would take only two hours to vaporize her. The bile roiled up Andie's throat. *Her father—the man who had carelessly wandered out of her life along a deserted Nebraska road—had just as carelessly wiped out his whole family.*

Filled with revulsion, Andie retrieved a notebook from her bag and wrote the details she was most likely to want: names, ages, the date of the front-page article. When she had recorded everything possible, she plowed through the subsequent issues of the *Ames Tribune,* looking for articles that would report details of the ongoing investigations. Maybe something—*anything*—would rule out the probability that this cold killer was her father.

A week later, there were obituaries. Apparently, relatives had been located, because the obituaries were too personal to have been written by a detached funeral director. The nine obituaries almost filled the paper's obit page. Andie devoured the details. William had done a brief stint in the Army before sustaining an injury that earned him a medal and kept him home. Nannette had graduated with honors from a teaching college. Jennie and Clare both played the violin. Hank had won accolades in a recent science fair. All of them were survived by just one family member: Drew Carlson. A single memorial service was held at the Ames First Presbyterian Church, under the direction of Pastor Clyde Barnett. The remains were buried in the City Cemetery on First Street.

Andie continued searching, a steady sense of panic rising with each edition of the news. What had become of Drew Carlson? Had he ever admitted what happened? Had he ever found words to describe the horror of that night?

Finally, in an edition several weeks after the obituaries, she found a rather small article, tucked inconspicuously on the fourth page under an article about a proposed bomb shelter being considered at the local elementary school.

Ames fire officials have released the results of their investigation into the November 8 fire that killed nine members of an Ames family. The lone survivor of the fire, 13-year-old Drew Carlson, was apparently trying to use kerosene in a homemade heating device to keep warm in a cellar bedroom.

Municipal electric officials have confirmed that the heat in the home had been turned off due to nonpayment of a bill that was nearly a year overdue.

The young Carlson had fashioned the stove in an attempt to keep the family warm. When it malfunctioned, flames rapidly involved a thirty-gallon container of kerosene that was near the homemade stove. Shocked by the rapid incineration, Carlson tried to wake Hank, 14, who was in the next room, but he was already unconscious. Carlson broke a cellar window and was able to pull himself to safety, but the rapid spread of the fire prevented him from reaching any other family members.

Killed in the fire were William, 39, and his wife, Nannette, 34; also killed were their children, Hank, 14; Jennie, 11; Clare, 9; Myrna, 7; Ann, 6; Teddy, 3; and Betty, 13 months.

Drew Carlson has been cleared of any criminal charges. He remains in the care of relatives in Newton.

Tears stung Andie's eyes. What a difference a few weeks makes! Had Maureen remembered *this part,* or only the fire? What about the rest of them? Andie felt as if she could see the neighbors circling the wagons, as it were...felt she could hear the gossamer threads of gossip carried on the bitter wind. Reeling in the aftermath of a blaze that had lighted up the November sky in a modest part of town, neighbors and reporters and fire officials had narrowed their eyes and looked only at the fact that a thirteen-year-old boy was the lone survivor—the only one left standing after an inferno that wiped out his entire family.

Andie wondered who had been the first to cast suspicion. Was it the fire chief? Was it the reporter, standing at the fringe of the horror and jotting down facts with the stub of a leaded pencil? Was it the efficient woman dispatched from social services who grabbed Drew roughly by the arm and pushed him into a dark sedan? Or was it the doctor who examined Drew, looking for traces of injuries, who saw only angry gashes caused by a frantic escape through a broken cellar window?

Then she realized with a wave of nausea that she had done the same. Had looked at the grainy photo of a charred house and had assumed the worst about a thirteen-year-old boy. A thirteen-year-old boy that would become her *father*.

Tucking her notebook back into her bag and switching off the projector light, Andie felt a sense of injustice on behalf of Drew Carlson—a man she had seldom felt *anything* toward. The article exonerating him, telling the tragic story of a thirteen-year-old worried about his baby sister trembling in the cold, belonged on the front page...should have had the same dramatic coverage as the fire. If it had happened today, she thought, it would have been the fodder of a good investigative journalist, who would have started her feature article with the irony of a company turning off the electricity of one of its own employees.

On her way out of town, she visited the City Cemetery on First Street. The sextant rolled out a large map covered with small plots and penned-in names and directed her to a far corner of the cemetery dotted with weathered headstones. There, along the edge of a narrow road, was a flat granite headstone bearing the names of the entire Carlson family—all but one. There were no birth dates, and only a single death date. Andie took a few minutes to brush the dead leaves off the stone and to offer a silent prayer for the souls whose remains lay beneath it. They were like all the other members of her family: buried and silent.

Driving back toward Minden to tie up a few last details, Andie clutched the steering wheel as the tears ran freely down her cheeks. Had Nora known about the fire? Had Nora ever wondered why Drew didn't have a family? Had Drew ever found the words, ever been able to form the ghastly picture of what had happened to the family he was trying to help? Had Drew and Nora talked about things like that on those steamy nights against the fertile soil between rows of corn, or had they only groped and explored with the unbridled passion of the young?

A good portion of her tears were tears of frustration. Andie would probably never know the answers. She straightened against the seat of the rental car. She had *some* answers—important ones. She knew a little about Drew's roots. She knew his father's name, and that his father had fought bravely in the waning days of a war on foreign soil. She knew his mother had once wandered up and down the narrow aisles between schoolroom desks, guiding small hands. She knew that he once had a large family, a passel of brothers and sisters who must have played night games and splashed in ditchwater and sucked air at the end of rope swings. Before leaving Ames, she had driven down the street where his childhood home had once stood, and she imagined hearing his laughter on the air. A strip mall now took up much of the block.

Winding her way across the border into Omaha, Andie no longer felt a driving need to know where her parents had married. She had new information that might help in that search. Maybe it was near Newton, where nameless, faceless relatives had taken in the boy who had put a match to the kerosene. Or maybe it was close to Ames. Or maybe it was somewhere in between. Somehow it didn't matter so much anymore.

She realized, too, that even though she hadn't seen a single photograph of Drew in the news coverage, a picture of him was for the first time engraved on her heart.

It was a picture mired in twisted conflict for Andie. It was the picture of a man who, despite an almost incomprehensible tragedy, had walked away from a wife and a little girl—had left them, alone and wondering, surrounded by fields that needed to be planted. How, having lost his entire family that frosty November night, could Drew have abandoned the little family he had managed to build? What would have possessed him to choose isolation over being part of a whole? Perhaps his utterly failed efforts to protect one family had left him stripped of confidence in his ability to protect another. Or perhaps the hurt from those nine lost souls had gnawed so mercilessly at his heart that he couldn't offer his heart to anyone else. Or maybe he was just selfish—trapped, as Mrs. Anderson suggested, in a loveless marriage he hated, and burdened with a child to which he felt no attachment.

Andie would never know. Drew had taken the answers with him out into the Nebraska plains, and anything that could give her a glimpse into his heart had vanished along with him the day he went off for a pack of smokes.

Pulling into the driveway of Nora's house long after midnight, Andie felt an odd sense of closure. She would fly back to Utah tomorrow...after she called Jack and Grace, and after she told Florence Anderson all about a thirteen-year-old boy and a homemade kerosene stove.

CHAPTER
20

Toweling off her hair and in a rush to get to her office, Andie heard the phone ring. Odd. She rarely got calls before she left for work. By the time she reached the phone next to her bed, it had stopped ringing. Within a minute, the message light blinked on.

With a sigh, Andie sat on the edge of the bed and punched in the code for her messages. *Please, don't let this be about Brock,* she thought. She wanted just a *little* time this morning without having to deal with him.

It wasn't about Brock. Far from it. It was Douglas Nelson, the attorney from Nelson & Brown in Minden who had helped settle Nora's affairs. He had some important information for her. Asked that she call him back.

What now? As far as she knew, everything in Minden had been settled. With Brock's case looming overhead, this definitely wasn't the time to have to deal with anything else. And it *definitely* wasn't the time to fly back to Minden to tie up any loose ends they had not noticed the first time around. Andie's life had been turned upside-down, and she couldn't imagine having to deal with anything else in Nebraska right now. It would simply have to wait, whatever it was.

Andie considered not returning the call until later, but figured it was best to just get it over with. Maybe it was something much simpler than she was imagining. Dialing the number, she was surprised when the secretary picked up on the first ring. Before Andie had any real time to get worked up, Douglas Nelson was on the phone, using his customary cool, emotionless tone.

"I've had a bit of an unusual thing happen. As part of settling your mother's affairs, we ran all the required legal notices in the paper—you know, giving people a deadline by which to notify us if they had a debt to file against the estate. Of course, your name was listed in the notices too since you are the executor of the estate."

Andie knew the kind. She wasn't an expert in estate law, but she knew what he was talking about. Sort of the speak-now-or-forever-hold-your-peace of assets. "And?"

"After the deadline for filing had expired, I got a letter from a woman who seems to think she is your cousin."

Andie involuntarily gasped. "I...I don't have any living relatives. What did she want? Did she think Nora was worth a bunch of money, and did she want in on the action?"

"That's the odd part," Nelson said. "She didn't want anything. Not from the estate, anyway. She said the family had been looking for your mother and didn't know your mother had any living relatives. She assumed *you* were a relative, and just thought it might be nice to make some connections—with family."

Andie was stunned. She kept waiting for a film crew from *Candid Camera* to jump out of the closet.

"Obviously, we don't give out any contact information without a client's specific consent—which I clearly didn't have from you. Instead, I took her name and number and promised to pass it on to you. In case you want to call her. You can do with that whatever you want."

Reaching for the small notepad on her nightstand, Andie penned the name and number. *Margaret Reid.* A Rhode Island number, according to Nelson. Before she called anyone, she needed to call Grace.

And Jack. This didn't have anything to do with the case they were working on together, but Andie realized with a glimmer of surprise that she also wanted to call Jack.

Andie folded the note in half and tucked it into her bag. The calls to Grace and Jack had gone about as Andie had expected. Grace thought she should call the woman. Check it out. See what was up. Jack was a bit more cautious; Andie could still hear his voice: *Once you make that contact, you can't ever take it back. She'll know you're there. What if she's nuts? What if she's not really your cousin—what if she's just trying to take advantage of you in some way?*

She weighed the options as she dressed for work. What if the woman *was* some sort of nut who just wanted to inch her way into someone else's family? But honestly, what were the chances she would have found Andie's family—a "family" that was scarcely there? That left a curious possibility: what if she actually *was* family? Andie had gone her entire life believing there *wasn't* anyone else. Nora had certainly never mentioned anyone. Yet according to this Margaret person, they had been looking for Nora. What on earth for?

Just as she was about to leave, her phone rang again. Not just one, but *two* phone calls before she left for work?

"Ms. Harrison? Gerald Oldroyd from the Minden Police Department." *Good. At least it's not someone wanting to talk about Brock Barlow,* Andie thought. *Not something I could stand before my first cup of coffee.*

"How may I help you, Detective?"

"Well, I'm hoping I have some information that might help *you.*"

Andie dropped with a thud onto the edge of her bed. "Did you find out anything about my father?"

"Actually, I did. And it was much easier than I was expecting; he used his own name and Social Security number after he left Minden. It's not clear what happened for the first month or so, but after that he settled down in Michigan—Detroit—where he worked in a plant assembling parts for Chevrolet."

Michigan. Of course. He headed for the familiar—for a place he had known as a little boy. A place where he had happy memories. A place where he snuggled into the curve of his mother's arm and caught a baseball pitched by his father. A place where there was no homemade kerosene stove, no fire, no smoldering ashes, no solitary headstone with its list of names. "That sort of makes sense," she said. "It seems he lived in Michigan when he was young, before his family moved to Iowa. I doubt he would have remembered any friends—I think he was only seven or so when they moved. But maybe he had extended family there."

"I don't know about that. Shame is, he wouldn't have been very hard to find at the time if your mother had looked very hard. Like I said, he used his own name and Social Security number. A fairly simple search would have pretty easily turned him up. I have no way of knowing how hard your mother or anyone else looked for him, but, fact is, Ms. Harrison, he didn't put much effort into hiding."

Andie could just see Nora, intent on keeping up appearances, simply avoiding the fact that her infant son had just died and that her husband had walked off into the sunset along a lonely stretch of flat country highway. Not asking for help. Not even calling the police, because what would people have thought of her?

Nora obviously hadn't even told the neighbors—not even the next-door neighbors, whose windows looked out on the yard behind the white clapboard house on Garfield Road. Andie remembered Florence describing how they just eventually noticed that the fields weren't being plowed—that the farm machinery was sitting oddly idle, that no one remembered having seen Drew for weeks. Or was it months by then?

He didn't put that much effort into hiding. Had he known that Nora's own inertia, fueled by an oppressive need to maintain appearances, would keep her from looking? Had he figured she would do exactly what she did—stay sheltered in the living room behind the big picture window, watching aimlessly for a figure sauntering down the road, but lacking the ambition to launch out on her own? Had he somehow known that Nora had too little drive, too little native curiosity, too few resources to scout out the trail he had so deliberately trod?

But that was only part of it. Most difficult for Andie was the fact that he had walked away from *her*—from a little girl not yet two. The fierce love she had felt for Beau at that age slammed into her with alarming force. Drew had wanted to escape Nora. Andie could deal with that—could even understand. Andie herself had wanted to escape Colin, and she had, but she had carried Beau with her every step of the way—first in the warm cocoon of her belly, then up and down the stairs of the white clapboard house on Garfield Road, then to Sanibel Islands, then from the fields studded with sunflowers to the rugged mountain peaks. It had never crossed her mind to leave Beau. And it came as an overwhelming sorrow that Drew Carlson had so effortlessly struck out along that two-lane highway, deliberately turning his back on *her*.

At quiet times, times when her thoughts drifted, she tried to imagine how desperate Drew must have been—how wretched a situation he must have endured. Could it have been that bad? What could drive a person to vanish, to leave without a word, to disappear along an isolated stretch of road without even so much as a change of clothes? Even in those quiet times, when those thoughts bounced off the inner curve of her head, Andie couldn't imagine Nora's part in it all. Andie herself had been on the receiving end of Nora's cold sense of righteous indignation plenty of times and knew it with a disconcerting intimacy. How much of it had Nora hurled at Drew? How badly had she crushed him?

He didn't put that much effort into hiding. Yet Nora hadn't put that much effort into looking. Had it not occurred to Nora that her little girl would always wonder about her father? That there would come a day when the very fact of his disappearance would haunt even her waking hours as she ran between rows of corn in the simple games of her childhood? Slowly, the sodden realization came over Andie that all those things—and more—*had* probably occurred to Nora. But that Nora hadn't cared. And that was perhaps the most disturbing of all.

"There's nothing I can do to change the past." Andie sighed loudly enough for Oldroyd to hear her disappointment on the other end of the line. "I can't understand why my mother didn't put more effort into finding him—or at least into finding out what happened to him. She never really talked about it. Never really talked about him leaving—or about him *at all*. You know, now that I think about it, I don't really remember how I found out that he left. It seems like it's always been part of my native consciousness. I truly can't remember a specific conversation about it."

"Hard to tell why folks do what they do. Like I said, it's a real shame she didn't seem to look, at least not very hard, because I think she would have found him without too much effort."

"To tell you the truth, I'm not sure it really would have changed anything. I guess I have to face the possibility that maybe she didn't *want* to find him—that maybe, on some visceral level, she was relieved. Up until the day she died, she was a woman almost pathologically concerned about what people thought of her. Maybe the prospect of a divorce was too much to bear—that having him walk away like he did, having him disappear across the desolate plains, was somehow more *acceptable* to her. Maybe being a victim—being abandoned—seemed better somehow. I don't know; I guess I'm just thinking out loud. Forgive me."

"No need to apologize. I guess you'll never know. I can't provide those kinds of answers. Now that your mother is dead, there may not be *anyone* who can give you those answers. What I *can* tell you is that Drew Carlson worked at that assembly plant for almost six years. Never caused any problems at all. Could say he was a model employee. Won some awards for safety on the job—all those years without any kind of accident or incident. Hopped around to a couple of different addresses; all rentals. Bought a few used cars—one a real beater. And that's where the trail goes cold."

"What do you mean?"

"Suddenly, he just dropped off the face of the earth—a second time, you might say. Records show he resigned his position at the assembly plant. Moved out of the apartment he was renting. Closed his bank account. There is no more activity involving his Social Security number."

The bile rose in Andie's throat. "What does that mean? Did he die?"

"Ms. Harrison, I don't think he died—not right then, anyway. It's not like he just vanished without taking care of things. He resigned his job. Gave his landlord notice before moving out of his apartment. Closed his bank account. Had he died, at least right then, he would have failed to show up at work. Failed to pay his rent, which would have sent his landlord searching. He wouldn't have closed his bank account; activity just would have ceased. Money would have sat there, not being used. No, I don't think he died at that point."

"Then what?"

"I think there are two possible scenarios. The first one—maybe he wanted to get married. And because he had never dissolved his marriage to your mother, he had to get a little creative. If that's what happened, he had a dilemma on his hands: If he wanted to do it legally, he had to file for a divorce, which means your mother would have been served with papers and would have found out where he was. If he was miserable enough to leave her like he did, you can imagine the thought of stirring up a hornet's nest years later wasn't high on his list. So if he decided against filing for divorce and getting married the legal way, he had to do it the illegal way. He had to take on a new identity—change his name, change his Social Security number, so he could get married with no questions asked. Then he was free to fill out the application and get the blood test and be on his way."

"But you have no way of proving that's what happened?"

"No. I'm sorry. Like I said, that's where the trail goes cold. And if that's what happened, he probably landed another job under his new name, at another assembly plant—Detroit was full of them—opened a new bank account, got married, and lived happily ever after without having to open up any old wounds out here in Nebraska."

Married. Happily ever after. That means a wife. And children.

New children. Children other than Andie, who had been virtually discarded that day, and Matthew, who never came home. "So if he used a new name, I guess there's really no way of tracking him down."

"I guess it might eventually be possible, given a lot of determined work and access to the right records and technology, but I'm afraid I've exhausted all my resources in that regard, Ms. Harrison. If that's what happened, I'm guessing that your father would be leading a very quiet existence somewhere in the Detroit area, likely with a wife and a bunch of kids and probably even a handful of grandkids, and I'm guessing that he wouldn't be real happy if someone—you, me, a private detective—showed up unannounced one day and reminded him of, uh, let's call them *his obligations* in Nebraska."

"You're a cop, and I'm a lawyer, and we both know that the scenario you're constructing is against the law. Plain and simple."

"Yes, it's bigamy, and it's plainly against the law. But there's nothing simple about it. If I've learned anything in my years in law enforcement, it's this: The human will is a force so powerful that we're more often than not helpless against a man who sets his mind to something. Even if we found him, Ms. Harrison, *you're* not looking at a happily ever after. He took pretty desperate measures to escape back then—and I'm guessing he wouldn't exactly welcome you with open arms. I'm not trying to hurt you; I'm trying to help you understand what you'd likely encounter even if we had the wild success of actually locating him. So a second marriage is one possibility. But we haven't talked about the other likely scenario."

"What's that?"

"That he is, in fact, dead. The fact that he quit his job and moved and emptied his bank account could be an indication that while his work record was exemplary enough, he was for one reason or another facing some instability in his life. And it's also been my experience that people who are in an unstable situation are at a far greater risk of dying."

"In what way?"

"Oh, every way—accident. Crime. Illness. But the most likely is suicide."

Suicide. The word drilled into the painful spot right between Andie's eyes. *Suicide.* She tried to maintain control, keep her voice even. "Suicide?"

"In fact, Ms. Harrison, people who decide to commit suicide often go through a peculiar series of activities in which they, in essence, settle their own affairs. They give away possessions and take care of paperwork and get everything in place so they can just exit without leaving other people in the lurch. That doesn't always happen—some people self-destruct in such a rage that they seemingly have no concern at all about how it will impact others. But many are quite careful, and I think that might have been the case with your father, considering Drew Carlson's last known activities. He quit his job instead of just failing to show up one day; his employer had a chance to hire a replacement so he wouldn't suddenly be without help. He gave notice and moved so his landlord had the chance to find a new tenant. He emptied his bank account—and it would fit the pattern for him to have given that money away, even anonymously. All those things fit with a suicide, Ms. Harrison. I know that's a terrible thought, but based on the last known activities of your father, that may be the case."

Andie squeezed her eyes shut against the dizzying spin of her room, just warming to the first slants of light coming through the tilted blinds. First Beau, now her father. Was it possible—even *remotely* possible—that a tendency to self-destruct could be *genetic,* even if two people were related but had never *met?* Her mind saw in vivid detail a scene her eyes had never actually beheld: Beau, dangling from the bare branches of a tree, situated at the edge of a vacant lot, the gray sky pressing against his last desperate act. Had her father done the same thing—looped a rope around the thickest branch of a tree, around a steel beam in a deserted building? Or had he chosen some other way to vanish, this time with no chance of being discovered?

"Ms. Harrison?"

Andie struggled to compose herself. "I'm sorry, but my son committed suicide last year, and the pain is still pretty fresh."

"Oh, I'm so sorry."

"This just—it just opens up all kinds of horrifying possibilities. I don't know enough about it, but—is there any evidence that the tendency to suicide actually runs in families? I mean, my son and my father obviously never met, so there couldn't have been any sort of behavioral influence. I'm just...boggled." *And where does that leave me? Will I someday wake up and just despair of it all and find myself fingering the frayed end of a thick rope?*

"I wish I could help you there, but I don't have any experience or background in that sort of thing. It certainly does seem—odd. It could be just a coincidence, especially since they never knew each other."

The hurt and the anger tore through Andie with a ferociousness that startled her. First her father walked away without a word of farewell—and in the ensuing years she was so far off his radar screen that he never came back to claim even the tiniest piece of her. And now—now, the picture a seasoned detective was painting consisted of broad brushstrokes of either indifference or brutal self-destruction. "So what you're telling me is that this is hopeless—that I should basically abandon any effort to find Drew Carlson?"

"I'd have to say yes. I know that's not the position I should take as a member of the police department who's working on a missing persons case, but, yes—if you were my daughter or my wife or my friend, I'd advise you to give up the search. Put the thing to rest. I know that's easier said than done, but that would be my advice."

"I appreciate your candor."

"I need to tell you why in your case, especially, I'd advise giving up. A few months after Drew Carlson 'disappeared,' the body of a John Doe washed up on a beach along Lake Superior. The body was in such a state of decay that it could not be identified; apparently their attempts at collecting DNA failed because it was so compromised. He was buried at the state's expense as a John Doe.

But his general build and what hair remained matched your description of your father. I believe it was him."

Andie clutched her stomach and rocked on the edge of the bed, tears sliding down her cheeks.

"If you would like, I can arrange for an exhumation of the remains. I'm not sure how much we'd accomplish, but if it would give you some peace, we can make it happen."

Andie rolled the possibility over in her mind a few times. "No. Thank you, though. No."

"I just can't see a happy ending on this one, Ms. Harrison. In the unlikely event that he's alive, he's probably created a whole new family, and if you find him, you would almost certainly be seen as an unwelcome interloper—not just by him, but by the rest of the family. I can't imagine there's a single player in that game who would welcome you with open arms...or welcome you at all. And if what I believe is true, and he's dead—well, there are no more options. Either way, you're at a dead end."

"And if I give up the search—"

"If you give up the search, *you* create the end. *You* decide how you want it to be. It really doesn't matter if your version of things isn't accurate to the smallest detail—or accurate at all. If it can become your reality, that's all that matters. You might find the greatest amount of peace by simply imagining what you want. That might seem sort of silly and stupid, but I've seen it work in lots of cases—and work fairly well."

"Well, I guess that's it, then. Thank you for spending the time you did in trying to locate him. And thank you again for your candor. I'm sure you're right. Whatever happened between the time he left and the time he died, I'm certain he did. Die, that is. Not that you need my permission, but I'm assuming you can consider the case closed."

"Actually, I do sort of need your 'permission.' Not *permission*, exactly, but protocol requires that I report my findings to you and that I clearly indicate what the next steps are. And the next step in this situation, sadly, is to close the case. Some might consider that giving up, but I don't. I think we've found what we can reasonably find, considering our relatively limited resources in this department, and now it's time to close the book. To let Drew Carlson rest in peace, so to speak."

Rest in peace. Like the charred remains of nine people under a single granite stone at the edge of a quiet cemetery in Ames. Like Nora, incinerated to a pile of crumbly ash in the bulging belly of a roaring oven. Like Beau—cut down from the tree, dressed in a new suit, tucked in a lonely grave. *Does anyone ever really rest? Did my father ever really rest? Will I ever really rest?*

Now she knew what had happened. And now it *was* time to rest.

CHAPTER 21

Rushing into her office, Andie was startled to see Jack sitting across from her desk.

"Andie, I hate like anything to pounce on you the minute you're back, but there's more." Jack glanced at a blue folder in his lap. "It's the last thing I expected, but there's more."

Andie lowered herself into her chair and hesitantly picked up the folder Jack slid across the desk. Andie was shocked at the heft of the file; it had to be thirty or more pages long bound with a large black clip. She set the file on top of the blue folder and placed a trembling hand over it. "I'm not sure I can read it, Jack. Not sure I *want* to read it. Is it just more of the same?"

Jack cleared his throat and gazed out the window before looking again at Andie. "Pretty much, unfortunately. Same crap, different state. Texas."

"How about you just give me a summary?"

"Seven murders over a four-year period in and around Arlington, situated almost exactly between Dallas and Fort Worth. Cops and residents alike knew they had a serial killer on their hands, and a sheriff lost reelection in the middle of it because he hadn't solved the cases and arrested a suspect. Texas has two well-known characteristics: a vigilante spirit and a fairly swift execution rate. Our man Brock is lucky he avoided arrest in Texas, because if lethal injection doesn't get you, the locals will."

"Were the Texas cases similar to the others?"

"Mostly. All boys in their early teens; in fact, if I remember correctly, all but one were thirteen. Cause of death was strangulation in all cases; one was garroted with a strip of his own shirt and a broken piece of lumber from a building site. All were sodomized, and all but the garroting victim showed signs of object rape. All but one were buried in shallow graves; the last one was tossed into a huge irrigation culvert. He was discovered the day after his murder. And yes, Andie, all the hands were burned."

"And the DNA?"

"Brock Barlow, in every case."

Andie stared at the folder. "Any more?"

"No, that's it. But now we have *three* states vying for extradition. North Carolina still appears to be the oldest set of crimes and jumped on it first, so it will likely get the first shot at him. I obviously have no clue what kind of defense will be mounted there, but it will be very difficult to overcome DNA evidence. And I imagine the prosecution there will do some sort of legal maneuvering to allow at least some mention of Brock's evident crime spree in two other states. Not to mention inadvertently leaving a live victim here. I'd say your wish has come true, Andie—I don't think you're going to be responsible for defending Brock Barlow much longer."

Wish? She *had* wished to be rid of Brock Barlow, to never look at him again. But she had definitely not wished for a trail of boys in three states to be littered across the landscape, torn from their parents and stuffed into crude graves. No. That hadn't been part of her wish at all. And faced with that horror, she would gladly barter for having to deal with Brock forever if it could only mean that Jameson Harper was his only victim.

"Like I said, Jack, my focus will be on getting Brock sentenced before any of the states can extradite him; then at least he'll have a sentence on the records here, for whatever that might be worth down the road. And once the sentencing hearing is scheduled, extradition will be delayed until that's finished. Obviously, the only way I'll be able to do that is to get him to plead guilty and skip the ordeal of a trial."

"From what I've seen of Brock Barlow so far, his absolute

arrogance is going to be the biggest thing to overcome. I'm not sure you'll ever be able to get him to plead guilty—not even on temporary insanity."

"It won't be easy. I think the only chance I'll have of getting him to plead guilty will be if he sees the absolute mountain of evidence stacked up against him...if he becomes convinced beyond any doubt that he has no chance of succeeding with a jury."

"Wave the death sentence in front of him too, Andie. Obviously, the prosecution can't go for the death penalty here; the nature of his crime here wasn't severe enough to warrant it. But the nature of his crimes in the other three states *does* warrant it, and they'll almost certainly go for it. Especially Texas. Texas tosses everyone they can on death row and eats the inmates for breakfast. And they don't take years to do it, either."

Because of what he did elsewhere, this nightmare might still be over in a relatively short time. Sloan was right. I can do it.

DESPERATE FOR A DISTRACTION, Andie decided to check out the mysterious "cousin" who had suddenly surfaced in response to the series of legal notices. Grace had offered to sit with Andie while she called Rhode Island. So had Jack. In the end, she decided to do it alone. But first she needed to find out what she could about Margaret Reid in the few precious minutes she had. Rhode Island was two hours ahead of Utah, so she knew she couldn't spend too much time on research—not if she wanted to call Margaret Reid tonight.

She decided to use the two quickest, easiest sources of information. Facebook wasn't too helpful. There was one Maggie Reid—but she looked way too young. Her profile contained only a sparse description: Female. Single. Interested in men. And she didn't live in Rhode Island, but Vermont. Chances were next to nothing that she was the right person.

A Google search turned up another New Englander, but this one wasn't in Rhode Island either: a New York social worker named Margaret Reid was listed on all kinds of professional registers. She looked much more age appropriate and was certainly impressive, but again probably not the right one.

Andie snapped her laptop shut and nestled back in her pillows. It seemed so easy on the surface: punch a few numbers into her phone, hook up with a woman in Rhode Island, and check out what the woman had to say. But there was nothing easy about this call. Somewhere in Rhode Island, all the way across the country, was a woman named Margaret who had all kinds of hope connected to this call. Was convinced she might have found a cousin. Andie suppressed a small snort—maybe a fourth or fifth cousin three times removed, if that, but *nothing* remotely close enough to start setting up a family reunion. It simply wasn't possible; once her teenage brother drowned, Nora was essentially an only child—none of it the sort of stuff cousins are made of.

And now here was Andie, about to dash someone's hopes.

And it wasn't just that. Andie realized *she* had entertained the very slightest of hopes herself—that maybe, just maybe, there *was* a cousin. *Was* a reason to start setting up a family reunion. But even as those thoughts skittered through her mind, her heart seemed to skip a beat. No, it wasn't possible. This wasn't a cousin. And once Andie pointed out the cold reality of the situation to Margaret Reid, there would be *two* sets of hopes dashed against the jagged rocks of disappointment.

Might as well get it over with. Andie pressed the series of numbers into the cell phone and punched the call button before she had a chance to change her mind. Two rings...three. Just as she decided to hang up, a smooth voice answered.

It was now or never. Jack was right; there was no turning back. "Margaret?"

"Yes?"

"This is Andrea Harriso—"

"Andrea! Thank you so much for calling! You probably think this is a bit...well, odd...but we've been looking for Nora Carlson for quite a while, and I think she might be your mother. And if she is, you are my cousin."

Andie decided to set some boundaries right off, and tried not to sound hostile or suspicious as she responded, "My mother's name was Nora Carlson, but I can't imagine why you would have been looking for her. She died fairly recently, and I'm an attorney, and I made sure that all the estate issues were appropriately settled. There really wasn't much to speak of in the estate, anyway. Did you have some kind of claim you wanted to make?" There. That would dissuade any gold digging.

"No! I didn't want to make a claim. Mom lost track of Nora—her sister—decades ago. Unfortunately, Mom died not too long ago as well, but before she died, she was trying to find Nora. Was hoping she was still alive. Just wanted to talk to her...to reestablish family ties, I guess you'd say."

"Look, Margaret—"

"You can call me Meg; everyone does unless I'm in trouble." Andie detected warmth and humor in the voice. And that made it even more difficult to disappoint this woman, who seemed genuine. She was probably a very nice person.

"And you can call me Andie. But, look, Meg—I don't want to disappoint you, but I think you have the wrong Nora Carlson. My mother was one of only two children in her family. And the only other one—her brother—drowned in an irrigation ditch when he was fifteen. Nothing I ever heard even hinted that he fathered a child before his death."

"Yes!" the enthusiasm was almost electric. "What was his name?"

Andie felt heat race up her neck and across her cheeks. She'd never really thought about it until now, and only now realized she didn't even know her uncle's name. "Wow. I'm very embarrassed, but I don't know his name. My mother had a very dysfunctional upbringing, and she never talked much about her family. I don't think she ever told me his name."

"Do you know her parents' names?"

Andie sighed. *Here comes the final descent, followed by the brutal crash.* "Yes—Elizabeth and Jonathan Gray. He was a Methodist minister. They lived somewhere in Iowa."

The voice on the other end of the line might as well have belonged to a cheerleader bellowing into a megaphone in a crowded football stadium. "That's *them*! You *are* my cousin!"

Andie pressed herself more deeply into the pillows, her brow furrowed. "Okay, wait. I don't see how. My mother's only sibling drowned when he was fifteen, so—"

"His name was Robert Harvey Gray. And he *did* drown when he was fifteen. But he was *not* your mother's only sibling. There were two others, both quite a bit older. Della, my mother and the oldest of the children, was already leaving for college when Nora was born. Nora probably didn't remember much about her...but I wonder why Nora never at least *mentioned* her. And their second child, William David, died a few weeks after birth. Apparently, he had some sort of congenital heart defect. He never came home from the hospital. To be fair, Nora might not have even known about him."

Andie felt as though she had been kicked in the chest. *Their second child—a baby boy—had died a few weeks after birth.* Just like Matthew. Just like the little boy Nora had lost, the little boy who had never come home from the hospital to be snuggled in the bundle of baby blankets so carefully stitched for him.

"That...that same thing happened to my mother." Andie felt the tears gathering in the corners of her eyes. "Her second baby, a little boy named Matthew, died when he was about six weeks old; never came home from the hospital."

"Wow. What a wild coincidence. Did you have other brothers or sisters?"

"No, I was the only other one. My parents became estranged right after Matthew died, before I turned two, and my mother never remarried. They're both dead now—as are my grandparents—and I honestly thought I was the last surviving member of the family. So you need to appreciate that this is a little...so, how did your mother lose track of Nora?"

"I don't know how much you know about what was going on in their family, but after Robbie drowned, my grandmother sort of checked out of life. Your mother was still at home, but mine had left to attend college. Elizabeth became an emotionally and often physically absent mom, just letting Nora go her own way and do whatever she wanted. And, well, you probably know how *that* turned out..."

"You mean her getting pregnant?"

"Well, yes. The whole thing made my mother really angry. Elizabeth didn't give two hoots or a holler about what Nora was doing until she suddenly wanted to marry a *seventeen-year-old boy*—a kid who was three years younger than she was and hadn't even graduated from high school. Anyone could see it was bound for disaster. I guess there were some pretty bitter arguments over the whole thing. But Nora was determined, and she finally admitted that she was pregnant."

"I can only imagine how well *that* went over."

"Well, according to my mother, Elizabeth didn't believe it at first. She thought Nora was lying—making it up so they would *have* to let her get married. But before too long it became obvious; she started to show. At that point, Elizabeth had only one choice: desperate to keep up appearances with her minister husband and his congregation, she completely cut Nora off. Kicked her out. Refused to talk about her. Acted like she'd never even been born. Mom thought it was horrible —how do you just turn your back on your own child?"

There it was again in living color: the almighty façade. So it hadn't started with Nora. She had learned it from the best—had even been a victim of it. Andie was starting to wonder if it was in the DNA.

The rest of the story, at least from Meg's side, was fairly simple. Della finished four years of college, snagged a diploma, and got engaged to a handsome engineer named Lloyd—a man also scorned by Elizabeth, for no apparent reason. Once Della said her nuptials, Elizabeth vanished from the picture. Della and Lloyd moved to Georgia. Meg—their only child—was born. Throughout those years, Della tried corresponding with her parents, but they never answered. The last letter she wrote came back stamped *Return to Sender— Addressee Moved, Left No Forwarding Address.*

"At that point, Mom gave up," Meg explained. "Figured she would never have any sort of relationship with her mother. Truth be told, I don't think she was horrifically sad about it, because she claimed her mother had always been very difficult. But she always worried and wondered about Nora. She tried writing letters to some government agencies in Iowa, trying to find out where your parents had gotten married and where they were living, but no one was able to track them down. Years went by, and Mom never really mentioned Nora. But I guess once she realized she was dying, she wanted to make one last-ditch effort to find her sister."

"Believe it or not, I'm not completely sure *where* they got married," Andie admitted. "They moved to a small farm in Nebraska right after they married. Mom was still living in that house when she died."

Andie could hear the exasperation in Meg's sigh. "Oh, I wish she had tried harder. Maybe with a little more effort... So, your father... you said he's also dead?"

"Yes. I don't have a lot of detail, because, as I mentioned, they were estranged when I was very young. In fact, there was apparently no legal divorce, and it appears he committed suicide at a relatively young age, probably in Michigan."

"Oh, Andie, I'm so sorry. My dad died of colon cancer when he was forty-one, when I was just ten. I think they had always wanted more children, but the chemotherapy and other cancer treatments made him sterile. Once my dad died, it was just me and my mom— kind of like you and Nora, I guess. The things we have in common are pretty wild."

As they continued talking, though, it became apparent that there were *many* things they *didn't* have in common. Meg had attended the Georgia Institute of Technology, graduating in intercultural studies after completing a semester abroad in London. The summer after graduating, she married John Reid, a graduate of Georgetown University; Meg met him while working in Washington. They moved to Providence, Rhode Island, where he took a teaching job at the Center for Biomedical Engineering at Brown University. Meg kept in close touch with her mother, visiting her in Georgia three or four times a year.

John was now just a few years from retirement, and they were weighing various options about what to do once that happened. Meg, it seems, had stopped working once her first baby was born. Kathryn, that firstborn, had gone to Brown, taking advantage of her tuition discount as the child of a full-time faculty member. She had studied at the Center for Gerontology and was now throwing herself into a rewarding career in Arizona, where she focused on the emotional and psychological needs of the state's aging population. She was still single, Meg explained, though she'd had a few long-term relationships.

"You said *firstborn*," Andie said. "Does that mean you have other children too?"

"Two other daughters. Emily and Jordan both graduated from the Rhode Island School of Design—Emily specializing in ceramics, Jordan in metalsmithing and jewelry."

Quite the eclectic bunch, thought Andie. And even in her limited circles, Andie remembered hearing at one time or another how prestigious the Rhode Island School of Design was. Before she could take a breath, Meg continued explaining the pedigree with what sounded like a stifled laugh.

"I don't quite know what to tell you about them. They...well, you know how artists are. I think they're both trying to 'find themselves.' Emily loves making pots and is associated with a small artists' colony in upstate New York. And yes, Andie, you can read whatever you want into the term *artists' colony*. And Jordan...well, Jordan is...

making jewelry, I guess! Her stuff is gorgeous, but I'm really not quite sure how she markets and sells it. Thank heaven they both got sizable scholarships, and I guess I should be grateful that neither of them has come to us for money. I'd hate to think we spent all that tuition for..." Her voice trailed off, still punctuated with laughter. "What about you, Andie?"

Andie blanched. A thousand explanations ricocheted across her mind. After what seemed like hours but was actually no more than a few seconds, she decided to tell it like it was. If she truly had found someone who shared a few strands of her DNA, she couldn't cover up the past in a bid for a possibly promising future.

"I was married briefly—for less than a year—to a man who committed adultery. I left while I was pregnant with our son, Beau, and I haven't seen or heard from my ex-husband since then. After my divorce was final, I finished school, got a law degree, and started practicing law at a top firm in Lincoln. When my boss moved to Park City, Utah, and begged me to join his firm there, Beau and I moved. I thought we were doing great, but apparently the move was harder on Beau than I could have ever dreamed; he took his own life when he was thirteen."

From the sound of things, Meg tried very hard but not completely successfully to muffle the gasp that leaped out of her throat.

Meg finally spoke. "Andie, you sound like a remarkable woman. You've overcome such hard things. I can't even imagine the strength and courage it has taken. I'm so glad I found you."

Glad? Someone was *glad* to lay even partial claim to her, a woman whose life consisted of such chaos? Andie fought to keep her voice even. "You can't begin to know what that means to me. My mother judged me until her dying breath—never thought I was good enough. Was completely ashamed of me and my disloyal husband and my failed marriage and my suicidal son. Didn't even attend my law school graduation. In fact, she wasn't even there when my son was born."

Andie could hear Meg's ragged breathing across the several

thousand miles. "I'm so sorry. She sounds...how hard for you. And how hard for *her* before you. It sounds like her own mother rejected her in every possible way. She probably didn't know any better. But that still doesn't make it any easier for you. And until now, you've been all alone with it."

For a tattered split second, Andie didn't comprehend the real meaning of that handful of words. *You've been all alone with it. Until now.* Until now—until a simple phone call bridged the years and wiped away the remoteness.

There was a prolonged goodbye. Exchanges of addresses. Promises of eventual visits, and more—lots more—phone calls. Emailed pictures. But most of all, there was a connection.

At last, a connection that spanned the crushing sense of isolation.

She *had* been all alone with it, Andie realized. *Until now.*

She picked up the phone to dial Jack.

CHAPTER 22

Two days later, in the middle of working out a strategy to delay or prevent Brock Barlow's extradition, Andie arrived at the office to a voicemail message from Brady Young. She readily heard the tremor in his voice: *Listen, Andie, we've had some more information come in here. The cops brought it over this morning. I want to comply with the disclosure requirement, so I'm going to send a runner over to your office with the file; I've made plenty of copies, so you can just keep what I send. Good luck.*

Andie glanced at the file on her desk already crammed with copies she had taken from Brady's office a few days earlier. She still hadn't summoned the courage to study the faxes from Texas. She was afraid of what she'd find there; already *knew* the basics but abhorred the details. Every name that jumped off the page took on a life of its own in her mind, became a kid who would have hung out with Beau, became a void in a mother's heart so ragged it defied any effort at ever being filled again. But if she were to convince Brock Barlow to enter a guilty plea, she had to know the details. *Every sick detail.* She had to be conversant in *him*, in what he'd done. She had to get inside his sick, twisted head—and hope she could get back out again.

Andie took a deep breath as she flipped open the folder. The Montana files were still on top; she knew those details, almost by heart, after hearing them only once. They were seared into her mind. Where had he *found* Kevin Duncan and Riley Marshall? Had they voluntarily climbed into his life like Jameson Harper had? Andie shuddered as she realized once again exactly how lucky Jameson was. Normally, no one would label the horror that happened to Jameson as *luck,* but that's exactly what it was: Jameson was at home playing video games and eating his mother's handcrafted pizza instead of being stuffed into a shallow grave in the woods somewhere. And these days, in Andie's estimation, that was its own special brand of luck.

She remembered being flabbergasted when the funeral director called her *lucky* for being able to dress Beau's body. Luck, it seemed, was a creature of circumstance. A matter of perspective.

Andie gingerly pulled the first of the Texas files from the folder and straightened it on the desk in front of her. Rhett Lewis. He had been just a month from his fourteenth birthday on that early August morning. The last time anyone saw him alive—anyone other than his killer, that is—he was with five friends at the popular Six Flags over Texas amusement park, screaming his lungs out on "Pandemonium," a five-story, spinning roller coaster that was one of the most popular attractions in the park. "Pandemonium" occupied the central piece of real estate in the park's Boomtown, and the people that were always clustered around the coaster gave new meaning to the term *crowds.*

Rhett and his five friends scrambled breathlessly off "Pandemonium" and huddled to talk about where to go next. A handful of adults sitting in the "parent swap" area next to the coaster remembered seeing the group—particularly remembered Rhett because of his distinct, brightly colored cotton shirt, a wild pattern punctuated with the color of tangerines and limes. Apparently, the group couldn't agree on what to do next; a couple wanted to grab something to eat, while three wanted to go to an adjacent section of the park to ride a roller coaster with suspended cars. Rhett was the lone dissenter: He wanted to head halfway across the park in the other direction to ride "Shock Wave," once the world's tallest roller coaster. After a minute or two of attempted negotiation, the six decided to go their separate ways and meet up again in the Old South area of the park. The last his friends saw Rhett he was jogging in the direction of "Shock Wave" and yelling something about a hamburger.

Carl Wright and David Stratton arrived at the designated

meeting spot first; after waiting a few minutes for the others, they ducked into Ben & Jerry's and bought two cones. Within a few minutes, three others tumbled up, still pumped with excitement over the thrill of the suspended roller coasters.

None of the five knew exactly how long they had waited before they got really annoyed at Rhett. After almost an hour, they decided he'd gone off on his own—the lines for "Shock Wave" were shorter, and they figured he'd gotten bored waiting for them. So they took off, too—no problem. That morning, they'd all agreed to meet at six in the evening at a specific spot in the parking lot, where David's mother was supposed to pick them up. None of the five gave it a second thought.

By six-thirty, Karie Stratton couldn't decide if she was more angry or worried; chances were good that Rhett Lewis was still in the park, stuck in line for an attraction he just *had* to ride before leaving the park. By seven, raw panic gnawed at her heart. She knew something was really wrong with Rhett Lewis. Records show her initial report to park security at 7:13. Then she called Rhett's mother. And that's when panic turned to terror.

Security guards fanned out across the park; Rhett's mother, a single parent, held vigil in the security office, intermittently sobbing and screaming at the dispatcher, demanding more decisive action. Andie could scarcely imagine the feelings that must have held court in her heart during those fretful hours. Once the park closed, security personnel did a thorough sweep of the more than two hundred acres; there was no sign of Rhett. The Arlington police department was alerted but responded with a jaded lack of concern: Anyone older than ten had to be missing for more than twenty-four hours before a case could even be opened. After all, an overworked dispatcher droned, lots of kids Rhett's age run away.

What if I hadn't received that horrible phone call? What if I hadn't been summoned out of court and told that my son had been found dangling at the end of a rope? What if he had simply disappeared and I had never been able to find him? It was a thought too terrible to even consider.

Late the next day, some kids playing along a cement culvert behind some new construction found him. Rhett Lewis had been hastily discarded, thrown over the edge and into the concrete culvert built to collect storm runoff and prevent flash floods. The culvert was bone-brittle dry that day, and Rhett Lewis lay in a crumpled heap at its bottom, the stiffness of rigor mortis set in. He was naked from the waist down, but a strip of his unmistakable tangerine- and lime-colored shirt had been torn away and used with a rough piece of wood, likely from one of the construction sites along the edge of the culvert. The garroting had been twisted so tightly that his face was hideously bloated, almost unrecognizable to the officers who responded to the scene, clutching his seventh-grade school picture so they could tentatively identify him. The palms of his hands were severely burned.

This couldn't have been a garden-variety abduction, no grab-and-run. There were simply too many people around. Anyone could have heard his screams, and Rhett certainly would have screamed. So how had Brock convinced a bright, energetic, confident boy to come with him without the slightest protest? What could Rhett have been thinking? How many times did that same dialog run through his mother's mind? What if? If only...

This murder—the last of the seven linked to Brock Barlow in Texas—was different...so different, in fact, that at first investigators thought it was not the work of the serial killer they'd been hunting for the past four years. The palms of his hands were burned through several layers of tissue; the other victims had burned hands too, but their burns consisted of only a trace of blackened skin. The other six victims had all died of strangulation. Rhett was the only one who had been garroted—not only shutting off his air supply, but completely interrupting blood circulation to the brain. All seven had been sodomized, but Rhett was the only one who had not been the victim of object rape. *Maybe the piece of wood used in the garroting had originally been intended for something else. What had happened in the course of the assault to so enrage Brock that he grabbed the wood and used it instead to strangle the life out of Rhett Lewis?*

That wasn't all. The other six victims had all been buried in shallow graves, likely in an effort to delay anyone from finding them. Rhett had instead been tossed out like a piece of garbage, thrown into a steep-sided culvert where he was sure to be discovered right away. But maybe *discovery* hadn't been the ultimate goal. Maybe—especially since he was the last of the seven murders—Rhett had for some reason posed a threat to Brock. Maybe, because of an unknown cascade of circumstances, Brock feared getting caught and didn't have time to find a spot suitable for the kind of shallow grave he had used before. *The fear factor makes the most sense, because he clearly left Texas soon after dumping Brock into the culvert.*

Based on the unidentified DNA, officials knew the same man who had assaulted and murdered six young teens in the Arlington area had now claimed his seventh victim. And it was now clear that man was Brock Barlow.

A newspaper clipping of the police announcement was attached at the end of Rhett Lewis's file. A grainy black-and-white photo showed a haggard chief of police behind a large cluster of television and radio microphones, announcing to a panic-stricken public that the latest murder had likely been committed by the same suspect—a suspect they were no closer to identifying than they had been after discovering the first body four years earlier. They'd hired an FBI profiler and knew that the suspect was likely a fairly charming and good-looking loner who was not married, had lost a parent during his childhood, fell into a middle-income bracket, was a blue-collar worker, and was not college educated. They had all the evidence they needed, the chief said, and were just waiting to match the DNA to a known suspect. All registered sex offenders in the area had been cleared of the crime; their DNA didn't match. The article ended with a plea to the public to maintain careful vigilance and report anyone who raised suspicion.

Andie couldn't even imagine living like that. She thought of all the times Beau had walked along the narrow streets with a friend, or even by himself...all the times he had gone to snowboard by himself for just an hour or two...all the times he had run through a meadow of wildflowers on a shortcut to a friend's house. She hadn't had to worry every time Beau left the house—hadn't needed to look for any murderous malice hidden behind the faces that passed her in the simplest of places. *Or should she have looked?* It was obvious now that such a monster had indeed roamed the streets of Park City—the very streets where Beau had innocently played out the fantasies of childhood.

Andie missed Beau so badly it hurt...so badly that his memory still occasionally stung her eyes with penetrating force at unexpected moments. But now, pushing Rhett Lewis's file aside and taking out the next paper-clipped set of faxes, she felt an odd sort of peace that Beau's life had ebbed out by his own design. Remembering the face of Jameson Harper's mother, imagining the face of Rhett Lewis's mother, she wondered if she could have survived knowing that a monster like Brock Barlow had twisted a length of shirt and grabbed a rough scrap of lumber to irrevocably snatch what wasn't his.

She stared at the next file, but the words seemed to be swimming on the page. She couldn't read it. Didn't want to. Hadn't the stomach to read one more description of depravity exacted against an innocent boy. Andie decided to find just the barest details, just enough to convince Brock that the deck was stacked solidly against him. She shuffled through the remaining paper-clipped files and quickly put them in chronological order. Then she glanced at the top file, found the name of the first victim, and jotted it on her legal pad. Caleb Chandler. Thirteen. Vanished on his way home from school. Found three weeks later in a shallow grave in a swampy field nine miles from where he was last seen.

Just a month later, Dallas Maxfield. Fourteen. Walked casually away from a video arcade downtown, apparently alone. Found a week later in a shallow grave in the same swampy field that yielded up the remains of Caleb Chandler, a field that straddled the river running along the west side of Love Field. The only connection investigators made between the two was their watery graves.

Almost a year went by before Matthew Hall, thirteen, never arrived home from a high school football game. It took detectives more than two months to find his body, buried in the muddy soil near the shores of Joe Pool Lake, just south of Duncanville. Fishermen discovered the grave when several weeks of drenching rains washed the mud into the lake, exposing part of the body.

A day after Matthew Hall's body was found, circuit court judge Colleen Whittaker joined other officials at a press conference announcing measures to step up the search for the Arlington killer. Officials stopped short of giving him a nickname but released a few salacious details to the public in a desperate hope that someone might recognize the work of a neighbor, friend, or family member. No one came forth with a potential identification—but a week later, Colleen's thirteen-year-old son Zach Whittaker disappeared. The friends he had been skateboarding with accompanied him to the parking lot of the condo where he lived with his single mother, but he never made it to the door. His broken and battered skateboard had been thrown out the window of a vehicle clearly traveling at high speed along the highway to Garland. His broken and battered body was found a few weeks later, buried a few hundred yards off the highway almost halfway between Garland and Plano.

Andie scanned a newspaper article clipped to the Whittaker file. Investigators were alarmed at the brazenness of a killer who would move in on the judge's son. The county sheriff assigned a probable motive: The killer was mocking law enforcement. It was his statement that he held the power...that no one would be able to stop him.

And he didn't stop with law enforcement. Just a few months later, thirteen-year-old Will Peterson, son of the *Dallas Morning News* editor, disappeared from a laser tag arena in Arlington. His friends hysterically reported that one minute he was there, and the next he was gone. Business owners closed their doors for the three days it took to find his body, laid on black plastic garbage bags and covered with a smattering of soil at the edge of the city dump. Tucked under his head was the edition of the *News* featuring the press conference. Flames from some sort of striker had danced around the edges of his palms, leaving a trail of blackened flesh.

Almost two years went by without another murder; authorities breathed a little easier when suddenly thirteen-year-old Quinn Reynolds disappeared from a bike path on his way home from his best friend's house. The path was tucked into a secluded subdivision and wound through a thick stand of flowering trees; biking after dark, Quinn would have been an easy target for someone acquainted with the trail. When investigators found his body a few days later in a shallow grave just a mile away, they knew the same killer was back: Quinn had not only been sodomized and strangled, but the skin on the palms of his hands had been burned. It was a match to the DNA left behind in the other five murders.

Hyper-alert, authorities waited for the other shoe to fall. Still without solid leads, they held seminars at local middle schools emphasizing safety tips for young teens and sponsored segments on TV news programs warning parents against high-risk situations for their children. Almost a year went by before Rhett Lewis, the last of the Texas victims, was taken from the Six Flags amusement park.

A brief fax included in the file reflected investigator concern about the Rhett Lewis murder: The killer had become much more violent. The garroting was almost over the top from a man who had merely strangled his other victims; the burns on the hands were unusually severe. He had also become much more brazen, leaving Rhett Lewis's body virtually out in the open.

As it turned out, Rhett Lewis was the killer's farewell note. The terror had ended, but seven families were left without answers and a community continued to hover on the edge of terror, never quite able to move past the dread that someday he'd be back—or that, in fact, he had never left. Andie could imagine it in the eyes of the mothers who pushed carts down the grocery store aisle or waited to pick up their kids from school: *My son could be next. He could come back, and my son might be next.*

Andie closed the file. Considering North Carolina, Brock had been at this for almost a decade. His predilection for young teenaged boys...when exactly had it started? In North Carolina? Or had he struggled with it his entire adult life? Was his sexual behavior like that of other rapists—not the sadistic lickings of lust, but a forceful expression of rage? Power?

Her thoughts were interrupted by a knock on her door. "A runner just brought this over from the county attorney's office." Kristen handed Andie a thick manila envelope.

Across a post-it note affixed to the front of the envelope was Brady's hasty scribble: *Three more between North Carolina and Texas — Virginia, California, Colorado. Call if you have questions.*

CHAPTER
23

Three more states. Three more places where single mothers—mothers just like Andie—found themselves unwittingly searching crowds of faces for the one they missed. Andie remembered the time, months after she tucked him into a grave beneath a nestle of blooms, that she thought she saw Beau in a mass of concertgoers at a downtown Salt Lake venue. She pressed frantically through the crowd, her heart pounding against her ribs so hard it hurt, trying desperately to reach the boy with the chestnut hair and the mouthful of braces. Suddenly it came crashing back—the shattering realization that Beau would never again attend a concert. The realization that the boy she saw belonged to somebody else. The realization that hers was a pain that would never end.

Andie bent open the prongs on the oversized manila envelope and tugged out a new set of faxed documents. Andie put the stack of papers on the desk and decided to call Brady before starting through the litany of horror. Because it was still early in the day, he hadn't yet left for court, and he picked up on the second ring. "Not quite the way I had hoped to start my day, Brady."

"I'm pretty flabbergasted myself. Okay, so we knew about North Carolina. Right on the heels of that nasty revelation, we found out about Montana and Texas. That was plenty bad enough. But this—"

"I'm afraid we might never stanch the flow of this thing. In fact, you know what I feel like? I feel like that little Dutch boy who saved Holland. I feel like I'm shoving my finger into a hole in a shoddy dam, and that millions of gallons of roiling water are on the other side...and that as soon as I stop concentrating for even a millisecond, all that water is going to burst through the dam and drown me."

"Even before the faxes from North Carolina, I suspected Brock had been involved in the system—he seemed to know far too much about the whole procedure. I remember you mentioning the same. But here's the strange thing: He was never arrested for any of these assaults or murders. Until we put his DNA in CODIS, these people never even knew his name. All they had were little collections of dots and dashes in a unique pattern, hoping and praying for a match. So where did Barlow's experience with the criminal system come from?"

"Good question, Brady. I'm still convinced he's been around the block a time or two when it comes to getting arrested and needing an attorney. But if he'd ever been booked in jail, they would have had his fingerprints, right? They would have already been in the database. North Carolina would have already had their man."

"I know. I can't figure it out. Maybe we were right with our cynical hunch that he's nothing more than a *Law and Order* junkie. Maybe that's all there is to it."

"These files you sent over...is there anything new or exceptional? Because—I have to be honest—I've already spent an hour this morning going through the Texas files, and I'm not sure I can stomach much more."

"No, they're disturbingly similar. All had single mothers. Everyone got sodomized, and most were also the victim of object rape. The ones who lived had their shirt sleeves singed with one of those strikers—the kind people use to start fires or light candles. The ones who died were strangled and had their palms burned. And in this batch, at least, all of them were buried except one. That one was wrapped in black plastic and tossed into a swift river that eventually emptied into the ocean; investigators were lucky that he was catapulted toward the riverbank and got snagged on a bunch of construction debris."

"How many, total?"

"Let's see...three who were assaulted but survived; eight homicides."

Andie penciled a series of hash marks on her legal pad. Before she went to see Brock, she needed to add all of them up. She needed a final count.

"Oh, and Andie, I think we found ground zero."

"Ground zero?"

"The first one. The one in Virginia. It predates the North Carolina crimes by about a year, and we haven't yet found any earlier. That means that by the time Brock Barlow got to North Carolina, he was experienced. The one in Virginia survived, but so did most of the victims in North Carolina. While he was in North Carolina, his fury escalated, and he started killing his victims—and that became the pattern. In the ensuing decade, only a few survived."

"Has anyone from Virginia moved to extradite?"

"Not yet, but as you'll see from my fax, the authorities there are well aware of Brock and want to close their case. The Virginia one, Dixon Barnhurst, is in his mid-twenties now, engaged to be married, pursuing a graduate degree at William and Mary. He was nabbed from a busy skateboarding park and taken to a heavily wooded area not far away. In his original statement, he claimed that despite the horror of the assault, he never felt in danger of losing his life. In fact, his assailant let him get dressed and then dropped him off a few blocks from the skateboarding park after the assault."

"Just out of curiosity, did he burn Dixon's hands?"

"Not his hands—the hem of his t-shirt. Used a cigarette lighter. Just sort of flirted around the edge. Nothing serious."

"Did he use an object to rape him?"

"No. I don't mean to reduce the severity of what had to be a horrific situation, but it was just a straightforward sodomy...other than the little dance with the cigarette lighter, nothing really out of the ordinary for a sexual predator. And now, all these years later, Dixon said he's prepared to make a positive identification. He's certain the ensuing decade hasn't dulled the memory one iota. Said he'll never forget the guy's eyes—cold and calculating. It would likely do the poor kid a world of good if they could charge and convict Barlow. Even if they didn't extradite him and try him in Virginia, at least he'd have some closure."

"Okay. Let me skim through these and jot down the names and dates and a fact or two about each. My primary goal here is to get a total head count and enough facts and figures that I can convince Barlow to plead guilty. Beyond that, I don't want to make a detailed study of the files."

"If he pleads guilty, you won't ever have to."

"That's my plan."

Ground zero. Virginia. A nicer, gentler Brock Barlow. A guy who picks up a kid at a skateboard park, maybe buys him a burger, then takes him to the woods and sodomizes him. Doesn't use a flashlight or the handle of a sledgehammer in his assault. If Dixon never felt in danger of his life, could he possibly have thought it was just a sexual act? Which would have the worst long-term effects on the psyche— being the victim of a crime, or thinking you had been hit on by a guy old enough to be your father? How on earth could a thirteen-year-old process *that*? How on earth does he tell his mom—his friends? His fiancé?

Almost polite...not a label you'd normally stick on a man who brutalized people. But there it was: A boy who was never really afraid for his life because he was being assaulted by someone who was *almost polite,* at least part of the time. How can one be *almost polite* during an assault?

And if he was almost polite as he traveled south and drifted over the state line into North Carolina, what made him snap? What took Brock Barlow from a man who almost politely sodomized young teenagers to one who snuffed out their lives afterward and then stuffed them into crude, shallow graves? What happens in the course of events to cause that kind of cataclysmic shift?

Maybe one had offered up resistance, had yelled so loudly that Brock feared getting caught. Maybe that boy had posed such a threat that Brock had to wrap his hands around his neck to shut him up. And maybe the force required to stop the yelling had also stopped the very life force ebbing through his veins. There Brock would have been, without malice of forethought, kneeling beside the heap of a corpse. Could there have been some desperation then? And could the ease of shoveling out a little soil have provided such a simple solution that Brock decided he never again wanted to risk leaving behind a witness?

Andie couldn't quit thinking about one other thing: How did Brock convince so many kids to get into his car? Some might have been taken by force—perhaps like the boy who was riding his bike along an isolated path. But so many were taken from public places, places where there were plenty of people who would have heard a kid screaming—like the skateboarding park in Virginia or the amusement park in Texas or the laser tag arena.

She reflected on all the times she had talked to Beau about never getting into a car with someone he didn't know, about screaming at the top of his lungs if someone tried to force him. She thought of all the programs at school that taught the same thing. It positively baffled her that people like Brock Barlow were able to get so many of those boys with what seemed like such little effort.

Grace glided into Andie's office with a cup of Starbucks and saw the new pile of faxes as she lowered herself into the chair. "Oh, that doesn't look good—new stuff on your boy Brock?"

"Here's what I don't get, Grace. All these boys—a few of them were prime targets. Riding a bike along a dark, isolated path. Walking along the side of a little-traveled road. But a bunch of these kids were taken from well-lighted places with lots of people around. Didn't they yell? Didn't their mothers warn them about people like Brock Barlow?"

"I'm sure the mothers were right on top of it," Grace said. "But you know kids—especially kids that age. They all think they're invincible. They all think it's never going to happen to them."

"And here's the other thing I don't get: In some of these cases, kids were disappearing one right after the other in the same town, sometimes with as little as a month or two between killings. Entire communities had to have been in a blind panic. And still Brock Barlow somehow managed to convince these kids to go with him. Look at Jameson Harper—no, there hadn't been any sign that a killer was on the loose here, but Jameson just climbed into Brock's SUV. Had seen him hanging around the school a few times and never gave it another thought."

"That might be the key, Andie. Brock might have moved to various places and taken a little time to work his way into the community. Maybe he hung around other schools too. Maybe he loitered on the sidelines at baseball games and wrestling matches and football practices. Maybe he sat in the waiting area at the laser tag arena. Maybe the kids who went with him had seen him before, evenly briefly, just on the periphery. And you know how the adolescent mind works—see him once or twice, and he's no longer a stranger."

"You might be right. I wouldn't put something that devious past Brock. It would certainly help explain why so many kids just climbed into the car with him. I'm just a little freaked that there are people in the world like him. Obviously, he's sick and twisted. He's a murderer, for crying out loud. But he's also very bright and calculating and determined. And until now, he was smart enough to get away with it for a very long time."

"Do you have a body count yet?"

"No; that's one of my priorities this morning. Before I confront Brock and try to convince him to plead guilty, I need to know the collateral damage. I've got to go in with both guns blazing, and he's got to know that he doesn't have a chance in hell of beating any of this if my strategy is going to work. And I've got to do it today. Every hour that goes by is another hour in which we could receive the official petition for extradition from any one of these states. I've got to get down to the jail, work a miracle by convincing Brock to plead guilty, and then get an emergency hearing in front of a judge. Today."

Grace stood to leave and shook her head. "I admire Sloan in all sorts of ways, and I've got to admit that the strategy he gave you is probably the best one. But I've got to say, I'm glad I'm not the one trying to help this guy."

"Don't think it's easy for me, or that I like it. I've lost a lot of sleep over it, and I'd give just about anything if Brock had never called my name that night at the Sinclair station. But it is what it is, and I think Sloan's right to do everything possible so he can never come back later and pull the 'technicality' card. I want this guy locked up so tight he never sees the light of day again."

"Think about it, Andie—I'm not sure he'll survive his initial sentence. There's real honor among thieves, as they say. Look what happened to Jeffrey Dahmer."

Dahmer had been sentenced to fifteen life terms—a total of more than nine hundred years—for killing, dismembering, and eating parts of seventeen boys and men; while most were in their late teens and twenties, his youngest victim was fourteen. He even kept some of their body parts as grisly souvenirs. Just two years after his incarceration at the Columbia Correctional Institution, he was bludgeoned with enough force to crush his skull; he died in the ambulance en route to the hospital.

Prison officials eventually found out which inmate was responsible for the attack, but the inmate was never punished. In fact, officials had to act decisively to prevent the inmate from being considered a folk hero. Not a soul there mourned Dahmer's loss. If there's one thing most prisoners don't tolerate, it's a child molester— even worse, a child killer. Grace was right; Brock might not stand a chance behind the bars meant to protect the community from him. All the states lined up with their extradition orders might never get a chance to bring him to justice.

Andie erased her penciled tally from earlier that morning and drew a vertical line down the paper, creating two columns. At the top of the first one she scribbled *Assaults Only*. At the top of the second she wrote *Homicides*. Pushing the legal pad aside, she gathered all the faxes Brady Young's office had sent over and put them in a single stack in chronological order.

She made the first hash mark in the left column boldly, decisively. It was for Jameson Harper, a living, breathing boy who was now virtually a prisoner in his own house in a nice subdivision in Park City. He no longer dared race along the shortcut through the field to his best friend's house. He no longer dared walk to school. Even if he did, his mother wouldn't let him; she was just as much a prisoner in that house as he. He could no longer stomach the thought of snowboarding...even if he could, he had surrendered his snowboard to the police. More evidence, even if the DNA was compromised. The last thing Jameson Harper needed was evidence that his life would never be the same.

Andie grabbed the first paper-clipped file. Virginia. *Ground zero*, Brady had called it. Brock's first foray into an evil that would occupy him for the next decade. Another hash mark in the assault column—this one for Dixon Barnhurst, now cracking the books at William and Mary and getting ready for his wedding. As repulsive as the assault had been, it occurred to Andie that Dixon just might be the "success story" among the victims. The one to be envied, if such a thing was possible. He seemed to be moving ahead with things. At least he was alive.

Tossing the Virginia file aside, Andie grabbed the next set of files. North Carolina. Eleven more hash marks in the assault column, and the first two marks in the homicide column. It was North Carolina that most baffled Andie. It was North Carolina where Brock morphed from assault to murder. Jotting the marks on the paper, Andie realized she would likely never find out why. Brock wasn't likely to tell her...and maybe he didn't even know himself. It would be a question that would always breeze through her mind like the scent of pine carried on the early autumn wind.

The next time Brock surfaced was in California, where he added two surviving assault victims and five homicides to his tally. Andie penciled hash marks in the appropriate columns. Six of the cases were typical Brock, but the details of the seventh—thirteen-year-old Rob Andrews, the one swathed in black plastic and tossed into the swift waters of a raging river—were so out of character that officials were certain the crime had been committed by someone else. When they at last succeeded in getting a viable DNA sample, made possible in large part to the tight plastic wrapped around the body, the verdict was clear. It was the same man who had assaulted and murdered the others.

The next series of crimes was committed in the forested Rocky Mountains surrounding Denver. There were no assaults; Andie made three hash marks to denote the trio of murder victims found there. The only remarkable one in terms of distinguishing characteristics was fourteen-year-old Austin Hart. His body was found almost two hundred miles from where he was abducted— possibly on Brock's way to Texas.

Texas...seven bold hash marks in the homicide column. Seven single mothers wild with grief who, like Andie, would never see their boys grow up. Seven mothers who, until now, could never put a face to the horror that had robbed them of their sons. How would they react when they saw the first photo of Brock—undoubtedly his mug shot—and looked into those black, unyielding eyes? Andie pressed the tip of her pencil into the paper so hard it tore as she made the last mark, the one for Rhett Lewis. It was a mark for every boy who ever climbed aboard a roller coaster, innocence intact...every boy who didn't vanish into a hot August Texas afternoon.

Andie fingered the last set of files...Montana, the most recent to die. Two hash marks in the homicide column. Kevin Duncan and Riley Marshall, both crammed into makeshift graves. Brock eventually made his way south, driving along a highway that wound like a ribbon into the idyllic hamlet of Park City. Only two victims in Montana...one of his shorter stays. She remembered the barren earth atop Kevin Duncan, no effort to scatter pine needles or rocks or dead leaves over the grave. Brock Barlow had been on the verge of being discovered.

Maybe as he fled from the scene at the edge of the popular campground in Montana, he just kept driving...drove until he found Park City, with its crowds of transients, just there to ski for a few days. People in Park City were used to seeing strangers—took their tickets in the lift lines, served them at coffee shops, navigated around them in parking lots, waited on them in gift stores, saw them milling about on the streets at dusk. No one here would give a second thought to a stranger. And until now, no one had to.

CHAPTER 24

Andie ran her finger carefully across the hash marks, adding them up in her head. There it was in black and white—the terrible toll exacted by Brock Barlow: fifteen assaults, nineteen murders. And those were only the ones they *knew* about.

The numbers dulled her senses. Fifteen assaults and nineteen murders, all with solid matches to DNA evidence or witnesses. It should be more than enough to convince Brock to plead guilty. *Let's just hope he sees it that way.*

It wasn't quite ten. Andie wanted to confront Brock and secure his plea in enough time to get in front of a judge that afternoon. First, she needed to talk to Brady Young and find out what concessions the prosecution was willing to make in exchange for a plea that would save them the time and effort of a trial.

It took Andie some time and a visit to the courthouse to locate Brady, who was already off and running on a day full of hearings and motions. After waiting for him outside a courtroom on the second floor, they ducked into a small break room for court officials and each grabbed a cup of coffee.

"Okay, Brady, I'm on my way over to talk to Brock. You know the plan: I'll work to get him to plead guilty so we can move forward to the sentencing phase."

"Yeah, that's what you told me you were going to do. With all the evidence against him here, he'd be crazy not to plead. So where do I fit in?"

"*Crazy* might be a good description, because I think that's exactly what we've got here. But I need another incentive to get him to plead

—I need to offer some sort of reduced sentence here, some sort of compromise from your office."

"Whoa, Andie. My office gains absolutely *no* benefit if Brock Barlow is sentenced here instead of being extradited to another state to face charges there. Why on earth would we agree to a compromise at this point? Face it, Andie—we have nothing to lose and everything to gain if someone extradites Brock Barlow."

Andie bit down on the inside of her cheek as she set her coffee cup on the table. She hadn't expected this response. Hadn't even considered that at this point she'd be left without a bargaining chip.

"Andie, he's going to be found guilty no matter what. In Utah, we have witnesses, including his victim, as well as DNA evidence. Elsewhere, they have irrefutable DNA matches, and with a little work, prosecutors there can track his movements and place him near the crime scenes. This guy doesn't have a chance. I simply don't need to play this time around. I want to see this guy locked up as long as humanly possible, and offering some sort of compromise on the sentence isn't going to contribute to that, is it? I can't even offer a dramatic gesture like keeping the death penalty off the table, because his crime here isn't serious enough to get him a death penalty—and if you're doing your job, you won't allow the evidence from the other states to be admitted."

"Obviously, you're right. I guess I was just hoping that—"

"What? I'm not really on board with your strategy to save him from extradition...extradition is a given. And look at it from *my* point of view, Andie—*I want him extradited.* I *want* him out of my jurisdiction. I'm afraid I really can't help you out with any sentencing compromises. Best of luck." Brady stood up, buttoned his jacket, and left for his next hearing.

Andie crumpled her Styrofoam cup, a slight sense of embarrassment creeping into her cheeks. Brady's position was obvious. *How did I let myself get so caught up in this that I failed to see the prosecution's side?* It wasn't like her. Her thoughts raced. She still had to face Brock, and she had to face him without any concessions from the prosecution. Brady was right—Brock would be crazy not to plead guilty here so they could move toward sentencing, winning a possible delay in extradition. Except for Virginia, his chances elsewhere were downright bleak.

JACK PUSHED OPEN the outside door of the jail and crossed the waiting area with a purposeful stride to where Andie sat. "Okay...are you ready to do this?"

"As ready as I'll ever be. He didn't know we were coming, so someone has gone up to get him and take him to an interview room. I wanted to catch him off-guard so he'll possibly be a *little* more pliable."

"Brock *pliable?*" Jack erupted in a sardonic laugh. "*This* I've got to see."

"Hey, as far as I'm concerned, a guy facing thirty-four serious criminal charges in seven states—charges that will be extraordinarily easy to convict and that will likely carry the death penalty—should be groveling for *anything* that will even potentially save him. But you've seen him in action. He's not your typical individual. Not by a long shot."

"Oh, but he is, Andie. He's been shoved into a corner and he knows it. He's *completely* desperate. And desperate people do desperate things. He won't respond to you with cool logic or a calm demeanor. There's nothing logical or calm about the spot he's in, and he knows it. That's pretty typical if you ask me."

"Awesome," Andie drawled. "Well, all I can do is go in there with both guns blazing and hope he surrenders. Just make sure you have my back."

"I *always* have your back, Andie." Jack's eyes met hers and locked onto them, swimming into their depths. "Yesterday, while you were plowing through those sickening files? I came down here. Alone. I tried to see Brock. Wanted to talk to him."

"Why?" Andie asked in a voice not much more than a whisper.

"Because I know how much this case has been haunting you. Because I know that you initially wanted nothing more than to get him extradited so you could wash your hands of it. Because I know you—and I know you're worrying about all that space that's still ahead, about never being able to forget this, about it dancing around the edges of your brain as long as you breathe. And I wanted to convince Brock to let *me* take the case."

"Did Sloan know you were going to see Brock?"

Jack shook his head almost imperceptibly. "No. I knew he'd try to stop me. But I knew it was an acceptable legal maneuver. I just... wanted to help you, Andie. I wanted to save you from a horror that seemed to be spinning out of control. I wanted to prove to *myself* that I had your back—and that I always will have."

And he was here now, not making her do this alone. A slight smile crept across Andie's face as a guard motioned for them to follow. This time the thud of the door closing behind them was even more sickening than usual for Andie. She was about to be locked into a room with a man who might as well have been the devil himself.

As the guard let her and Jack into the narrow interview room, Andie immediately noticed that Brock Barlow sat at the table without restraint. A pool of panic churned in her stomach and spouted up her throat; she swallowed hard to keep from throwing up her cup of coffee. Barlow narrowed his eyes and glowered at her; it was as if he didn't even see Jack. Hate laced through his voice as he asked, "What are *you* doing here? Did you finally decide to get off your high-paid ass and help me?"

"Mr. Barlow, you and I have something very important we need to discuss. I need your full attention. I need you to forget about everything else that might be agitating in your mind so you can focus completely on what I'm saying. Can you do that?"

Brock turned toward Andie and spat a foul wad onto the floor.

Jack stepped toward Barlow. "Okay, Mr. Barlow, that's not a good way to start this out. We're going to insist that you conduct yourself appropriately, or we'll demand that you be restrained for our safety."

"I want to speak with my attorney *alone*," Brock demanded. "I want you out of here. I refused to talk to you yesterday, and I'm refusing to talk to you today. I have the right to talk to her privately."

"I'm sorry, Mr. Barlow, but you lost that privilege the day you grabbed your attorney's arm and injured her. You have certain rights, and we're here to make sure those rights are protected. But Ms. Harrison has rights too, among them her safety. And because of your previous actions, I'm here to make sure *her* rights are protected."

Barlow spewed out a sound that reeked of derisive laughter. "You don't think I couldn't take *you* down in an instant?"

Jack took two steps backward and rapped firmly against the door of the interview room. It instantly flew open and two guards pushed their way past Jack and Andie. "Is there a problem here?" the larger of the two asked.

"Mr. Barlow is implying a threat of physical harm to one of us," Jack said in a calm tone that belied his apparent upset. "Ms. Harrison and I would feel much safer and better able to conduct our business if Mr. Barlow is restrained."

"You got it," the guard said. In one fluid motion he pulled a set of handcuffs from his pocket and slapped them over Brock's left wrist. An unmistakable click sounded the reassurance that at least he wouldn't be *taking anyone down*.

The very act of restraint always sent Brock into a fury. Chest heaving, he faced Andie. "What do you want?" he seethed.

"I want to talk to you about your situation, Mr. Barlow. As I'm sure you're well aware, it's not good."

"I'm well aware that there were people over at that Sinclair who are willing to identify me and testify against me. And I'm sure that kid will do the same. I'm guessing you don't hold a lot of stock in your ability to get me off."

"No, Mr. Barlow, I don't. I've interviewed Jameson Harper, the young man you assaulted, and he is very mature for his age. He remembers even the tiniest details of that evening, and he's never wavered in the telling of those details—not to the police, not to the hospital, not to the prosecution, and not to me. He's ready to testify, and that testimony is going to be a powerful witness against you. But that's not really what I'm talking about right now."

Brock pushed his chin into his chest and raised an eyebrow. "Oh, really? What, then?"

Brock was going to make this even tougher than Andie had anticipated. She and Jack cautiously sat down in metal chairs across the table from Brock. "Well, Mr. Barlow, you remember that someone from the forensics team got a sample of your DNA."

Again, Brock chuckled derisively. "How could I forget?"

"Well, your DNA was entered into a national database, and I'm sure it will come as no surprise to you that we've since heard from officials in six other states who have matched your DNA to evidence that was found at crime scenes there—and that they're very anxious to talk to you."

"I don't care." Brock's jaw was set with steely determination.

"I'm suggesting that you care. That you care a lot."

"Why? I'm not being held on any other charges. I'm being held on charges related to that Harker kid."

"Harper."

"Whatever." His eyes narrowed again with cold hatred. "It doesn't really matter about the others now, does it? Because I'm here and they're there, and they can't touch me. Not if you do your job. And that's why I hired you."

"I can tell you know a lot about the legal system, Mr. Barlow, and I'm not trying to be condescending in the least when I tell you that several of those states are preparing right now to extradite you so you *can* face the charges they've connected to you based on DNA evidence. You're completely wrong in believing they can't touch you."

Brock blanched. A slight tremor crept into the hand that was cuffed to the arm of the chair but just as quickly vanished.

Immediately he regained control. "What's that? They can't make me go anywhere. Hell, I can't even step onto the sidewalk out front."

"Oh, but they can, Mr. Barlow. And as I said, they're preparing to do that right now. Which is what I've come to talk to you about. We've got to act quickly if we're going to delay those extraditions."

"What are you going to do to stop them?"

"I *can't* stop them, but I may be able to delay them. And the only way to delay extradition to another state is to have you sentenced in the state of Utah for the crime you committed here. They can't extradite you as long as that sentencing phase is still underway."

"*Sentence?* I haven't even been *tried* yet."

Andie glanced at Jack long enough to solicit a nod of support, then turned her attention back to Brock. "That's what I want to talk to you about—what I want to advise. I'm advising you to plead guilty, *today*, so we can get a sentencing hearing on the docket."

"You call that *counsel,* counselor? *This* is what I paid big bucks for?" Brock strained against the cuff that bound him to the chair.

Jack stood up. "Take it easy, Mr. Barlow. I'd suggest you give Ms. Harrison a chance to explain."

"Explain *what?* That she's throwing me to the wolves?" The veins on Barlow's neck stood out and his face turned crimson. He balled his hands into fists and clenched his jaw.

"In plain and simple terms, Mr. Barlow, here's what you're facing: The forensics team came and took a sample of your DNA because the state of North Carolina subpoenaed it. You already know that. I'm sure you also know it is a match. The sheriff there is busy getting his motions filed to—"

"A match to *what?*" Barlow bellowed.

"Come on, Mr. Barlow. We don't have time for this. A match to the DNA you left behind when you sexually assaulted eleven boys and killed two others."

Barlow jumped to his feet, nearly overturning the table, the metal chair dangling from his wrist. Already on his feet, Jack pressed into the door, banging the palm of his hand against it. Within seconds, two guards struggled to get Brock back into the chair. Hot tears stung the back of Andie's eyes.

"Stay back!" Brock shouted, trying to wrestle his free arm away from one of the guards.

"Not an option, buddy!"

Brock lunged and twisted but didn't prove a match for the guards. Almost before Andie knew what had happened, Brock was back in his chair—this time manacled, both wrists cuffed. While one guard held him down, the other buckled the cloth restraints, securing both arms firmly to the chair, both ankles to the chair legs. As a final insult, the guards looped a flexible restraint around Barlow's chest, holding him ramrod straight against the back of the chair.

"That ought to do it." The guard was winded; perspiration dripped down his face and stained his shirt in thick wedges under his arms. "Or would you like us to remove him?"

"No, I need to talk to him. We've got an issue that needs to be resolved today, and I still need to discuss the details with my client. Thank you for making that possible."

"We'll be right outside if you need us, but I don't think there will be any more problems."

The last guard to leave the room shot Brock a threatening glance. "I think Mr. Barlow has been reminded that he needs to behave." Brock tried to lunge forward, his teeth bared in a menacing snarl. The latch clicked shut, and Andie turned to face Brock again. She could feel her resolve crumbling.

"I'm not quite sure what that was, Mr. Barlow. I'm certain you're upset and possibly even frightened, but the best thing you can do right now is calm down and hear me out, because what I'm offering is the only advantage you're likely to get. If you plead guilty here, you'll be sentenced on a single assault and attempted homicide. Once North Carolina gets you, you'll be up for the death penalty if you're convicted. And with the DNA evidence they have, you *will* be convicted. I guarantee it. So you need to decide if you want us to try to delay that."

Brock sat completely still. Their eyes locked but Brock didn't speak.

"That's the situation as it stands, Mr. Barlow. When those extradition papers arrive, we will have no choice but to send you to North Carolina. The only thing that could delay the extradition at this point is if you plead guilty and we are in the process of getting a sentencing date on the docket. Once that process starts, it will effectively delay any effort by any state to extradite you."

"So they can never get me?" Brock's voice was surprisingly childlike—the first sign of real vulnerability Andie had seen.

"No. That's not true. They just won't be able to extradite you *now*. They will have to wait until you have been sentenced here. They'll monitor the sentencing process here, and once your sentencing hearing is over, they'll file the extradition request. But you'll buy time. You'll avoid having to face multiple charges right now. And there's always a chance—though slim—that North Carolina will lose interest in the interim. And you need to understand that other states have also expressed interest in extraditing you, though North Carolina was the first."

"But that wasn't the first place..." Brock mouthed in a whisper.

"I know that, Mr. Barlow. I know about Virginia. You should know that your victim there, Dixon Barnhurst, is going to college and preparing to get married. And you should know that he is certain he can identify you—says he'll never forget your eyes. Even if he *can't* identify you, your DNA can."

Brock stared straight ahead, almost in a daze. He didn't appear focused on anything. Icy fingers of dread moved rapidly up Andie's spine. *He's reliving it. He's remembering. He's assaulting Dixon Barnhurst all over again. Right here in front of me. I am witness—mute, but not blind.* She wanted to run screaming from the room.

"Mr. Barlow?"

Brock's eyes gradually came into focus and he looked directly at Andie.

"We need to put this all out on the table. We've received faxes from four other states as well. California. Colorado. Montana. Texas. They've all matched your DNA to murders committed in their jurisdictions. They will all line up to extradite you as well. By our count, Mr. Barlow, we have fifteen assaults and nineteen murders—which includes the crime you committed here. Is that the extent of it?"

Barlow sat completely silent. The only indication he was still alive was the slight flaring of his nostrils as he took slow breaths. "Maybe." He gradually lifted his eyes to stare at Andie. "Maybe not."

"Let me state this clearly, Mr. Barlow. I'm the only person you have in your corner. Everyone else wants to see you go down in a blaze, the sooner the better. You've got parents and friends and family members of thirty-four victims who want to see justice done. You've got investigators and law enforcement officers in seven states who want to close the cases on their books—including a former sheriff who lost his reelection bid in Texas because he hadn't found the killer who was terrorizing his community. You've got news reporters in those same states who can't wait to sink their teeth into this thing and to hold you up like bait for the pit bulls. I would suggest that you seriously consider what I'm advising, because I think it's your best chance to at least delay the inevitable."

Barlow brooded for a minute before making a sound. "Seven states? That all?"

Andie almost visibly recoiled. "You tell me. *Is* that all? Are there more? Because I don't like being blindsided, Mr. Barlow. It's time for you to come clean with me."

"Why bother? What if there *are* more? What would it matter? According to you, I'm hosed anyway. Would it really matter if there was another one? Or ten? Or a hundred?"

It can't be. Could there be more? More innocent boys snuffed out? More mothers devastated?

"Mr. Barlow, it would matter immensely. Because every boy whose life you took belonged to someone. You owe those families closure. I'm going to ask you one more time: Are there more?"

"Maybe. Maybe not."

Andie scrambled to her feet, trembling inside so severely she doubted her ability to walk. "Okay, Mr. Barlow, I'm done here. You're obviously not interested in helping yourself, let alone in accepting my help. You've got a big decision to make. I'd suggest you give it some serious thought—the most serious of your life. At eleven tomorrow morning, I'll be back to hear what you've decided. I have an appointment with the judge tomorrow at one. And if you're a fraction as smart as you want us all to believe, you'll be there with me in that courtroom promptly at one to enter your guilty plea."

"You'd like that, wouldn't you?" Barlow sneered.

"I would, Mr. Barlow, because I have been hired to help you. That's what I'm trying to do. And based on my own legal background and what I've been able to learn from my colleagues, the solution I'm offering you is your best chance. A guilty plea suggests to the judge that you are feeling contrite—or, barring that, you are at least accepting responsibility for what you did. If the judge can see that, he might be a little more lenient in your sentencing. That would obviously be in your favor just in case no one tries to extradite you; you'd serve less time here. And I would like you to reach out and grab hold of that chance. You won't get another like it. And you won't get this kind of leniency anywhere else. I can guarantee that. I'll see you tomorrow at eleven."

Jack beat Andie to the door. The second it opened she pushed her way into the hall and to the outer corridor before Brock could see her calm façade crumble.

CHAPTER 25

Maybe. Maybe not.

There could be more. More mothers scarcely able to breathe, hoping every day for answers. More investigators pressed against unyielding dead ends, wishing for a single lead. More boys—perhaps some still living—plucked from neighborhoods and parks and the ordinary days of their lives to face an unimaginable evil.

The possibility of more was bad enough. But it wasn't the worst. The worst, Andie decided, was Brock's cavalier attitude. His apparent detachment. *So what if there are more?* He seemed to taunt. *I don't care.* Taking even one life was inconceivable to Andie. Taking dozens, so many you might even lose count, defied comprehension.

Andie turned on the ignition to heat up the car. She looked across the cemetery from her vantage point on the narrow roadway near Beau's grave. The ground was studded with granite headstones; at the far end were a large cluster of markers more than a hundred years old, almost stark in their beauty. Silent drifts of snow settled between the headstones. Andie's mind danced with stories that must have filled the days and hours of those now tucked forever into soundless graves.

She often came here when she needed peace. She felt an odd sort of attachment to Beau in this dappled resting place, as if he were just around the bend in the road, on his way home for his favorite dinner of pork chops and potatoes. Her head dropped back softly against the headrest. Letting her eyes fall gently closed, she could see his smile. Could almost hear his laughter above the hum of her engine. She could still make absolutely no sense out of that last defiant act. He had seemed so *happy*. If only she had known—if only she had seen some indication of a sadness licking at the edges of his heart, maybe she could have done something to change his mind. Maybe she could have gotten him some help. If only...

If only. She wiped at the cold tears sliding down her cheeks. *I'm not the only mother dancing around those two lonely words.* She thought of the mothers of Brock's victims, of the thorny phrases that must have still come unbidden at the most unexpected times. *If only I had picked him up from school. If only I had made him leave the video arcade an hour earlier. If only his friends had waited for him. If only.* They had to be the two saddest words in the English tongue—words that hinted of an entire future, gone forever.

Sloan had insisted Andie take the rest of the day off when she returned from the jail. Jack had beaten her there and given Sloan the entire grisly rundown. Knowing Jack, no detail had been spared. Sloan had intercepted her in the lobby and had walked her back out to her car.

"You've done everything you can, Andie. You made him the offer. You explained clearly why it was in his best interest to take it. You've earned a break. See you in the morning." With that, Sloan had tucked her back behind the driver's wheel.

Sitting in the cemetery, Andie watched as Beau swept back across the panorama of her mind. He was still, and would always be, thirteen—full of fun, brimming with prospects, just waiting for the next adventure to come around the corner. Nothing seemed impossible. At least that's how it appeared. His was a life interrupted, one he chose to end, and the pain of that reality was almost too much to bear.

Andie's mind wandered to the thirty-four mothers who were part of that sorority of grief. She felt a peculiar sense of comfort in the fact that thirty-four other women knew the details of her heart in such an intimate way. There they were: at a salty beach in North Carolina, on a forested hillside in Montana, along a sandy trail in Texas—the women whose very lives had been shattered by the loss of their brave sons. The details were different, but the outcomes the same. Their boys were taken by a depraved monster; hers had been taken in a haze of confusion and misplaced determination by his own trembling hand.

Even the fifteen boys who had survived their assaults were taken. Their lives would never be the same. Their mothers would never be the same, either, keeping a constant and unrelenting vigil in an effort to prevent any further tragedy.

It was dusk. The setting sun sucked the warmth out of the air, and Andie knew the caretaker would be closing and padlocking the wrought-iron gates at the entrance of the cemetery any minute. Today of all days, she wanted to stay. Wanted to keep watch, to listen for just another imagined hint of Beau's voice on the winter breeze. Instead, she pulled slowly away, her tires crunching the gravel at the edge of the narrow roadway where an irreplaceable piece of her broken heart was tucked alongside her beautiful son.

THE NEXT DAY was blustery and cold, even for Park City. Andie had been at her desk only a few minutes when Jack burst through the door. "Less than three hours to go before your date with the judge, Andie, and you're going to *love* what I found out."

"Love it? That's going to take some work, Jack."

"*Love it,* Andie. Call it a hunch, but after you left the office yesterday, I decided to track Barlow's movements around the country —see if he'd lived for any length of time anywhere other than in the states we know of. You know, see if we might find some news reports of some unsolved assaults or murders. Maybe beat this guy at his own game."

Jack paused, a smug look of satisfaction on his face.

"Okay, Jack, I'm almost afraid to ask. Besides, why would I *love* the idea of more victims? I dread it with every shred of my being."

"That's just it, Andie. I don't know of any additional victims.

Here's what I *do* know: The guy in that cell over on the second floor of the Summit County Jail is not Brock Barlow."

Andie's jaw dropped. "What? Who is he?"

"Who knows? I just know it's not Brock Barlow."

"And how do you know that?"

"Like I said, I decided to track his convoluted path around the country—see if we might be missing anything obvious. First thing, I ran a check on his Social Security number to see where he'd lived, worked, applied for credit, opened bank accounts—that sort of thing. The Social Security number belonged to Brock Barlow, all right: a Brock Barlow who died a couple of years ago from a cerebral aneurysm in a Miami area hospital with his wife and three grown children at his bedside. They had to make the agonizing decision to turn off the life support after three long days of watching him languish."

"*What?*"

"That's right. The Social Security number went 'dead' for about a year, and then roared to activity again in Montana, attached to our guy over at the jail. He undoubtedly got it from one of those 'mills' that provides fake Social Security cards. It was used when he applied for a rented townhouse, opened a bank account in Missoula, secured a credit card, and got a job as a security cop at a place outside town that manufactures backhoes and other large machinery."

"Oh, that's rich—a criminal landing a security gig."

"Yeah, the irony is amazing. Anyway, *they* had no idea he was a criminal; they figured he was the same Brock Barlow who had worked at several security jobs in Florida. The employment check breezed through. After all, he had the same Social Security number, and the overworked office personnel at the firms where the real Brock Barlow had worked didn't know he had died."

"So—"

"So we don't have Brock Barlow at all. We have a guy who has spread his DNA all across the country, but he sure isn't Brock Barlow. And he's only been 'Brock Barlow' for about a year—a time he spent in an area of Montana that put him in perfect proximity to kill Kevin Duncan and Riley Marshall."

"This is fascinating—yet disturbing—information, Jack, but how is it going to help me this morning at the jail?"

"Don't you see, Andie? The more we know about this man—the more we can start to crack the veneer around the activities he's tried to hide—the more vulnerable he becomes. And the more vulnerable he becomes, the greater your chance of persuading him to plead. I think you should go over there at eleven, as promised, and see what he's decided. If he's decided to plead guilty, great—prop him up in front of the judge, tell him to speak up loud and clear, get his sentencing hearing scheduled, and make sure they lock him up and throw away the key. If he won't plead, then you hit him with the we-know-you're-not-Brock-Barlow card, and see how he reacts to *that*."

"You might be right. It just might work."

Brock was ready for Andie and Jack this time. He was seated in the interview room as they were escorted up the corridor at an angle so that Andie could see his face, and it was clear he would make no concessions. The old arrogance was back with a vengeance. He immediately locked eyes with Andie and glared at her as she walked in and sat down at the cold metal table across from him, next to Jack.

"Good morning, Mr. Barlow. I think we can skip the pleasantries this morning, since we covered everything pretty thoroughly yesterday." A tight pain started at the center of Andie's chest and spread with the memory. "I guess we need to know how you've decided to proceed."

He scowled at her, his head tilted and his mouth pressed into a thin line. He looked like he was memorizing every detail of her face before his words suddenly erupted from what seemed like a churning cauldron deep in his stomach. "I've decided to proceed as originally intended."

Andie waited for more, but it didn't come. "And that would be...?" Sitting across from her, unrestrained, he could have lunged across the table at her—something she fully expected—but he maintained a strange, almost brooding sense of control.

"I'm referring to my intention to have a fair trial before a jury of my peers in this jurisdiction on the charges that have been filed against me. And my intention is that you will actually defend me against those charges like I have paid you to do. *You,*" he said, jabbing his finger in her direction, "not *him.*" He released his gaze from Andie just long enough to stare briefly at Jack.

"I'm very clear that you have retained me to defend you, Mr. Barlow, but as I explained yesterday, there are mitigating circumstances that have seriously complicated this case. Those circumstances, as I have explained, have stemmed from your criminal activities in other states—crimes against which I have no power to defend you."

"You can defend me *here,* and that's what you're going to do."

"As I explained to you yesterday, I don't think we'll get that far. Officials in other states, North Carolina chief among them, are preparing to extradite you to stand trial for crimes that predate your assault charges here. Those requests are already underway. We are talking *hours* before those extradition requests reach us. And by law, we will have no choice but to extradite you immediately unless you have entered a plea and a sentencing hearing has been scheduled. They'll need to wait until that process is complete and that sentence has been handed down, which will offer you a delay. So if you want to delay any potential extradition, this is your only option." Jack nodded in agreement as Andie went on. "I don't know how much clearer I can explain it."

"And I don't know how much clearer I can state it. No. *I will not plead guilty.*" His voice was as hard and unyielding as marble.

It was almost as if he was being intentionally defiant—acting like a child who refused to do something positive just because an adult asked him to. A child who would rather put himself at a disadvantage than do what the grownups wanted.

"You're making a big mistake. I wish I could feel confident that you understand exactly *how big* the mistake is."

"Don't treat me like I'm some sort of moron," he growled, clutching the arms of the chair so hard his knuckles blanched. "I get it. I get what you're saying. I've heard your rambling explanations and your attempts to get out of defending me like you were hired to do. I—"

"I am *not* trying to get out of defending you, Mr. Barlow. And let me be very clear about one other thing: I have not taken one single second of this case lightly. It occupies every waking minute and haunts every sleeping one. But unless you take my advice and enter a guilty plea, my hands are going to be tied in trying to help you. It's that simple."

"No!" The sound of his shout ricocheted off the cinderblock walls. "I've heard enough!"

"Well, maybe I haven't finished. You've been cooling your heels in here for no more than a couple of weeks. But in that short amount of time, a veritable mountain of information about you has come cascading in. Most of it has been as a result of your DNA sample, but we've received additional information—some of it just yesterday—that is deeply troubling. Almost every hour that goes by, your case gets worse."

"What information?" For a split second, his careful façade crumbled. Andie thought she caught a fleeting glimpse of panic.

CHAPTER
26

As usual, Brock recovered quickly. His sneer sickened Andie. She shifted in her chair and sat up a little straighter, trying to gain a position of power and control before she delivered her punch line.

"Just yesterday, we found out your name isn't Brock Barlow. We found out you've been using the Social Security number of a man named Brock Barlow who died in a Miami area hospital. And we learned you used that falsified number to gain employment and credit in Montana, where two of your victims were murdered. Your use of falsified information alone represents serious charges. And I suspect it's not the first name you've used fraudulently in your cross-country murder spree. Your case has just gotten a whole lot more complicated."

"I don't care." He slumped back against his chair in a display of forced nonchalance. In a show of steely grit, he somehow managed to erase all hints of emotion from his face. Andie was completely unable to read him—a skill she had honed early in her career, one on which she heavily depended. But it was useless against this man.

Andie leaned slightly forward and raised the level of her voice. "You'd *better* care because things between you and me are about to change. If you want me to help you, you're going to have to be straight up front with me. No more games. No more false names. No more failing to reveal the extent of your past criminal activity. I need to know exactly who you are and what you have done. Those are my terms. You can take them or leave them."

His laughter punctuated the air, startling Andie. "You don't seem to get it. I've already paid for you. And when your boss took that money, it was my guarantee of your services. It might as well have been a contract signed in blood."

The analogy was revolting, and Andie hated it. In a last-ditch attempt, she decided to call his bluff. She stared directly at him, willing herself to avoid even a simple blink of the eye. "That money can be refunded, and I can walk away. *How am I supposed to defend you if I don't even know your name?* I don't even know what to call you."

He rose to his feet slowly and deliberately. "How about *Dad?*"

An electric jolt rammed through Andie with a force that threatened to knock her out of the chair.

A menacing smile spread across his face. He extended his hand across the table toward her.

"Drew Carlson. Nice to meet you. *Again.*"

CHAPTER
27

Andie reeled back as though she'd been shoved. Her eyes were wide, ringed with terror. She clapped her hand over her mouth as the bile churned up her throat. Her breaths were shallow, ragged.

Jack stared in surprised confusion, his mouth hanging open. "What the—"

Andie let out a strangled cry and stood to face the prisoner. Her rage was apparent. "*How dare you!* How dare you pretend to be my father! My father is *dead!*"

"I don't know who told you that, but it's obviously wrong. I'm right here. And I'm very much alive."

Andie trembled violently; grabbing the edge of the table for support, she leaned toward the prisoner. "How do I know you're telling the truth? You've lied about everything else!"

He breathed out an anguished chuckle and sat back down, resting his hands flat on the surface of the table. His voice was laced with sarcasm. "What kind of proof would you like? Oh, wait... I don't seem to have my wallet with me. Can't produce any ID right now, I'm afraid. But I can tell you anything you want to know."

Andie collapsed into her chair and pressed her palm firmly against her chest. Focused on slowing her breathing, she stared into his face, scouring every detail for even a flicker of some ancient recognition. "The names of my parents and where they lived are a matter of public record," she said. "And you seem to be a pretty smart guy. How do I know you didn't just do a little research?"

"Oh, I can go way beyond the basic facts. Try the chicken coop."

Andie visibly blanched. "Go on."

"Right after that bitch of a woman trapped me into marrying her —while she was pregnant with *you*—we lived in a converted chicken coop. It was disgusting, but better than she deserved. I made her shovel all the chicken shit. She hated that. Retched up most of what she ate."

Jack put his hand on Andie's shoulder and squeezed gently. "Are you sure you want to do this, Andie? Because I can—"

"I think it's time I find out the truth." She narrowed her gaze but never let it leave the prisoner's eyes. "Go on."

"The truth? You want the *truth*? Fine. I was seventeen—no family. Trying to work my way into something better. Took a job with a co-op of corn growers in Iowa. It was hot and muggy that summer, and your mother kept hanging around the corn fields with her friends, complaining of the heat and wearing these gauzy little shirts that skimmed those full tits of hers. She was three years older and knew her way around, that's for sure. Knew exactly how to get into my pants. I was in it for fun—loved the feel of it, the diversion from the backbreaking work, the softness of her thighs against—"

"That's enough!" Andie cried. "You can spare me the details."

He smirked. "Damn, it was good. Every other night or so, sometimes out in the dirt between the corn stalks, sometimes on the thick grass behind the equipment shed." A slow smile spread across his face as he seemed to relive the lusty nights, then abruptly vanished. "Didn't really care for her—*at all*—but loved what she put out. Loved the way she helped me feel normal, even if just for a while. I figured I'd finish up the corn harvest and head somewhere else, really get a good start, and just put her behind me.

"But as summer petered out, damn if she didn't turn up *pregnant*. Whined and cried and said she couldn't possibly go back to her parents—her uptight, holier-than-thou, Methodist parents—they'd kill her. Demanded we get married. I couldn't believe it. I was *seventeen*. But I had nowhere else in particular to go. I got tired of listening to her endless tirades, and I stupidly gave in. Went to a local justice of the peace. Got married. Figured I could just deal with it later—you know, figure out how to get away before she got used to it. Biggest mistake I ever made."

Andie straightened up in the chair. "Really? *The biggest mistake you ever made?* I find that hard to believe, coming from a man who has murdered at least nineteen people."

"Listen to me and listen closely: Yes. Marrying Nora Carlson was the biggest mistake I ever made. It was a living hell. But it was done, and I was stuck, and I couldn't figure out how to get away, so I tried to make the best of it—decided to see if it was something I could learn to tolerate, even if I couldn't stand—"

Andie was on her feet before he could utter another word. "Why were you all alone at seventeen? Where was your family?"

Drew Carlson's skin turned ashen. His expression was void. He almost snarled his one-word reply. "Gone."

It was a powerful emotional tug-of-war, and Andie felt she had finally gotten her fists full of the thick end of the rope. "What do you mean by *gone,* Mr. Carlson? Gone where?"

A look of what could only have been panic brewed with confusion washed across his features. He set his jaw and for the first time gazed away from Andie, his focus scattered. It was clear he wasn't going to speak.

"I know more about my father than you think I do," Andie taunted. "And I know what happened to his family. So unless you have that information—"

"Then you know they went up like a torch!" he cried, almost spitting out the words. Narrowing his eyes, he stared at Andie with contempt. "Do you know what it's like being only thirteen and trying to pull your brother—bigger and older and heavier and all but dead—out a cellar window when your hands have been burned? Can you even *begin* to understand what it's like knowing that your baby sister is upstairs in your mother's arms, dying? Do you have any idea how it feels to have flames licking at you as you take the only way out? *Do you know what it feels like to die inside when you find out you're the only one still alive?* There are things a lot worse than death, *Ms. Harrison.* Sometimes it's living that's the real hell."

Trying to save your brother when your hands have been burned. He wasn't trying to obliterate the fingerprints of his victims. He was reenacting his own searing pain.

Only thirteen. He wanted to die when he was thirteen. So most of the ones he touched *did* die when they were thirteen.

"So, what happened then, Mr. Carlson? If you were only thirteen, where did you go?" He probably still thought it was a test... didn't know that she was now seeking answers.

"I got sent to live with my father's cousin. He turned out to be a twisted bastard; raped me almost every night while his wife fell asleep in front of the TV downstairs. I could hear her snoring. She looked like a big wad of overripe bread dough propped in that chair of hers. I finally told someone at school what was happening, but they didn't believe me. He kept raping me until I finally got big enough to threaten him—to scare him. He crept in one night, ready to go, and I came out from behind the bedroom door with a big metal bat I got from a kid down the street. Told him if he touched me again, I'd break every bone in his body then tell his wife. Then I rammed that bat into his nuts. He never bothered me again."

"And then?"

"As soon as school got out, I ran off—didn't say goodbye. Hitchhiked a couple of counties over and got a job at the co-op. Met your mother...well, I think you got that part of the story already. Came as far as Minden and bartered with a guy for that little farm out on Garfield Road. Worked my ass off. Just tried to grit my teeth and steer as wide a path around that bitch as I could. Then *you* were born, and I knew I would never get out. You *disgusted* me. I couldn't even *touch* you. The prison I'm facing now is *nothing* compared to the prison you created by being *born.* Then your mother turned up pregnant again—has to have been someone else's, because I hadn't touched her in more than a year. That little whelp got lucky and died, but the two of you were still there. That's when I decided to—"

Andie's words erupted staccato-style as she walked briskly to the door and banged on it with the flat of her hand. "I'm finished here, Mr. Carlson. I am canceling the one o'clock appointment with the judge, and I am declining this case. It would be completely unethical for me to continue representing you now that you have revealed your relationship to me. Jack will be in touch with you to let you know who will be taking my place."

As the guard pulled the door open, Drew Carlson leapt to his feet. "No! *You* will represent me!"

Walking away from Jack, Andie quickly crossed the threshold into the hallway and didn't even turn to face her client as she responded. "I'm sorry, Mr. Carlson. That won't be possible."

The door latched shut. Jack thrust the door open and managed to catch up to Andie partway down the corridor. "Look, I don't know what just happened in there—"

Andie spun around to face Jack. "I just found out that the monster in that room, the man responsible for a string of assaults and murders all the way across the country, is *my father*. The father who walked away, disappeared before I turned two. Abandoned me and my mother. The fact that he walked away from us has haunted me for years—and *this* is where I find him!"

Andie suddenly veered toward the wall and collapsed against it, sliding down the rough cinderblock and crumpling into a heap at Jack's feet. Barely discernible above Andie's guttural sobs were the muffled and unintelligible shouts of Drew Carlson. From the sound of it, he was hurling himself against the locked door of the interview room.

It couldn't be true.

Every cell in Andie's body fought against the possibility that the animal in cell 209 was her father.

He certainly knew the details—certainly had bits of information he couldn't possibly have pulled out of thin air. He even told the raw story of the fire that destroyed his family, a story that had never been uttered by Nora. Had she even known?

But what if the facts he so brazenly articulated had been *lived* instead of *discovered*? Was it remotely possible that this man, whoever he was, could have *known* Drew Carlson those decades ago —and now be living in his skin? He chose Brock Barlow...why not now choose Drew Carlson?

It would be a cruel charade. But this man—a man who plucked up innocent boys and brutally annihilated them—was well acquainted with cruelty.

Splashing cold water on her face, Andie consumed her image in the mirror. She couldn't deny the resemblance. She had never looked like Nora—short, plump Nora with her soft, rounded face, her nondescript eyes (sometimes slate, sometimes blue), her dishwater-blond hair. Tall and lean, Andie had high, sculpted cheekbones; eyes the color of dark chocolate; thick, chestnut-brown hair—just like the inmate in cell 209. Grabbing a wad of paper towels and blotting her face, she suddenly bolted into one of the stalls and vomited at the recognition.

Having responded to a call from Jack, Grace met Andie at the front door of the jail. "I heard, Andie. Are you okay?"

Andie felt as though her throat would close off. "No. I've rarely been *less okay* in my life. What if he's lying? *Oh, Grace, what if he's not?*"

"What do *you* think?"

"I don't know *what* to think. He knew things—things about my mother that happened early in her marriage. He knew all about the fire that killed my father's entire family. That's not stuff that would be easy to unearth...but then again, I did. What if he and my father were friends decades ago? Maybe even during their childhood? He'd know those things—and if the detective in Minden was right, and my father is dead, my father would be a perfect target for stolen identity. Especially by someone who knew him—knew his story."

"What does your gut say?"

"I can't face it enough to *feel* much of anything. The possibility is too horrific."

"You can find out for sure, Andie. You know that, right?"

"How?"

"DNA. You've already got his."

That simple fact had completely escaped Andie. In all the visceral drama of the interview room, she hadn't processed the fact that this man's DNA had been gathered on the end of a swab and entered into the system and now held all the answers. A simple swab of her own cheek—a solitary strand of hair—and she'd know. She could expose him for the liar he was.

Andie called in a favor with one of the forensics lab technicians she had previously plied with free legal advice. He swabbed her cheek, snapped the vial shut, penned her name on the label, and promised results overnight. It almost seemed too easy. It was the same simple act that had started a landslide of grief for her former client—a simple act that had brought cops and sheriffs swarming from all over the country, licking their chops for a piece of the killer.

THE NEXT MORNING Andie parked outside the lab and clung to the steering wheel long after she turned off the engine. Her measured steps to the technician's desk belied her desire to run raggedly in both directions. When he looked up and saw her, his eyes said it all. She couldn't manage to speak.

"The test was positive, Andie. He's your father."

Her heart plunged precipitously toward the cavernous void in her gut. It couldn't be.

"Are you sure?"

"As sure as is scientifically possible. I ran a simple paternity test, Andie. There's less than one in about a hundred billion chance you are *not* the child of this man. The results are so accurate that for legal purposes, they're considered 100 percent."

So that was it. He showed up in Park City, nabbed a boy that he intended to murder, slipped up at the Sinclair, and shouted her name. His *daughter's* name. More than three decades after walking away.

It didn't make sense. None of it made sense. How did he know she was an attorney? How did he know she was an attorney *in Park City?* A creeping dread started under her scalp and devoured her, inch by inch.

She had to know how he found her.

CHAPTER
28

Andie perched nervously on the hard stool on one side of the glass barrier. A grimy telephone sat in its cradle on the half-wall to her right. The small Formica countertop in front of her needed to be wiped down with lots of hot, soapy water; she leaned her forearms carefully against the edge and folded her hands tightly. Now that she no longer represented Drew Carlson, the interview room was off-limits. Any discussion she had with him now was limited to the phone, a heavy slab of reinforced glass mounted solidly between them.

At last a muscled guard led Drew by the elbow to the stool on his side of the glass. Drew yanked his arm away from the guard and sat down hard on the stool, facing Andie. It was easy to see, even through the thick glass, that he was angry. His jaw was clenched, his mouth in a straight line. The veins in his neck stood out, and he narrowed his eyes as he studied her every feature. He stared at her with the same look of calculated hatred she had seen in every encounter with him. He sat, unmoving, stewing in what appeared to be a simmering rage.

Andie reached for the phone and held it against her head, never breaking eye contact with her father. He continued to stare, never moving a muscle. After several minutes, Andie realized he was unwilling to talk. She started to return the phone to its cradle.

Suddenly Drew slammed the palm of one hand against the glass and reached for the phone with his other. Still maintaining a level of eye contact that caused physical pain, Andie eased the phone back to her ear.

"What do you want?" Drew snarled.

"I want you to answer some questions," she said in a voice bold enough to cover the terror that held residence in her heart. "I think you owe me that much."

"I don't owe you a damn thing, *Ms. Harrison,* but go ahead. What do you want to know?"

"When you were arrested at the Sinclair station, you shouted my name—told the police that you wanted me to represent you. Said I was your attorney. How did you even know my name? Or know I was here?"

Drew angled the phone away from his head and laughed riotously. At first Andie feared he was not going to answer, but he eventually brought the phone back to his mouth. "I've been watching you, you stupid bitch. Ever since the day I went away, I've watched you from afar. Kept track of you. Known where you were and what you were doing."

Andie's chest constricted, and hot tears seared the back of her eyes. In a flash across the surface of her memory, she imagined a sad little girl keeping vigil at the living room window with her mother, waiting for her daddy to come back. "If you always knew where I was, why didn't you—"

"What? *Let you know?* Because *I hated you,* that's why."

Helpless to stop it, Andie felt a single tear slide down her left cheek. It felt cold against her flushed skin. "I was a *little girl,* Mr. Carlson. Not much more than a baby. What on earth could I have done to you to make you hate me so?"

He lunged toward the glass. "*You were born!* That hideous bitch of a mother of yours used you as a pawn to trap me into marrying her. All that hell—all the time in the converted chicken coop, all the days in the fields under the blistering sun on that run-down farm, all the nights in that stifling house, *they were all because of you.* Did you know *I never touched you?* You made me sick!"

"Wait a minute! If I was such a *trap,* why on earth did you let her get pregnant?"

"You think I *wanted* that? I didn't want *that.* I wanted to get my rocks off—what guy doesn't? But a *child?* With *her?* Are you *kidding me?*"

"Then why did you let it happen?" It was agonizing to squeeze the words out, but she asked again. Reduced her existence to an *it*, something this twisted man had dreaded since those days back in the corn field.

"There was no *letting* about it. Crazy bitch—she lied about that like she lied about everything else. Told me she was messed up. Couldn't get pregnant. Would never have kids. You think I would have kept banging her if I thought *that* would happen?"

That. The tears came unrestrained, and Andie slumped against the Formica. "So why did you stay at all? Why didn't you leave the minute you found out she was pregnant?"

"I *wanted* to, believe me. But I was young and stupid. I had nowhere to go. I panicked. It was the path of least resistance." A dark, brooding mood seemed to cross his face but vanished with startling speed. "I had no family. No one. Found a guy on a work crew on the other side of town who said he knew someone who could take care of it. Not a coat-hanger job or anything, but something more—you know, safe. But Nora would hear nothing of it."

"You wanted her to get an abortion?"

"Hell, yes!" Drew exploded. "It would have solved it all. But, oh, no—not prim and proper Nora. She'd spread her legs on a whim, but when things went wrong, would she consider an abortion? No. Wasn't the *moral* thing to do. The alley cat suddenly got religion."

"That didn't mean you had to *marry* her, Mr. Carlson. You could have cut ties right then and there. That probably would have been the kindest thing—for all of us."

"Think I don't know that now? Married her because I didn't know what else to do. Kept promising myself I'd figure something out in a few days, but the days kept coming and going and then I was trapped. *You* came, and I was out of options."

"But you *did* leave. Just walked away. Couldn't you at least have told my mother you were leaving?"

The twisted laughter pulsated again through the crackling phone connection. "What? So she could follow me? Continue to make my life a complete misery? No. I'd served my time. I was *through,* and the only way to get out was to walk out. Walk away. Never look back. Leave no forwarding address. And that's what I did."

Andie took a few slow, deep breaths. "But you *did* look back. You just admitted it. I don't understand...if you hated me so, and wanted so desperately to get away from me, why did you watch me—why did you keep track of me? Why not just cut all your ties and *truly* never look back?"

Drew leaned as close to the glass as he could get; one of the guards behind him stopped pacing aimlessly and focused in on Drew, his gaze fixed. Drew slowly, cautiously, sat back a little. "Don't you get it? I've been waiting all these years—all this time—to make your life the living hell you made mine. I knew I'd eventually get the chance."

Andie felt the smallest measure of indignation creep into her heart. "Oh, come on. Seriously? You didn't have anything better to do with your time than *that*?"

"Oh, it's been worth it." He tapped his index finger rhythmically against the Formica on his side of the glass. "And besides, as you've found out, I came up with some interesting ways to occupy myself in the meantime."

It was too vague to be considered a confession...just enough to taunt and sicken her.

"How long have you been here? In Park City?"

"Oh, off and on, as long as you have. I followed you here. Left a few times for a while, but always managed to come back, just to make sure *you* were still here."

"Then why have I never seen you?"

"How do you know you haven't? I sat on the back row at your kid's funeral."

Andie stood up suddenly, sending the stool skittering across the hard vinyl floor. "*I don't believe you!*" she screamed. "My mother was there! She would have seen you—would have *recognized* you!"

"Hell, no. That was easy. She was as self-absorbed as she's always been. Don't think she *ever* focused on anything other than herself. It was simple staying out of her line of vision. I don't think she even once turned around. By the time the bagpiper pumped up to play his first notes at the end of that funeral, I was out the back door and down the hill...free and clear."

Somehow the thought of him in the same room with Beau—even though they were only Beau's remains—sickened her. Beau, she remembered, had taken flight...had drifted far beyond that chilly spring day in a gesture too heartbreaking to comprehend anymore.

"So you've just been hanging around, waiting to torment me?"

"Pretty much."

"I just can't help asking, Mr. Carlson. If you were so angry at *me*, and so determined to make *my* life a living hell, why all the boys? What was with *that*?" She took in a sharp breath and held it; this could be as good as a confession, though it no longer really mattered from a legal standpoint. She just wanted to hear it. Wanted to hear it from him.

He locked onto her gaze and one corner of his mouth turned up almost imperceptibly. "No special reason. Just wanted to."

Andie felt as if she was going to vomit. Thirty-four lives ruined on a whim. A sick, twisted whim. "That's it? Just because you *wanted to*?"

Drew visibly relaxed and smiled. "Why don't you ask that stupid shrink that's been poking around? *He* seems to think he has it all figured out."

"What shrink?"

"The one the half-assed prosecution hired. He's exhausted me with all his questions—all his theories."

Andie hadn't known anything about a psychiatric evaluation. It stood to reason—get a profiler or a therapist in there right up front, get a handle on what kind of crap was really going through this guy's head.

"And what theories might those be, Mr. Carlson?"

"Total horse shit."

"Could you be a little more specific?"

The phone went silent. Andie could see a physical change in Drew's demeanor—an expression that looked like agonizing pain. He hadn't often demonstrated any vulnerability, but she remembered a few fleeting moments of panic in the interview room. It was etched now in every line of his face. Then, as suddenly as it had come, it vanished.

"It was the fire."

"Fire?"

"The fire that killed my family."

"What about it?"

"They're blaming it on the fire. At least most of it. They think I kill because the people who meant the most to me were killed. In front of me. They think I kill thirteen-year-old boys because I was thirteen, and I was there, and I should have been able to stop it. I should have been able to save them. That's the theory. Like I said, total horse shit."

The grainy black-and-white images that dotted the front page of the newspaper slapped across Andie's recollection. "Has someone actually *said* that to you, Mr. Carlson—that you should have been able to save your family? Because I think that's unrealistic. You were thirteen years old, sleeping in the basement, barely able to get out of the house yourself. That fire spread ferociously; I don't think anyone could have expected you to outrun or outsmart the flames that took that house and your family with it."

Drew Carlson's eyes narrowed, and his expression hardened. "How do you know so much about it?"

"Because I looked for you—for a long time. Isn't it ironic? I was looking for you, and you've scarcely let me out of your sight. When my mother died, I drove through every hamlet in Iowa trying to find some record of your marriage. During that search I found a woman who had lived in Ames when the fire killed your family. She gave me the clue, and the rest was easy. I went to the newspaper office and read the articles on microfilm."

His stare was icy. "Then you know I was the suspect. That they blamed the whole thing on me."

"I do, and I can't imagine how horrible that must have been for you. I also know it was totally unfair. I also know that within a few weeks they realized how stupid they had been, and they placed the blame squarely where it belonged: on a faulty kerosene stove. I know you were just trying to keep your family warm. And I know the electric company for which your father worked had shut off your power. I know you had nothing to do with it."

"I was the one who lighted the stove. So, I guess I *did* have something to do with it."

Andie shifted uncomfortably. "I didn't mean *that*, Mr. Carlson. Clearly you lighted the stove. But clearly you had no intention of harming your family."

His gaze was menacing. "How do *you* know?"

A wave of nausea swept over Andie with sudden intensity. The lines of newsprint flashed across her memory. "I know because the newspaper article said you were trying to keep your family warm, and that you tried to save the brother who was sleeping in the basement with you. I know because it would never even occur to a thirteen-year-old boy to set his house on fire and kill his family."

"You don't know *shit*."

A suffocating panic squeezed Andie's chest. What *had* really happened on that frigid Iowa night, a family scattered through a chilly house, two boys cocooned in the basement? Was this just jailhouse bravado?

Andie set her jaw. "Then why don't you tell me what I don't know."

CHAPTER
29

It seemed Drew didn't even blink—never broke eye contact as he slowly pushed the phone toward the wall. Her muscles aching with the strain, Andie pressed the handset against her ear, watching for even the smallest crackle in the unyielding plaster of Drew Carlson's face. Still he stared, holding the phone less than an inch from its cradle. Less than an inch, and the conversation would be over. The sweat trickled down Andie's back, carving a path along her spine.

Part of her wanted to hang up. Wanted to pretend she didn't care. Wanted to walk away, never knowing, not caring. But a bigger part of her wanted to hear it directly from him. Wanted to know, against all hope, that just one thing in his broken life had been exactly what it seemed: a tragic accident.

Muscle, sinew, flesh. All of it remained so immobile that he might as well have been sculpted of marble, an emotionless effigy slumped onto the stool and propped against the grubby Formica countertop. His eyes seemed black, not a single flicker of light betraying any emotion. They bored into Andie's eyes with painful intensity. But she refused to snap her eyelids shut against his sinister stare. Two could play this game.

Drew's fingers blanched where they wrapped around the phone, and at last she detected the slightest tremor in his hand. Registering absolutely no emotion, he finally moved the phone slowly back against his ear. He held it there, saying nothing at all, for what seemed like forever. Only by concentrating ferociously could she hear his jagged, irregular breathing dancing across the line.

Then, without warning, he spoke.

"You think you know it all. Think you know how I felt and what I did. You should walk up and down the aisles of this hell-hole and listen in on the things that are said. It'd blow you away. I don't think you have a *clue* what goes on out there, outside your neat and tidy little bubble. Outside your perfect little world."

Andie felt the anger starting to simmer. "My world is *not* perfect, Mr. Carlson. It never has been. I grew up in a home where my father walked away without leaving a forwarding address, and where my mother never got over it. I had to fend for myself almost from the time I could walk. I married a man I thought I would spend the rest of my life with until I found him in our bed with another woman. I gave birth to a little boy who also grew up without a father"—the tears were stinging, threatening to spill—"and he was the only part of me that made any sense. I lost him, and it was the hardest thing that ever happened to me. Now I find that the father I thought was dead is instead a serial killer. I can't think of anyone who would consider that a *perfect* life."

"Oh, so you blame me too?"

"I don't blame you for anything in my life. I won't lie—it was tough. You left us in an untenable situation. But that's not who I am. I chose a different reality, and I've made it work. The thing that makes me sad is that *you* could have chosen a different reality too. Your situation didn't have to define you any more than mine had to define me. The people who blamed you were *way* out of line, but they didn't have to define you."

"Maybe it was the truth."

"What? That you were at fault?"

"Yes."

"I know you didn't purposely set that fire, Mr. Carlson." She was doing it again. Grasping at straws. Hoping to shape what she wanted to hear.

"And how do you know that?"

There it was again—a question too horrible to consider. The one she wanted answered. She locked him into her stare and slowly shook her head. "Because I know you wouldn't do that. And because you almost died yourself trying to save your brother."

He visibly slumped, resting his elbows on the counter and leaning his forehead against his clenched fist. "It wasn't supposed to be like that."

"Like what?"

"Hank wasn't supposed to die. We were supposed to get out together."

Bile roiled up Andie's throat, and a horror squeezed her chest until she almost couldn't breathe. It took every shred of courage to ask what she didn't want to know. "Exactly what are you saying, Mr. Carlson? *Did* you set the fire?"

He slowly lifted his head and looked squarely at her. His jaw muscles rippled. His mouth was drawn into a tight line. He once more moved in what seemed like slow motion toward the phone cradle on the wall. Andie heard the guttural scream ricocheting off the walls of the visitors' room before she realized it was coming from her own soul.

Drew Carlson slowly brought the phone back against his head. "What's the problem? Too much for you?"

"*Did you set the fire?*"

He cocked his head as the corners of his mouth crept upward into a sinister smile. "I'd do it again. But this time I'd make sure Hank got out first. It was his idea, and we had plans. It wasn't supposed to end that way."

The horror trapped Andie in a fierce grip. The grainy newspaper images flashed through her mind again—the tattered little girl in the wagon. The dark-haired mother with her haunting eyes. The skeletal remains of a house, only one wall left standing, the bicycle leaning against it. It seemed like hours before she could form enough words to speak again.

"Tell me. Right now. About the fire."

"Why?"

"Because I think it matters."

"To you, maybe. Not to me." Drew shook his head as an almost troubled expression splashed over his face. "But I guess I have nothing to lose at this point."

Drew shifted on the stool, rubbing his elbow. "Hank? Hank and I were the oldest of that horde of kids. And we took the brunt of it all."

Andie concentrated on keeping a level tone, a cool expression. Any betrayal of emotion, and Drew might shut down completely. She stuck to the obvious. "The oldest kids in the family always have to do most of the work—"

"Not that!" Drew interrupted wildly, his words coming in staccato phrases. "My mother. What a wreck! Worn to a frazzle. Lashed out at Hank. Slapped him, pulled his hair, kicked him, pushed him into the wall—even bit him once. One day I saw her pummeling him with her fists. Beating the shit out of him. It made me crazy because he never fought back. Just looked at her like a beat dog whenever she started in on him. I hated her.

"One day he said something that set her off. Or maybe not. Didn't matter. She never needed a reason. She lunged at him and wrapped her hands around his throat and shook him so hard his head snapped back and forth on his neck. His face was purple, his eyes wild." Drew's eyes narrowed with hatred. "I lost it. Jumped onto my mother's back. Dug my heels into her. Tore at her hands. Guess it startled her because she let go of Hank's neck. Spun around, knocking me flat on my ass, and told me that if I ever did that again, she would kill me. Thing is, I knew she meant it. After that, we were *both* her whipping boys." A line of sweat broke out across Drew's forehead with the brutality of remembering.

Allowing herself to blink for the first time, Andie wiped her mouth with the back of her hand. "Why didn't you tell your fath—"

Drew slammed his fist against the Formica. "That bastard! He was beating us too—pummeled me so hard one time I got a concussion. My mother *had* to have known."

And there it was. Having the city turn the heat off barely even registered on the scale in that house of horrors. Andie's widened eyes rimmed with shock. Drew was undeterred.

"It was Hank first thought of it. All we wanted to do was save those kids. From *her*, from her fists, her wild fury. And from *him*. Sooner or later, he would have nailed Betty. And she was only a baby. They were better off dead. All of 'em. Figured we'd send *them* to hell, and the kids to the angels. So we made a plan. We'd start a fire, using the kerosene heater. We'd climb out the window while the whole place went up like a torch. I did my part. But Hank—Hank wouldn't wake up. I got out, but I couldn't pull him out. He wasn't supposed to die. Not him. Not Hank."

Andie's mouth felt like it was filled with cotton.

Drew *had* set the fire.

The abuse was brutal. But it didn't change the fact that Drew had snuffed out nine lives. Nine people who choked and died in a scorching inferno. Realizing the dread of it all, she watched as Drew once again assumed his arrogant demeanor. His eyes blazed with challenge.

Something in Andie snapped. "Then I guess I misjudged." Hot tears splashed over her cheeks. "I thought your list of victims totaled thirty-four. I guess there were nine more."

Drew Carlson snorted with a derisive laugh. "No, Ms. Harrison. Ten."

"Ten?"

"You're missing one."

"I don't know what you mean."

"Your precious little Beau—the one you found dangling from a tree. And you were so stupid that you *actually believed* he put *himself* there."

Andie slammed the phone into the cradle and stood so suddenly that her stool flipped onto the floor. There was no way to know if

Beau had also been sodomized; since his cause of death had seemed an obvious suicide, no one had done an autopsy or checked for that. Andie would never know—and maybe it was better that way. Trembling, she pulled her cell phone from her pocket. Taking the last ounce of power away from her father, she dialed 9-1-1. "I need to report a murder."

EPILOGUE

ndie slowly ran her index finger along the date carved into the speckled gray granite. The stone was smooth, unyielding. *March 20.*

There it was, etched into forever: Her birthday. The last day she saw Beau, jogging backward away from the condo, waving. The day her world skidded to a halt. The day she wondered if she would ever be able to make sense of anything again.

She brushed the powdery snow off the flat headstone. Across its surface she gently laid a bundle of bright yellow sunflowers studded with curly willow branches, punctuated with deep purple iris, tied with a crimson ribbon. It was the fifth March 20th she had visited this solitary grave, nestled at the corner of the cemetery along the edge of the gravel road. The fifth March 20th she had also laid a piece of her heart against the smooth gray granite.

Beau had been cruelly taken from her. That much was clear. But somehow knowing he had expired at the hands of Drew Carlson was a peculiar comfort when compared to the dread of believing he had *chosen* to leave.

He *had* taken flight that day, just as she had always imagined. But she knew now that flight had not been a tortured escape from an existence he could no longer bear. It was knowledge that gave Andie the ability to bear all he had left behind.

THE DECAYING REMAINS of Drew Carlson had been tucked away in their own grave in a prison cemetery somewhere in north-central Texas. The extradition order from Texas had arrived before the one from North Carolina; it reached Summit County mere days after Andie learned that the prisoner in cell 209 was her father. All things considered, Sloan had abandoned the effort to protect Drew Carlson with a rapid guilty plea. Texas had done what it does best—extradited and tried and executed without fanfare. Somewhere in the vast eternity that stretched beyond the sky, the ethereal bits of Drew Carlson now floated, desolate and gauze-like and harmless.

He was gone. And with him all the horror and the pain were gone.

Andie stood, wiping the snow from the damp knees of her pants. She moved her hand slowly over her swollen belly before wrapping her heavy sweater snugly around it. Taking a step backward, away from the grave, she leaned up against Jack, feeling his warmth as his arms encircled her.

"Ready?"

"Yes." She slipped her hand into his, and they turned toward the car. Pausing, she looked back toward the solitary grave, covered now with the bright yellow sunflowers that tied her childhood home in Nebraska to the cottage where she now lived, nestled against the hills on the sunny side of the canyon. She wiped away a single tear, startled at the realization that it was a tear of joy.

Resting her free hand on her belly once more, she smiled at Jack. "Beau would have loved this little girl."

ABOUT THE AUTHOR

Cassandra Grey has authored a number of nonfiction books, but this is her debut novel. Her first brush with a real-life criminal came when she took a criminology class in college—a requirement for journalism majors, who might later be assigned the police beat. Class members learned how to rob banks, crack a safe, and hijack an airplane. And what do you know? One of the class members—Richard McCoy—did exactly that: hijacked an airplane, ala D. B. Cooper style, parachuting out over Utah with his haul.

When he was tried, Cassandra was assigned to cover his trial for the college newspaper. Meeting your friend in the elevator at the courthouse when one of you is in an orange jumpsuit and manacles? Awkward.

But that's nothing compared to her later exploits. During her first post-college job, Cassandra and her roommate used to give Ted Bundy rides to church. That's right. *That* Ted Bundy. They both thought he was cute. And, happily, they both lived to tell the story. Finding out he was a serial killer who had been killing women during the time they had been shuttling him to church? Takes awkward to a whole new level.

Cassandra has more than forty years of professional experience in corporate and internal communications, public relations, media relations, marketing communications, and publications management and has held communications management positions at a variety of national and international corporations. (A series of criminal-free environments, to her knowledge.)

She wrote an award-winning book-length poetry manuscript recognized by the governor of Utah. A former member of Sigma Delta Chi, she was named an Outstanding Young Woman of America.

Her interests include reading, writing, cooking, traveling, and doing family history. She has met five presidents of the United States, sailed up the Nile River, prayed in the Garden of Gethsemane, eaten tempura in Tokyo, and received a dozen long-stemmed red roses from a stranger on the street in Athens.

Cassandra is the mother of five and the grandmother of four.

This has been an
Immortal Production